The Heavy Butterfly

by Mark Gomes

Copyright © 2024 Mark Gomes

All rights reserved.

ISBN: 9798224189908

For
ENMAH

Part I: BROKEN

Chapter One

Amber died in the sky.
No, try again. Amber died in my arms on the road.
Then I saw her in the sky.
Sitting on a yellow door.
Floating on an endless sea between the clouds.
She looked at me and...
No, stop. Don't go there.

The journey to Amber's football practice was 4.7 miles. To Java Jane's coffee shop was 0.9 miles. All other distances are immeasurable. What is the distance from loving father to hated parent? How far did I travel to become a bigot in the eyes of my wife and daughter?

Outside Java Jane's, in the middle of the road, as I cradled Amber's broken body, my senses were flat and grounded. The steaming radiator of the indifferent truck hissing behind me, screaming patrons on the sidewalk outside Java Jane's, casual strollers stopping as if smashed in the face by a cartoon hammer when they see Amber and me in the road. Was I already wrong to say this? Should it have been Amber's body and me? Siren's, soft in the distance, their meaning deafening. An image on a cracked and bloody phone screen silently accusing me.
    Like a torch turned from wide angle to focus beam, my senses lasered onto a single image. Amber in the sky. Sitting on a yellow door. Floating on an endless sea between the clouds. She looked at me and said,
    'Why Dad? Why did you do it?'

Chapter Two

Hugh recovered from his physical injuries quicker than expected. The mental injuries were a little trickier. Grief and loss he knew would eventually lessen over time, allowing him to join the unfortunate club of zombie-parents who have lost children. Lost. A subtle attempt to soften tragedy, except death doesn't do subtlety, death's a kick in the teeth with steel-capped boots. Hugh already thought of himself as a zombie-parent, someone who lived in the world but now destined to forever participate in it differently. Less than. The expression spoke to him. Less than. He couldn't place it. It was a side effect of the accident, as though someone had emptied all the drawers in which he kept his memories and put them back in a hurry, all messed up.

Grief, loss, jumbled memories, none of that mattered to Hugh. Guilt was the Big Bad and no amount of time could out-wait guilt, no distance far enough to get away, no speed fast enough to out-run guilt. Big Bad was an ever-present vicious prison guard, snarling, 'You will not hide, you will 'fess up to your deed, here, drink this dirty water filled with broken glass then repeat after me, I'm the reason Amber is dead.' Hugh knew Big Bad was a bastard but a liar he was not.

It felt like a month since the accident, he couldn't be sure, time had lost all meaning, the days having no purpose, except for the equation of course. Somewhere in that month he had left Laura, too cowardly to remain in the presence of her unspoken accusations. They both knew what had been going on before the accident, Hugh didn't need Big Bad to fill in those details. Sometimes Hugh wished Laura would say what he knew she was thinking, pull the trigger and let the bullets fly, it would be better than living with the gun constantly to his head.

She wouldn't understand why he really had to leave, that he had to find the soul of Amber because he believed he had seen it in the sky when the accident happened, and that if he could find her soul, he knew it would help to fix them. He had to try. If only he could understand his equation.

The equation was all he thought about. He worked on it in his room, when he wandered the streets, it was all he thought about and now, sitting on a park bench, he was staring at one of the hundreds of pieces of paper on which he had scrawled the equation.

(Amber dying in my arms on road)+(Amber on door on sea in sky)+(Amber could see me)+(I could hear her) = X

Answer: X = Amber's soul
Find Y, where Y = the place where souls go.

In the bottom corner was another part of the equation, the negative part that Hugh didn't want to acknowledge, didn't even know where to place. He couldn't not write it down, so he put in on the paper in a way that he could look at the main X and Y statements without seeing the troubling statement he wanted to ignore,

-(Why Dad? Why did you do it?) = Z
Where Z means

Hugh could not bring himself to write down what Z means, could not even add a question mark at the end of the statement because that would suggest it was a question to be answered. Hugh Mann did not want to answer this question.

"I can help you solve for Y."

Hugh looked up to see a tall man with the air of a schoolteacher, someone more used to blackboards and chalk than white-boards and tablets.

"C'Farer's the name, Gerald C'Farer," he said, extending his hand in greeting, which Hugh belatedly shook.

"And you are Hugh Mann." It wasn't a question.

"How do you know who I am?"

"A little detective work after the reporting on your daughter's accident."

Hugh was finding the encounter akin to stumbling through an overgrown jungle; something important was behind all the leaves but no matter how many he pushed aside, there were always more in his way. All he could manage to say was,

"Seafarer, like for boats?"

"Not quite," said Gerald retrieving a business card from his jacket and handing it to Hugh.

The card was the cheap kind, one step up from home-made, many steps down from good for business. Gerald seemed to notice Hugh's unspoken criticism.

"We don't have much of a marketing budget," said Gerald. Hugh said nothing but wondered what kind of company had a marketing budget that couldn't run to business cards. The card had a simple typed font that read, The Soul Comfort, Hiking Instructors & Puzzle Architects Partnership.

Hugh took a few reads of the card before saying, "That is not a combination you see every day."

"My partners and I don't do everyday things. And we would like to help you, if you will let us."

"You can't help me. I don't need to sit in a circle and share, a hike in the mountains won't fill my soul with anything good and...puzzles, no time for them," said Hugh.

"May I?" said Gerald indicating a spot next to Hugh on the bench.

"It's not my bench."

"Quite," said Gerald taking a seat next to Hugh, holding his hand out for Hugh's paper.

The leaves in Hugh's mental jungle cleared; I can help you solve for Y.

Why had he forgotten as soon as Gerald had said this? Hugh realized it was because the idea of finding a soul was crazy, but it was his crazy and keeping it to himself allowed him to keep it real. Sharing his equation opened him up to the risk of being quickly told it was a trauma induced hallucination, followed by advice to seek grief counseling.

Hugh gave Gerald his piece of paper with the equation as Gerald retrieved a retractable pencil from his jacket. In the space between Hugh's main equation statements and the negative Z statement at the bottom, Gerald proceeded to draw a diagonal line from bottom left to top right. He then drew two stick figures at the bottom of the line and three small houses spaced along the line, the last at the top. Next to the first house he wrote Astrophysicist, by the middle house he wrote Jigsaw Maker, by the top house he wrote Deejon's Freedom Club and in the space to the right of the line, a little lower than the top house, he scribed a large Y and then gave the paper back to Hugh.

Hugh was having a bit of a goldfish moment, his mouth working making no sounds, as he struggled to compute any kind of map that offered a solution to his equation, let alone the preschooler effort Gerald C'Farer had just drawn. Gerald, who was now pointing at the map with his pencil and explaining it to Hugh.

"These two fellows at the bottom are you and me. After I've explained the process, you will travel up the mountain, this diagonal line being the mountain, where you will meet my associates, Leonora, The Astrophysicist, Beli,

The Jigsaw Maker and Deejon, who runs the Freedom Club. They will help you."

"Are you serious?"

"Of course, what could be more serious than matters of the soul?"

"And this Y floating on its own over here, this is the place where souls go?"

"They have to go somewhere Hugh Mann. If you want help with your math that has no numbers come to my office at 4pm today." He stood and walked off without looking back, leaving Hugh once again, in goldfish mode.

Hugh remained on the bench staring at Gerald's ridiculous solution, I can help you solve for Y, Hugh snarked a laugh at the very idea. Then he looked at the statements above, about seeing Amber in the sky, on a door, on a sea and sadly saw the irony in the ridiculousness of his own equation. Before he knew it, he was laughing, as close to happy as he'd been since the accident. His equation and Gerald's solution were a perfect match. He felt it in the depths of his own soul. In that moment, alone on a bench in park holding a piece of paper with an equation and a solution, he was convinced the likes of which had never been penned before, Hugh Mann made a decision to seek Gerald C'Farer's help to find the soul of his daughter.

As he walked home he mentally wrote the letter he would leave for Laura, he'd tell her what he saw at the time of the accident, that it was so vivid he was convinced he could find or at least connect with Amber in some way, to give Laura and him some comfort, something to hold onto so that they could be less broken. He would end by saying he was going in search of Hope.

He couldn't tell her the other half of his truth, that every day he died a fresh death because of the guilt he felt over Amber's death. Because he could never truly be with Laura again if he didn't try to fix what he had broken.

Chapter Three

AMBER

Amber remembered the crushing pain, her Dad screaming and then darkness. Absolute darkness and silence. Water trickling, then rushing faster, then fast and deafening, the sound of water all around her, but not on her, yet she felt as though she was rushing along with the water. Light penetrating the darkness, resolving to a blazing sun above a deep blue sea and the yellow door upon which she floated. There was no more pain.

She sat up, the sea stretched forever in all directions...except down. As she looked into the water next to her door she could see her Dad on the road cradling her body, her body that was half crushed underneath a truck. It was like looking through a window. The scene played out with everyone oblivious to her watching from wherever she was. Her Dad saw her. It was long enough for her to see him and remember what he did. He half reached out to her, but she looked away, and like an old-time cartoon, the window closed from the edges to the center, and she was alone on the sea.

Amber sat in the middle of her door, she thought of it as her door because wherever she had arrived, it was here with her, *for her*. Arrival. That is what it felt like to Amber, she had arrived somewhere. She was on her own, more so than she had ever been in her entire life, alone floating on a calm sea, yet she was not scared. The scene on the road was scary, the way her body looked in her Dad's arms, and still, here she was, without a scratch. Amber concluded she was unconscious, her vision of the accident a part of her unconscious dream. She couldn't imagine another explanation, this made sense to her, let her feel calm like the sea, and in her dream, ready for whatever came next.

No sooner than she had the thought and a breeze picked up, moving Amber and her door.

It wasn't long before a beach crept onto the horizon, a sliver of gold in the distance. As she was gently blown across the calm sea the sliver of gold resolved into a sandy-white beach that seemed as wide as the sea upon which she sailed. Nearer to the beach she could see it was not very deep, with a tall wall of sand grass about 60 feet back from the shore. The door was close to making land when Amber saw someone walking out from behind the sand grass, someone who was walking purposefully towards Amber.

Chapter Four

The door came to rest in the surf, the woman standing a few feet away in the sand. She had on a rucksack and carried a long thin branch as a hiking stick. Colored strands of ribbon were tied to the belt loops of her cut-off jeans. She wore two silver band rings on her left hand, and a gold one on her right hand. On her right wrist was a double-loop rope bracelet.

Amber stood motionless on her door. Alone on the sea she had felt calm. It had been a feeling of inner peace the likes of which Amber had never known, like the fuzzy warm glow when waking from a perfect dream on a summer morning with no plans except to be yourself in whatever way you choose. Now the woman's presence was like a jab to the gut, taking her breath away. Amber wasn't simply motionless; she was paralyzed as the meaning of seeing her Dad holding her broken body on the road hit home, as the meaning of this stranger in a strange place told her that all the people who weren't strangers in her life were gone.

Gone. Because she was dead.

If the woman's presence was a punch in the gut, realizing she was dead was the knock-out blow. Amber wanted to fall back into the sea and simply drift away, drift home would be best but away would do, as long as she didn't have to step forward into the reality of her death. As Amber felt herself embracing the wish to push the door back out to sea, the woman spoke, "Come to me." Her voice was more than sound, it touched Amber, wrapping her in its comforting warmth. Amber stepped into the surf. A burning sensation shot up the leg in the surf, she wanted to step back onto the door.

"Come to me," said the woman, as she reached out, encouraging Amber onward.

It was no more than eleven steps but with each step Amber felt she was burning and being crushed. She closed her eyes, saw flames everywhere, heard familiar voices lost in the noise of a raging fire.

"Come to me," the woman's voice pulled her forward.

As the pain threatened to overwhelm her, she was suddenly in the warm embrace of the woman.

"You made it. I'm Mia, your Helper."

Chapter Five

"Where am I?" asked Amber.

Mia sat on the sand and waited for Amber to join her.

"You are somewhere safe. Close your eyes, let the light warm you and listen to the waves."

Amber could see Mia was doing exactly this and recognized she would get no answers until she did as instructed.

Amber hadn't realized how bright the light was but with her eyes closed, instead of darkness she experienced brightness.

"Can you feel the light and the waves?"

Amber whispered, "Yes." It was as though the waves had moved from the beach to inside her, gentle waves of comfort, caressing and calming her.

She felt peaceful, not missing her parents, not feeling lost, just feeling there was nowhere else to be but on this beach, in the light by the sea.

Mia's words drifted into the light behind her closed eyes, "You have arrived from the Sea of Eternity at the Place Between."

Chapter Six

HUGH

Gerald's office, much like his business card, was one step above a home-office and a long way from anything remotely professional. It was nestled in the foothills of the local hiking area, densely wooded hills which at a mile high, could qualify as mountains. The office was a single story weathered wooden hut, with a look of permanence that suggested it was as old as the hills themselves. An old brass plaque beneath a bell covered in cobwebs read, *The Soul Comfort, Hiking Instructors & Puzzle Architects Partnership.* Ringing the bell dislodged a few cobwebs and created a mini dust-cloud which caused Hugh to sneeze but not much else. Shades over the windows prevented Hugh from seeing inside. He decided to sit on the steps and wait.

As the sun warmed his face he pondered what had brought him to be sitting outside a wooden hut in the middle of almost nowhere, waiting for a stranger he hoped would be able to help him find the soul of his daughter. He looked at the dirt road he had followed from the main road to get to the hut. Hugh knew it wasn't either of these roads that had brought him here; that particular journey started three weeks and a lifetime ago in June, just after Amber's 16th birthday. Hugh fell asleep and dreamed of the past.

Amber's birthday was in the middle of June, 2 weeks before the local Pride Parade, on 28th June. This is not something Hugh would have known if it wasn't for a special birthday request from Amber. It was a family tradition to go to the restaurant of choice of the birthday person. As they were having birthday cake for breakfast, another family tradition, Amber said she wanted to trade her birthday restaurant pick in return for the whole family going to the local Pride Parade.

"I'm all for live and let live but I don't need to go to a gay parade," said Hugh.

"It's not about being gay, it's about pride in your identity, whatever it is," said Amber.

"Hugh Mann, that's me identified, like it says on my driving license."

"Identity is so much more Dad, it's everything," said Amber.

"I don't know what everything means but it seems like identity for your generation is what therapists were for the baby boomer's. You've got the luxury of having 1st world lives and too much time so you navel gaze on questions that don't need to be asked, much less answered," said Hugh.

"Dad, will you come, it's a birthday wish from me?" said Amber.

"Only if we still go out for dinner tonight but I get to pick," said Hugh.

Amber's hand shot out quick as flash, "Deal..." Hugh shook her hand to seal the deal as she added, "...only if you choose Delila's Rib Shack." Amber laughed as she skipped upstairs to get ready for school.

"Do you know what all this gay parade stuff is about?" said Hugh.

Laura was between a rock and a hard place; she did have some ideas but they were her own ideas and not down to any conversations with Amber and the last thing she wanted to do was give Hugh any misguided inputs.

"Maybe she has friends taking part," said Laura. Hugh pushed the last piece of cake around his plate before getting it on the fork, then seemed to push the sugary mess around his mouth before finding his words.

"If it was a football game and maybe someone was playing she wanted to support, maybe get to know better, makes sense but how does that translate to a gay parade?"

"It's a Pride Parade not a gay parade," said Laura.

"Is there a difference?" said Hugh. Laura was glad to have distracted him from his own question.

"Whatever this is about, she's involving us and that's a good thing, so let's go and keep an open mind. It will be a knew experience, you remember what that's like don't you?" said Laura, getting up and giving him a quick kiss before disappearing upstairs.

Hugh quickly man-interpreted Laura's words and shouted after her, "Should I be reading something into that last comment, something funkaay?" The sounds of Laura and Amber talking suggested not.

"Did you ask them?" said Mich, short for Michelle, pronounced Mitch, aka Amber's best friend, a goth cyber-punk, sporting a single red braid in her otherwise jet-black cropped hair. They were in Mich's bedroom, a pit-stop on Amber's way home so Mich could give her a birthday present.

"They'll come but my Dad sounded pretty old school."

"Old school how?" said Mich.

"Like identity extends as far as your name on a driving license," said Amber.

"Damn, that's stone-age thinking," said Mich.

"Maybe but also pretty normal for a whole lot of people," said Amber.

Mich came over to Amber, rested her hands on Amber's hips, took a beat to take her in before saying, "And what's your normal?"

Amber lazily draped her arms over Mich's shoulder's, rested her forehead on Mich's and said, "I don't know." Mich pushed away from Amber, "Not the answer I was expecting."

"I didn't mean..." started Amber but Mich, putting a finger on Amber's lips, shushed her, "You don't need to know yet." She turned to pull a poster tube from under her bed and gave it to Amber, "Happy birthday."

Mich had given Amber a poster showing all the different flags of the LGBTQ+ community.

"I'm sure you'll find the one that works for you," said Mich. Amber stared at the poster of the multi-colored flags and their various descriptions.

"Thanks, it will get pride of place on my wall," said Amber with a smile that didn't quite reach her eyes.

Later, alone in her own bedroom, Amber again stared at the poster, now lying on her bed. She had meant it when she told Mich she would give it pride of place in her room but that wasn't the full story. The poster left Amber feeling conflicted. She liked the principle of gender diversity and inclusiveness that the flags represented, but she didn't feel a commitment herself to any of the labels. She felt attracted to Mich but didn't feel un-attracted to guys and didn't feel any need to find a label that covered her ambiguity on gender and sexual orientation. She turned the poster over so that only its bare white back was showing. The emptiness, the lack of definition on the plain white surface resonated more positively with Amber than any of the flags on the other side. Amber knew what she wasn't, but it didn't mean she knew what she was and that was OK for her.

She put Mich's poster on the wall above her bed, stood back and knew it wasn't working for her. She could understand how it worked for Mich, who identified strongly as gay, and she admired how well Mich seemed to feel in her own skin but that wasn't her. She rummaged around in *her cupboard until she found an old poster from a kids TV show, she stuck it back-side out next to the flag poster.*

Amber was happy she had found a solution that almost captured what she felt and a little sad she couldn't tell anyone how she really felt, not even Mich.

Brutus ruined the plans for a family birthday dinner. Brutus was a young dog, 120 pounds of muscle-bound uncoordinated friendliness, still coming to terms with his own power. When he ran it seemed that his back-end was trying to overtake his front-end which had the effect of changing his direction. Brutus's instinct when this happened was to run even faster, which only served to exaggerate the course direction error. Normally Brutus would end up about 20 feet to the left of where he wanted to be, bark excitedly at his original destination and then bound over to it, covering the 20 feet without further mishap. He was a gentle giant more likely to do himself harm than anyone else. Except on Amber's birthday, he managed to grievously harm Josh Grosse. Josh was about to impress Bianca with a standing-start back-flip. Bianca was bored but sensed some excitement might come if Josh made an epic fail, she didn't wish for him to hurt himself, but thought failing at something might stop him constantly talking about his successes at the bank or former sporting glories. The trajectory of the relationship was not looking good for Josh. The trajectory of Brutus, trying and failing to outrun his back-end, was looking even less good for Josh. Josh was hunkering down in final prep for lift-off when what seemed like a small bear bowled him up and over. Josh landed on his front, the wind knocked out of him and face first in a cake he had fake-baked (his Mom did it) to impress Bianca. Bianca had the event uploaded to multiple social platforms before Josh had finished his first groan. Twenty feet away Laura's Mom was rushing towards Brutus. Brutus could smell cake and was already returning for a second helping of fun at Josh's expense, which involved licking his face clean of cake.

The upshot was Josh calling the police, the police taking Brutus away and Laura being with her Mom at the vets with the police, establishing that Brutus was guilty of nothing more than clumsiness. And that Josh was a bit of a dick. It would eventually work out well for Brutus and Josh, who managed to show his human side to Bianca and actually ask Laura's Mom from where she got Brutus.

Laura gave Hugh a little pep talk, setting him up to listen to Amber more than mansplain any and all subjects. Hugh had asked if it was OK for him to still be the parent who maybe knew a little more than his 16 year old daughter, to which Laura pointed out all she was saying, was the man who only that morning had asked if there was a difference between a gay parade and pride parade, should maybe listen on subjects new to him.

"Happy birthday to me," *said Amber raising her soda to Hugh's beer.*

"Happy birthday honey, shame Mom and Nana can't be here but we'll fix that at the weekend."

"Gives us a chance to talk anyway Dad," *said Amber. Hugh was getting the feeling he wasn't the only one Laura had given a pep talk to.*

"Do you know what you're gonna have?"

"Dad you always ask and I always have the same thing."

"There's about a hundred things on that menu, I thought maybe you'd branch out, seeing as it's your birthday, you know, be adventurous."

"I'm a girl who knows what she likes," *said Amber giving the menu an unnecessary once-over and nodding to herself, as if to confirm the accuracy of her statement.*

The waitress came to take their order.

"What will it be folks?"

"Spicy wings to start followed by a rack of baby-back ribs finished with 3 scoops of chocolate ice-cream. Times two," said Hugh.

"Coming right up."

"No steak Dad, how come?"

"I want to know what my daughter finds so special about her choices."

As the waitress hadn't taken their menu's Amber stacked them together and moved them aside before saying, "So how do you feel about my choice of going to the Pride Parade?"

"I'm wondering why you want us to go, why can't we catch it on TV? I don't have a problem with the gays, I'm all for equality but I don't need to be so up close and personal with the gays."

"Dad you can't say, 'the gays', it's the LGBTQ+ community."

"Why do they have to be a special community, they're just people, like us, male, female, you can like guys or girls or both, it's not more complicated than that," said Hugh.

"It's not complicated Dad but it's way more varied, have you even heard of gender non-conforming, binary, non-binary, gender fluid, agender, bigender, bicurious, aromantic?"

"Well, I do like to consider myself a bit of a romantic, just ask your mother," said Hugh flashing his daughter a cheeky smile that vanished under her withering gaze.

"OK, tell me why this is so important to you," said Hugh.

Amber took a long sip of her soda, as she wondered how best to explain things to her Dad. She had always thought her Mom would be present when she told them how she felt, maybe even that her Mom would be present, and her Dad wouldn't first time round. She had finished her soda when remembering Mich's poster flag gave her an idea.

Amber took one of menus, a napkin and the salt & pepper mills. She placed the menu in front of her, a big vinyl edged laminated piece of card with circa 50 items on it.

"This is like all the variations of gender identity, it's great and everyone has to be acknowledged and valued. But only once all of this is really seen, can it not be seen. Am I making sense?" And in that moment before her Dad spoke Amber was a child who desperately wished to be understood by her Dad. Hugh only half disappointed her...that being a child's generous interpretation.

"I don't agree with these variations, but I understand the idea of them exists. What I don't get is this 'really seen before it cannot be seen,' and I don't get what any of it has to do with you," said Hugh.

Amber took the plain white paper napkin and spread it out next to the menu.

"This is me, a blank canvas..." she put her hand on the menu, "...against all these options."

Hugh rested a hand on his daughter's and said, "You're literally 16 years old today, you don't need to be clear on gender, if you feel there's some reason for confusion and about..." Hugh needed to take a beat before he could use the S word with his daughter, "...sexuality, time is on your side, there's no hurry."

Amber moved her hand from under her Dad's placed both of hers on the napkin, "I am cool with how I feel, it's not a confused position, it's just developing but you..." she picked up the salt and pepper mills and placed them on the napkin, "...have me and everyone else as either male or female and even though I'm developing my own thing on this napkin at the bottom here, you already have the answer, salt or pepper, girl or boy."

The waitress brought their food, forcing Amber to move aside her gender-explaining menu/napkin/salt+pepper model while Hugh tried to digest what he didn't want to understand. Hugh had taken a good look at the blank napkin while Amber rabbited on and he quickly put all possible descriptors that might find their way onto the napkin into a room in his head, which he now stood outside, door safely locked, key in hand, as he wondered what to do next. He realized Amber was talking again.

"...and if we can get to a place where everything is seen then maybe we can go to a place beyond, where we stop seeing and stop making judgments, everyone can be themselves and no judgment means no prejudice, right Dad?"

And the little Hugh Mann in Hugh's head put the key in his pocket because Hugh knew what to do. There was a problem that needed fixing, and he was going to fix it.

"Sure Honey, see it all, don't see it, everyone's going to be happy. I get it, we won't focus on our differences, makes sense."

Amber heard her Dad sort of say the right words but it was the way he took the napkin from earlier, blew his nose in it and scrunched it up, that spoke to her more.

Laura found Hugh watching a game on TV.
"Where's the birthday girl?"
"On her phone in her room, do you know a Mitch, and how did everything go with your Mom and Brutus?"
"Mom, Brutus all good, took a while to get this banker-type to calm down, by the end he wanted his own Brutus. Mich is Amber's best friend, you know this."
"Michelle is her best friend, I think Mich might be a boyfriend," said Hugh.

Laura looked at Hugh as though he had just arrived from Mars, which completely missed him as he'd returned to watching the game.

"Hi honey, sorry I missed dinner but Nana really needed support."
"It's cool Mom. I had an...interesting meal with Dad."
Laura sat on the bed, nodding to Amber's new flag poster.
"Discuss that did you?"
"Kind of. You know how sometimes Dad says what he thinks you want to hear but you know it's not what he's really thinking."
Laura couldn't help laughing as she answered, "You are seeing the refined version, I've seen that develop over the years. I think of it like your Dad speaking Chinese, he's making sounds but he doesn't know what they mean."
Amber high-fived her Mom, "Nailed it Mom."
"What's the backward poster about?" said Laura.
"Me. Work In Progress." Time stopped for Laura as she took in the glory of her 16 year old daughter. Amber was beautiful in the way all children are if you look at them long enough to see the splendor of their hopes and dreams.
"Take your time, and remember the answer is yours to write..." Laura stood, kissed Amber on the head, "...happy birthday beautiful."

Laura joined Hugh on the sofa as the game finished.
"Hey Hon, you know we got to get ahead of this gay problem," said Hugh.
Laura loved her husband but sometimes he really was a Martian from another planet.
"There is no problem, gay or otherwise. The only problem you need to fix is my empty wine glass."

As Hugh set about remedying the wine problem, Laura wondered how she would deal with the real problem of Hugh's attitude to the LGBTQ+ community. Houston definitely had a problem, and the fix wasn't assured.

Chapter Seven

"Have you ever been to Houston?"

Hugh drowsily woke from his dozing on the steps outside Gerald C'Farer's office to find Gerald peering down at him.

"Houston, have you ever been?" asked Gerald.

"No, is it important?

"I was thinking about the 'Houston we have a problem', people speaking across great distances, a bit like you wanting to reach out to your daughter."

"So I should go to Houston?" said Hugh standing, still not quite fully awake.

Gerald laughed as he walked past Hugh to open the door to his office, "You should follow me into my office and let me tell you all about the Three Big Questions and the puzzles you'll need to solve to get help answering them."

The inside of Gerald's office was different to any office or room Hugh had ever been in before. In the middle of the floor two old wooden rocking chairs were positioned either side of a table made from a section of old tree trunk. A recess had been roughly hewn in the center of the table, in the recess was a thick candle. Behind the chairs was the only modern thing in the office, a large white-board, which had a map on the side showing, at least Hugh thought it was a map. There was a legend showing a scale which corresponded to a faint grid overlaying the image. There was a slim border of blue running around the entire image, so Hugh assumed he was looking at an island, and that was as much as he could work out from looking at the map. The image was the problem. The image was of a dense forest from above, so dense it almost looked like a single blob of green painted by someone struggling, and failing, to find their inner Van Gogh. The chairs, table, candle, map, curtains constituted the entire contents of Gerald C'Farer's office.

"Take a seat," said Gerald as he occupied one of the rocking chairs.

As Hugh sat he nodded to the map, "Is that meant to be a map?"

"It's not meant to be, it is a map," said Gerald.

"It doesn't look much like a normal map," said Hugh.

"The journey to find the soul of your daughter is hardly a standard one, why would you expect the map that will aid you to be normal, as you put it?"

"So, you can help me find Amber, let's just say Amber shall we?"

"Our service has to start with you. We provide soul comfort, but one soul can't do anything for another if that soul is itself not well. And I don't think you are well Hugh."

"Apart from the accident, you know nothing about me."

"Do you know why you are really looking for *the soul* of your daughter, let's call it what it is, shall we?" said Gerald.

"Isn't it obvious."

"To me, yes, but is it to you?" said Gerald.

Hugh felt as though he was being interrogated, notwithstanding, Gerald's soothing voice and kindly nature, his questions poked at dark places. Once again Gerald seemed to be in tune with Hugh's inner thoughts, as he said, "There was a statement on your piece of paper, something like 'Why Dad? Why did you do it?'..."

Hugh started to protest but Gerald held up his hand to silence him.

"It's not my question Hugh. I simply asked if you know why you are really looking for the soul of your daughter and pointed you to a part of your equation. So, let's move on, shall we?"

Hugh nodded agreement and with a sprightly step Gerald went to the white-board, flipped it over, revealing a blank white canvas on which he proceeded to draw a bigger version of the picture he had drawn earlier for Hugh. As Gerald drew, Hugh was deeply questioning his decision to seek the help of Gerald C'Farer. However, as Gerald finished and stood to the side, Hugh could see the picture was not entirely identical to the one on his piece of paper. Next to Astrophysicist was written How? Next to Jigsaw Maker, What? Next to Freedom Club, Why?

"The journey to find a soul has three waypoints. Waypoint one is How, as in how does our physical self become whatever a soul is, how does something that can't be seen by the naked eye or any instrument exist inside our physical selves, how does it manifest when our physical lives end, if a soul is eternal, what is the nature of eternity with respect to a soul. People die at different ages, with different viewpoints, how does that work for a soul."

"That's a lot of how's," said Hugh.

"That's waypoint one, where Leonora the Astrophysicist will be your Helper. Waypoint two looks below the surface of the practicalities of How. Waypoint two looks at what you're not seeing, so where is the soul once it leaves the body, and what is the process that is going on? Beli the Jigsaw Maker will be your Helper at waypoint two. Once you know How and What, then comes the last question, the first amongst equals of the Big Three, Why? Why do we have a soul, and What is its purpose? If you get to the Freedom Club, you just might find out."

"And this Lennie, Beli and whatever the Freedom Club is all about, are going to explain all that to me?"

"They won't explain anything, but they will show you a path to achieve your own knowledge. There are rules, you can't go from one place to the next unless you solve the puzzles you are given."

"Why can't you just tell me what I need to know or where I need to go, why all the voyage of discovery stuff?"

"You just answered your own question, there's stuff you need to discover if you want any chance of finding your daughter's soul. Even if I told you exactly where her soul was, you wouldn't see it."

"OK. When can I start my journey to meet Leonora the Astrophysicist?"

"When you solve your first puzzle."

"Which you're going to give me now I presume."

"A simple question which should give you no trouble at all, I want you to tell me the most important difference between humans and animals."

"Our intelligence is much higher," blurted Hugh.

"While that is true, it doesn't answer my question. You have to tell me the *most important* difference between humans and animals," said Gerald.

"It's our intelligence that has elevated us to the top of the food chain, designed the cities we have built, our magnificent monuments, invented electricity, the lightbulb, cars, planes, computers. Not one animal anywhere at any time has even managed to make a single brick, let alone build in the world as humans have," said Hugh.

"True again and yet still not correct and I suspect you will not divine upon the correct answer no matter how many chances I give you."

Hugh was getting worried because he really had no idea where to start looking for Amber if Gerald wasn't able to help him and he was certain that human intelligence was the correct answer.

"I'll tell you the right answer because the real puzzle is yourself and how you use the information contained in the answer," said Gerald.

"I don't see what could possibly be a bigger difference than human intelligence," said Hugh.

"Maybe if you applied some of that valuable human intelligence you would hear me repeating that I want to know the *most important* difference," said Gerald.

"It's the same thing," said Hugh, crossing his arms and sitting back in his chair like a petulant child.

"The most important difference is our capacity for deception."

"You mean lying, which is something we use our intelligence to do."

"I don't mean lying and I'm not sure we're always using our intelligence when we chose to lie. I mean self-deception."

"Call it what you will, it's still lying, and it's still powered by human-intelligence," said Hugh.

"Animals are always true to themselves. By comparison to all the human inventions you mentioned their lives are simple, their relationships considerably less complex..."

"...it's because of that complexity we sometimes need to lie," said Hugh.

"...but they live in total honesty with themselves, in their simple lives, in their little tribes. I will provide for you, I will no longer provide for you, I will protect you, now go out on your own, I will work for the group, I will be your mate, I will not be your mate, and so on. There is no deception. For me that is the most important difference between humans and animals."

"OK, I accept your answer," said Hugh, thinking it would be the quickest way to get Gerald to let him start his journey up the mountain.

"Good, so you understand the need for self-reflection, a long hard look at yourself to get to the unvarnished truth, as they say."

"As who says?" said Hugh, suddenly feeling as though he was on the edge of a cliff, with a strong wind gusting at his back.

"Butterflies and the honesty of animals, that's what you'll need to understand if you want to find the soul of your daughter," said Gerald as he stood and went to the map.

And there it was, the gust of wind that pushed Hugh off the cliff; butterflies and the honesty of animals. Gerald C'Farer was not playing with a full deck. Hugh put his head in his hands as Gerald said, "Well, you are off to a good start. You can leave first thing in the morning once your guide arrives. I can give you a room for the night here."

"Guide. I don't really want company, can't you give me a map."

"Don't worry, you'll like Charlie, she's completely lovable. I'll show you to your room, we can discuss butterflies at breakfast."

Chapter Eight

LAURA

Laura ran through a mental checklist; avocados, cold cuts, cheese slices, bread, chips, melon, juices, a couple of the beers Hugh liked. All were present in her shopping cart, nothing out of the ordinary yet she couldn't help feeling people were staring. Making her way to the checkout she caught her reflection in a glass-fronted refrigerator. There it was. Woman shopping in pyjama's, slippers and fresh off the pillow sleep-hair.

Laura left the cart in the aisle, hurrying off to find a coffee shop.

Chapter Nine

"Ma'am, you can't park here," said the waiter. The woman inside the car was resting her head on the steering wheel she gripped with white-knuckled hands. He was about to knock on the window again when a voice of treacly sweetness froze the blood around his bones.

"Touch that window and Brutus will eat your balls, preferably spiced with a little cayenne pepper."

Moving back from the car the waiter was confronted by a woman more Golden Girls than T2 Sarah Connor, smiling sweetly at him. He wanted to push back with a smart response, but her harmless appearance and the cayenne pepper comment had him at a mental disadvantage.

"Say Hello Brutus," said the woman.

A growl like a pre-earthquake tremor shook the waiter to his core, his core being his balls, which he felt shrivel ever so slightly. The owner of the growl was a mean looking Rottweiler.

The waiter's fight or flight instinct was urging rapid flight when he noticed the woman holding a $20 bill in his direction.

"...corner table, two black coffees," said the woman.

As he was taking the $20 she quipped, "...and a little cayenne pepper, just in case." The waiter hurried off, not feeling any warmth from the woman's smile.

The woman instructed Brutus to keep guard by the car before getting in the passenger seat.

"Hi Mom," said a sniffling Laura, head still stuck to the steering wheel.

Gently stroking the back of her daughter's head, "I hear you've been modeling comfy sleepwear at the 711."

"How?"

"Dr. Midler's assistant called..."

"So, he's getting you to track me down now."

"I don't know about tracking you down, told his assistant he saw you leaving a full trolley in the store before making a quick exit."

"Is that all?"

"He might have mentioned your PJ's."

"Nothing else, you're sure?"

"It was not twenty minutes ago, I'm sure. Is there something else he should have mentioned?"

Laura sat up, face pale save for red-rimmed eyes and black patches beneath.

"Did I hear you scaring a waiter into getting us some coffees?"

Jean let the change in subject slide, she knew her daughter would get to the point when she was ready and not a moment before.

Inside the coffee shop the waiter had set them up on a corner table, coffees were waiting and a bowl of water for Brutus, which he hoped would be a seen as a trade against the cayenne pepper. Brutus drank as much water as he spilled, then spread himself on the floor for a snooze, his presence, even if asleep, ensuring nearby tables were avoided by customers while others were free.

Laura liked the warmth of the coffee mug in her hands, liked that it was too hot to be comfortable but not enough so she couldn't hold it; it stopped her thoughts wandering to the conversation she was convinced Dr. Midler wanted to have with her.

"I haven't been to the hospital today, that's why I thought Dr. Midler was calling."

"It's 9.30 in the morning. Dr. Midler had stopped to get a bagel to-go, saw you looking a bit lost so had his assistant get my number and call. They're not keeping tabs on when you visit, if anything they'd tell you to take a break, almost every minute since the accident, except when you've been sleeping and sometimes even then, you've been at the hospital."

"I don't want to go."

Jean took her daughter's nervous hands in hers as she said, "We can go together."

Laura seemed to look at someone outside the coffee shop. When Jean tracked her gaze there was no one there.

Laura pulled her hands away, stared at them resting in her lap, as she said, "Mom I was with Hugh and Amber in my dreams." Her hands were wet now, and as she looked up the tears kept flowing.

"Hugh and I had a picnic by the lake late in the pregnancy, there was something special about this moment so close to the birth. Hugh took the afternoon off and for a couple of hours we had the lake to ourselves. I was sitting against a tree looking over the lake and the biggest sky I had ever seen, Hugh was resting his head on the bump that was Amber. It was a perfect moment, my family so close and it felt like that big sky was full of expectation."

"A special memory and a good dream. It's your subconscious trying to give you some happiness because the days...well the days are not."

"But it wasn't just a dream Mom. When I woke it was like I was still in the dream even though I was awake. I could choose to stay in the dream."

"Baby, everyone wants their good dreams to never end and no one in this world has more reason than you but you can't go shopping for a picnic that happened more than 16 years ago."

"Why not? Why can't I stay in my memories, that's where all my happiness is."

Jean knew better than to argue. The best thing was to get Laura to the hospital, let her see what she still had to stay strong for.

"Let's finish our coffees. I'll drop Brutus at home then come by your place and we can go to the hospital together. OK?"

It took a while for Laura to nod agreement and Jean knew her daughter well enough to recognize when the affirmative nod and the steely eyes were not aligned.

Part II: JOURNEY'S

Chapter Ten

HUGH

Before going to bed Hugh had moved from feeling Gerald's comments about butterflies and the honesty of animals had pushed him off a cliff, to a feeling of camaraderie with Gerald. Clearly Gerald was off his rocker but was Hugh himself any different? He was trying to find the soul of his daughter because he had seen her floating in the sky. And because of the things locked away in the dark room in his head. Hugh made a decision; it was time to step up, shut up and just go with it, whatever *it* was.

Hugh didn't often dream anymore, only wished the millisecond before being fully awake, when the reality of Amber's death was still hidden in the fog of unconsciousness, could last a little longer, about forever would be fine.

His room was sparsely furnished, apart from the bed, there was an old wooden chair for his clothes and a metal sink fixed to the wall with a cracked mirror above it. Hugh sat on the edge of the bed, wiped the sleep from his eyes and crossed his arms over his knees as he wondered if seeking help from Gerald C'Farer was an attempt to extend that millisecond of ignorance into long-term denial, to lose himself in an activity, no matter how futile, so long as it allowed him to keep Big Bad locked up.

He shuffled over to the sink to splash some water on his face. As he blinked the water from his eyes the cracks in the mirror gave the impression someone was behind him, a shadow presence watching him. Hugh dried his face, dressed and went to meet Gerald for breakfast. He knew he was alone, no matter the deception of a cracked mirror.

In keeping with the style of general disrepair, breakfast was laid out on a somewhat clean molded plastic table, with matching somewhat dirty chairs. Breakfast was a box of donuts and take-out coffee.

"It's not five-star but it is free," said Gerald as he chomped into a jelly donut, indicating for Hugh to join him. The coffee was good, and he'd had worse donuts.

"I'm going to tell you about butterflies and you're going to tell me why you really want to search for the soul of your daughter."

"I already told you; I believe I saw Amber in some place other, somewhere beyond the world we live in, and I have to find her."

"You did say something about that, and all it tells me is *what* you want to do, not *why*."

"You're playing with words," said Hugh.

"And what are you playing at Hugh? Is it a game of Hide & Seek?" It felt like Gerald was picking at a scab and Hugh was the scab.

Gerald moved the box of donuts aside, lent across the table.

"It's not impossible to find a soul. Understanding a little about butterflies will help you. Imagine I asked you to find a Blue Morpho butterfly whose natural habitat is in Central and South America, what would you do?"

"I'd go to where they can be found to get one," said Hugh.

"Good. A simple answer to a simple question. And in this place where you find what you are seeking there would be hundreds of butterflies for you to choose from. Now imagine I ask you to bring me back a specific Blue Morpho, what would you do?" said Gerald.

"Butterflies aren't people, one Blue Morph thing is like any other," said Hugh.

Gerald smiled warmly at Hugh before saying, "Blue *Morpho*. Don't get lost in the detail, just think how it might be done if you had to find a specific butterfly."

"I'd have to capture them all and look at them one by one to find the one you wanted."

"OK, but now, I still want a specific Blue Morpho but all the butterflies are in their cocoons, completing their transformations before they rise and fly away," said Gerald.

"I'd wait till they emerge and..."

"There is a catch, the cocoons are spread all over the forest and you won't even know which cocoons have Blue Morpho's in them, and once the transformation is complete, they emerge and fly away," said Gerald.

"Then it's an impossible task," said Hugh.

"Terribly difficult but not impossible," said Gerald as he closed the lid on the donut box, which contained one last glazed sprinkles donut, before moving it to the center of the table and placing his coffee cup a little distance away. He placed one hand on the donut box, the other on the coffee cup.

"The box is the cocoon, the cup is you. It will take some skill to get to the right part of the forest but assuming you've got what it takes, once you're in the place of the Blue Morpho's..." Gerald gave the coffee cup a little shake, "...there is one way and only one way to find your butterfly. Can you tell me what that is Hugh Mann?" Gerald sat back, folded his arms and waited for Hugh to answer. Hugh had the feeling this was more than a general conversation on butterflies, he wasn't sure he'd get another word from Gerald if he failed to answer the question satisfactorily.

He sat back too, his mind racing through memories of nature documentaries, a visit to a butterfly sanctuary as a child. He had nothing except that butterflies were beautiful, fragile things that needed the perfect conditions to survive. Unhelpful memories, a donut box and an empty Styrofoam coffee cup. He wanted to laugh, felt like crying. Hugh closed his eyes...saw Amber on the door on the sea, turning *away from him*. Hugh had the answer.

He opened the box containing a glazed donut covered in multi-colored sprinkles, "She has to reveal herself to me."

Gerald looked at Hugh for a long moment, took the last donut from the box and proceeded to eat it.

"Very good Hugh. In this mountain forest behind my hut are my associates who can help you but the only soul you really have any control over finding is your own, you seek your daughters while you hide from your own." He finished the donut before continuing. "You'll have to find your own first. Do you have the courage to look behind the closed doors, because they are waiting for you in the darkness of the forest?"

"I'll do whatever it takes," said Hugh.

Gerald put a hand over Hugh's, "Everyone who sits in your chair answers as you have, but not everyone can climb mountains, they go as far as they can, then make their way down the mountain looking for others who can help."

"There are others that can help?" said Hugh.

"No."

"But you said..."

"There is only one way to find a soul, and it starts by going up the mountain," said Gerald, as he pointed again to the mountain behind his hut.

"The others provide help by taking away the fear of finding what is hidden, by making rules and providing safe places, places where there is less of a need to think, just to follow and have faith in hope."

"Is there something wrong with doing that?" said Hugh.

"Nothing whatsoever. But it's like boiling water to make pasta when you want rice, you could make perfect pasta, but you'll never have rice. So it is with the safe places, comfort and hope are wonderful things but there is a journey that every soul must make alone." Gerald reached under the table and retrieved a red rucksack, which he placed on the table. "Are you ready to make the journey up the mountain Hugh Mann?"

"I want to find the soul of my daughter."

Chapter Eleven

AMBER

Amber gazed at what she now knew to be the Sea of Eternity, it stretched as far as she could see in all directions save for the endless sliver of sandy beach on which she sat with Mia.
"You said you were my Helper."
"That's correct."
"Can you tell me if I'm dead?"
"Yes and no. If you think of your life as you knew it, then yes. Yet here you are, clearly not dead, so the answer is no."
"That's not much help."
Amber stared out at the sea again, pointed at it before looking at Mia, "Sea of Eternity, that's what you called it, and the Place Between. They are not real places, which means I'm dreaming or maybe unconscious but I'm definitely alive, just not properly alive like a normal human."
"That's true and it's because you are alive as a soul, a normal soul, which, when you are ready can be quite spectacular."
"Wh..." Mia held up her hand, cutting Amber off.
"As your Helper I need to make sure you have knowledge and not merely facts. For this to happen you are going to have to trust me at the beginning of this process. You will have many questions but first let me help you understand a little about your very special classroom. OK?" said Mia, spreading her arms in a way to suggest the beach and the island behind were all a part of Amber's special classroom.
"Is there another option?"

Mia smiled, stood up and said, "Let's go for a swim."

She stripped and walked to the water shouting over her shoulder to Amber. "No need to be bashful in the Place between."

After swimming out about 100m they were floating on their backs in water as warm as a bath.

"You were born in a hospital but the place you came from wasn't on any map. Inside your mother's womb, surrounded mainly by water from her body. This amniotic fluid protected and nourished you as you transformed from embryo to fetus to baby. Your soul traveled through the waters of the Sea of Eternity to arrive here in the Place Between. Of course you have questions about what exactly of you traveled here, where is here, how can you be here if you saw your body somewhere else, to name a few. Just know that you are your soul, let that knowledge seep into your being as you lay in the water. Let the Sea of Eternity nourish you as the waters of your mother once did."

Amber had been listening with her eyes closed, the sun, the warm water and Mia's soothing words enveloping her in a feeling of utter safety the likes of which she had never felt before. In fact, safety wasn't a good enough description for the well-being that she felt, but she didn't how else to describe it. Peace or tranquility suggested the removal of their opposites, such as troubled, chaotic feelings. This was different. She decided not to dwell on the description and to simply enjoy the feeling.

Too soon for Amber, she heard Mia start to swim back to the beach. She followed but with a longing for the feeling, of what she now thought of as uber-safety, to continue. Once on the beach Mia rummaged in her rucksack, pulling out clothes not dissimilar to her own and gave them to Amber.

"I think you'll find these more comfortable."

As Amber dressed, she looked out over the sea and felt its vast calmness replicated in her. Like rubbing sticks together to start a fire she felt the kindling of new knowledge, which for now, was clouded in smoke.

"Have I been reborn, you mentioned all that stuff about amniotic fluid?"

"No. It's more like a significant birthday. In many societies a person legally becomes an adult at 18, 20 or 21. Think of arriving here like one of those birthdays except it's about becoming a soul and 18, 20 or 21 is actually whenever you die."

"I feel different, older but not in a physical way, like I'm open inside, one big space. It's odd, I don't think I know more than before, but I feel capable of knowing more."

Mia smiled at her and said, "Then I guess you're ready to visit Sparky's Diner."

Chapter Twelve

LAURA

Laura left the coffee shop fully intending to go with her Mom to the hospital as they had agreed but there was a place calling her, a place between.

Between sleep and waking. Not conscious, not unconscious, whatever and wherever such a place could be.

The sky was an upside-down sea stretching away forever, hopes and dreams smashed on shores Laura could never have imagined. Yet she felt there was an edge to this place between, where something she had heard waited for her to understand it fully. She rested her head against the tree, closed her eyes and enjoyed a perfect summer picnic.

From a distance Jean watched her daughter, still wearing her pyjama's, close her eyes and drift into memories to relieve the brutal pain of her present. Jean poured herself a coffee from the flask she had brought, sandwiches staying wrapped for later. A Mom's intuition told her she was more likely to find her daughter by the lake than at home, and like all parents, she was the unseen safety net ready to spring into action at the first sign of danger.

After watching Laura resting by the tree for fifteen minutes Jean took out her cell phone, stared at it for a good five minutes, googled a number and made a call she never thought she would.

Part III: 3 WEEKS AGO

Chapter Thirteen

Teenagers. Sloths that meld to beds and sofas or hyperactive balls of energy. Toady was Parade Day and Amber was in hyperactive mode. Hugh was dressing, mid-trouser stage when Amber's head popped round the door, her words still reaching him after she'd disappeared again, "Dad, hurry up, we're going to be late."

Hugh checked his watch.
"It's not for two hours."
Amber's head popped back.
"Is that what you're wearing?"
Hugh looked at his half on chinos and favorite polo.
"This is my best stuff."
"It's so uncool Dad, you look like a store manager..." Her phone beeped and Amber was off to her room, shouting back, "...ask Mom for help, you need it." Hugh couldn't help smiling as he heard her laughing at her own wit, a trait she had from her mother.

"How come I'm the uncool one?" said Hugh to Laura as she entered from the bathroom, face flushed from a shower, towel wrapped around her.

"There's a mirror behind you hon, you'll find the answers there," and then proceeded to laugh heartily at her own joke. She was happy, Amber was happy, Hugh didn't need much more. Or did he? Laura's towel was on the floor as she fussed over what to wear.

"You know I could lock the door and we could..."
"...and you could wish upon a star while sliding down a rainbow, not going to happen now Mr. Mann," said Laura without taking her attention from her wardrobe.

"Harsh Mrs. Mann."
"I only said now, maybe just push the timeline to later," said Laura.

"OK but I got to warn you, there is a game on tonight." The smile hadn't made it all the way across Hugh's face before he was blind-sided by a thrown cushion to the head, which, due to his half-trousered state felled him in a flurry of limbs and flapping chinos. The thud of his backside on the floor and Laura's guffaws brought Amber running. She didn't need long to find her Dad's prone position hilarious.

"Good shot Mom," said Amber, walking across the room to high-five her now robed Mom, when Hugh caught her square in the face with the cushion that had downed him. Amber joined him backside down on the floor.

"Hugh, you'll hurt her."

"Oh, now you think it might be painful." But Laura needn't have worried, Amber was up for the fight.

"Game on Dad." She grabbed a pillow from the bed and took a good swing at Hugh, which he only partially avoided as he charged Amber and threw her onto the bed and grabbed another pillow. Laura watched as a pillow fight ensued, a throwback to times when Amber was younger, and all Hugh had to do was make a funny face or blow a raspberry to make her happy. She wondered if his reaction to the day's events ahead would also make their daughter happy.

Chapter Fourteen

Amber was hurrying them out the front door when Hugh's cell rang.

"It's my boss, let me take this and I'll meet you in the car."

"Don't be long Dad."

"I won't but Bob wouldn't let a work call come between him and the golf course on a Saturday morning if it wasn't important."

Amber made a funny eyes-on-you gesture with her fingers before leaving as Laura mouthed a smiling 'hurry up'.

"Hey Bob, what's going on?"

"Sorry to call on a Saturday Hugh but there's going to be an announcement on Monday and out of respect I wanted to give you a heads-up. We're giving the promotion to Sally. You've both got good numbers, a bit more tenure in your favor but in today's climate, Sally's the right call."

The decision didn't surprise Hugh, and he understood the reasoning. But it didn't make it any easier to hear. He had been wandering the hall as he listened to Bob, now we went to the dining room and took a seat.

"Hugh, you there?"

"Yeah, I'm here Bob. Look, I get it and thanks for the heads-up. I was half expecting the cards to play this way. I'll be fine and give Sally all the support she needs."

"Good to hear Hugh. Sally will give you the run-down on the new structure on Monday. Enjoy the rest of the weekend."

"Sure thing Bob, see you next..." The call was cut before Hugh finished, which was unlike Bob. Hugh wondered about the new structure and assumed Bob didn't want to get drawn on it, rather leave it to Sally. He sat with his head in his hands thinking he'd have to get used to not being VP of National Sales a while longer. He and Sally had been colleagues a long time and she deserved the promotion as much as him, he'd keep doing his job, VP Regional Sales, wasn't too shabby anyway. The narrative in his head played well, it just wasn't getting the required support from the frown on his face.

The front door opened.

"Dad, hurry up!"

There's nothing like excited happiness in a child's voice to cheer a parent. Hugh smiled as he left the dining table to join his family.

"Everything OK hon?" said Laura.

"All good, I'll tell you more later." Laura didn't like talking too much while she was driving so didn't push Hugh for more details.

"Mom park by the library then we can cut through the alley and get a good spot."

"OK boss, you got it," said Laura.

Amber was right, they had a really good spot to see the Parade. The only problem being it was the last thing Hugh needed. The frown he had on his face after speaking with Bob was controlling his inner narrative now, spicing things up with words and phrases like 'unfair', 'me-also', 'equality is a 2-way street'. So, the festival of colorful diversity was pushing every wrong button imaginable for Hugh Mann. There were standards, a tried and tested way of doing things, male and female, simple gender identities. He was bringing outdated templates to a Parade of glorious gender fluidity. To Hugh the Parade represented an otherness he didn't want to understand or accept, because it was pulling in a direction he didn't want to go, a direction he believed was taking things away from him, leaving him less than the Hugh he had been before the Parade and everything it represented. And Hugh's view was not considering that his daughter might see things differently, his view assumed she must have the same view as him, which if he only looked to his left, he would have realized was fundamentally flawed.

Amber was having a blast. She couldn't imagine the carnival in Rio to be any more exciting. The people on the floats, on the street, wild costumes and crazy body make-up, the noise, color, sounds, everything was so visceral and border-less. Without common boundaries. That is what Amber liked more than anything else. All welcome, all equal, a place to simply be who you are. On Parade Day, a time to celebrate loudly and just BE WHO YOU ARE.

Amber saw Mich go by in a sort of hot-pant-biker-body-glitter-rainbow costume. Amber had given Mich strict instructions not to pull her into the Parade, as she knew Mich otherwise would. Amber wanted the Parade to be a family day out, it was a birthday wish after all, but mostly Amber wanted to use the Parade as an opening to discuss some important things with her parents. In some ways she was more advanced than her parents in understanding gender politics and fights for equality of the 21st century and in others she was a child, naively assuming if she was having fun, so were her parents.

Laura could see Hugh was not having fun, she knew there was more to the phone call with Bob than he was saying, but the Parade was not the time for conversation. The Parade itself made Laura happy, to her it was a celebration of life, and she didn't really care about any further analysis. Her Mom and Dad had taught her well to live and let live, up close and personal included. She saw Amber screaming to someone she vaguely recognized in some sort of glitter rainbow costume, her daughter's joy rubbing off on her, Laura chose to be happy. She and Hugh could deal with the work call later.

Chapter Fifteen

Hugh wasn't sure how they had ended up in Delila's Rib Shack again. After a time the Parade had morphed into a slow-moving wall of color and sound, background to his musings on what the meeting with Sally on Monday would bring. He vaguely remembered Amber negotiating with Laura about where they should eat as they made their way to the car. They had turned to him for confirmation, he had said yes to a question he hadn't fully heard and here they were, at Delila's Rib Shack.

"What can I get you?" asked the young waitress. She wore skinny black jeans, a white T, green arms and a silver nose ring. At least that's what Hugh made of the tats covering most of her arms and her hoop nose ring. In fact, all he could do was stare at her nose ring. Laura ordered for herself and Hugh, followed by Amber placing her standard order.

"OK, I'll get that to you real quick," said the waitress turning to leave.

"Does that thing hurt?" said Hugh.

"I'm sorry..?"

"Your nose ring, does it hurt?" said Hugh.

"Not since the piercing, it's cool," said the waitress.

"But why would you..."

"Hugh, let our waitress place our order with the kitchen and bring the drinks, OK?"

Laura name-checked the waitresses tag, "Stacey, he's had a long day."

"No problems Ma'am, be right back with those drinks."

"Honey?"

"I'm sorry, I saw a lot of piercings today, it was just going around in my head."

"Really, that's what's going around in your head?" said Laura.

Hugh made eyes towards Amber who was at one with her cell and not paying them any attention. Laura took the hint and parked the topic for later.

Amber had been messaging with Mich about the Parade. Mich wanted her to come to a Parade party later on. Amber sent her last message, *'poss CU @ parT. Going 2 tell M&D wish luck'.* She got a screen full of shamrocks from Mich before she put her phone down.

"So, what did you guys think of the Parade?"

"I loved it, the people were so happy, carefree. I think I most liked the feeling of inclusiveness; I mean even watching and not being a part, I felt like I belonged to the overall diversity of everything," said Laura

"Wow, way to go Mom," said Amber giving Laura the obligatory high-five.

"Dad, any thoughts?" Their drinks arrived before Hugh could answer and his first thought was to take a large swig of his beer.

"I'm not sure I'll be getting a high-five. I don't share your mom's feeling about belonging. I didn't see anyone in the Parade like me. All the fancy costumes, the exuberance of it all, it's not my world and men being like women and women being like men. It's even more than cross-dressing, they're cross-bodying with all this trans bull..."

"Hugh, not so loud, people are staring." Laura was right, people at tables nearby had gone quiet, preferring to eavesdrop on Hugh's rant than their own conversations.

Hugh took a pause via another swig on his beer.

"Sorry. Amber, I think you get it's not me."

"It's OK Dad. I just wanted you to see..." Amber's mind was a blank, the conversation wasn't going anything like she had planned. Mom was way better than she expected and Dad way worse. She looked around as though she might find the words she needed lying on the table. The menu.

"...to see everything that's on the menu because it is m..." Hugh cut across her. Laura saw the hurt writ large on her child's face, she wasn't a violent person but when her Mother's Protector-Love was ramped up, she'd face-off against an army. And right now she had Hugh in her sights.

"The world has bigger problems than 'the gays'. Men wanting to wear high heels, women who wished they had dicks..."

"Hugh!"

"Mom, it's OK, I got this," said Amber as she placed a calming hand on her Mom's arm. The touch of Amber's hand stopped Laura from going to a wild place. She looked at her daughter and saw a beautiful grace in her bearing. Laura didn't know how else to describe it; Amber was in the moment as herself, ready to discuss on equal terms with her Dad.

"Dad it's none of those things you said, that's just willful ignorance. But you are right that the world has bigger problems than LGBTQ+ issues. I bet if you said to the whole LGBTQ+ community, put your fight on hold, stop all campaigning for equality in all its myriad forms for one year. Why? Because this year we are going to solve global hunger. We guarantee every child will have enough food and water after 1 year. Then after the year if you said, wait another 12 months with your fight because we're going to fix the planet, I bet the LGBTQ+ community would wait. But the world doesn't work like that does it? And if people don't fight for themselves, no one else will. Everyone has to pick their own battles and they're normally the ones right in front of you." Amber sipped her soda, eyes never leaving her Dad.

Their food arrived, providing the cover of cutting and chewing for a few minutes silence. The pause gave Hugh time to reflect on his situation, there were a number of things going on, the number of which was at his absolute maximum. He was chewing steak and drinking beer. He was mulling over not getting a promotion and a meeting on Monday he felt blindsided by. He was dealing with Parade images he just had no time for. He was aware he was disappointing his daughter, and his wife was staring daggers at him. He was looking for an exit ramp, but no matter how he viewed the Parade and 'the gays' and all that stuff, he was certain he was going the right way down a one-way street. He felt something shift inside himself, it was a settling-in as he traveled towards a destination he hadn't known he was headed for. Most of all he wished the list of things he was dealing with stopped at steak and beer.

"When I was your age I'd be into a band for three months and it was like no one else even made music, three months later it was another band. Girlfriends were forever and forever was 6 weeks. Everything was a phase. That's where you're at now with all this identity and LPQT stuff." Amber didn't bother to correct him, instead she said, "Dad, I'm not gay." Hugh sighed deeply, happily, until Amber followed up with, "I'm not not gay either."

"Huh. What does that mean?" He looked to Laura for support. She gave him a tight smile with as much warmth as a polar wind and continued eating.

"It means it's not a phase and I don't fit into the ready-made boxes you have in your world."

"My world. I'm pretty sure my world and your world are the same," said Hugh.

"I'm really not," said Amber, and that was the last thing she said to him all night.

At home Amber retreated upstairs. Laura checked Amber's door was closed before she proceeded to read Hugh the riot act.

"Our daughter wants to tell us something extremely important to her and you don't have the decency, the sensitivity to recognize this, to listen to her. You blabber on about bands and High School crushes..."

"...because that's what this is, a High School crush on an idea that will be gone before Thanksgiving."

"You don't know that, you didn't listen enough to know anything about what Amber is thinking."

"I know plenty."

"Really, you can't even say LGBTQ+ or gay. 'The gays' and LP whatever you say. I don't know who you are. These are people, same as you and me..."

"Not..."

"Don't you dare say it. These people, normal people, could be where our daughter feels most at home."

Hugh stared at Laura a long moment, felt himself traveling a little further down his one-way street.

"But you can say that, standing here in our home, it's OK for you to say our daughter feels more at home with the freaks we saw at that stupid Parade." Hugh was bellowing at the top of his voice. Laura knew there was no point talking any more tonight, not that Hugh was giving her the option, as he brushed past her, saying, "I need some fresh air." As he walked by the stairs he saw Amber sitting on the top stair. The tears on her face were the icing on the cake for the crappiest day Hugh had had in a long time.

Laura sat with Amber on the stairs. "Your Dad's got some things going on, that's not how he really thinks."

"What if it is?"

"He got that call this morning from work, I was so mad at him after dinner I forgot to ask him about it, but I'm sure that's at the root of your Dad's mood. He's just off, that call was bad timing. We're a family, we've got time to work things out."

Laura put her arm around Amber, pulled her in tight.

"How about some hot chocolate?"

"That'd be nice."

As Laura was halfway down the stairs she turned and said, "Did I see Mich in a quite interesting rainbow glitter outfit?"

"Maybe," said Amber, as she jumped up, ran to her room, shouting back, "Marshmallows too please Mom."

Laura smiled to herself, warmed in her heart by the way Amber could bounce back to feeling better so quickly.

The house was quiet when Hugh returned. In the bathroom he looked in the mirror, he knew as clearly as the image which stared back at him that he had messed up big time today. Walking past Laura's side of the bed, he bent over and whispered, "I'm sorry, I'll do my best to fix this tomorrow." Laura didn't stir. He kissed her on the forehead and went to bed.

The next morning Hugh was up early. He did a little internet research and prepared to mend bridges with the tried and tested method of pancakes, ham and eggs. Breakfast started to thaw some of the frost from both Laura and Amber but there was still work to do. Hugh knew if he could fix things with Amber, Laura would come round quickly enough.

"Amber honey, I know I demonstrated some less than enlightened views last night and I was shouting, for which I apologize to both of you, some not nice stuff. I'm going to try and be more understanding, I want to learn about the LGBTQ+ community, which I believe people in the know also call the queer community. As a first step I've made a reservation for next Saturday at Proud, a hip restaurant for the LGBTQ+ peeps. You should bring Mich and also invite her for pizza night next week."

Laura had frozen mid-chew on a mouthful of pancake, it wasn't a pretty sight but Hugh's moves had stunned her. Amber was nothing but pleased, she gave her Dad a quick hug then made for upstairs to message Mich, before leaving the kitchen she turned and said, "Dad, I don't think I can go." Hugh, who had been beaming at Laura, was crestfallen, "Unless you get some new clothes." She darted out of the kitchen just avoiding a flying pancake.

"What do you think?" said Hugh to Laura as he cleaned pancake from the door-jam. Laura didn't want to burst Hugh's bubble, but she didn't think learning the acronym and a dinner reservation had changed his views, which she had found unexpected and shocking.

"It's a start and I'm glad you didn't let any of this sit." It seemed to work for Hugh, so she moved on.

"What was the call from Bob all about?" Hugh told her and said he'd know more after meeting Sally tomorrow.

Chapter Sixteen

After running her first Monday 9am team sales call, Sally asked Hugh to stay behind in the conference room.
"How was the weekend Hugh?"
"Good, eventually."
"Sounds like there's a story to be told."
"I can't say I didn't spend a moment or two thinking about the changes going on here."
"Yeah, I wish it could have been different but there can only be one VP of National Sales and there's two of us, the math just doesn't work for one of us."
"For me you mean," said Hugh.
"Hugh I don't want to get into things now. Could you make it for Monday Night drinks at the Old Tavern, like the old days, say 6, straight from the office?"

Hugh had ordered his second JD and coke when Sally finally arrived at the Old Tavern, thirty minutes late.
"Sorry, Q3 forecast call ran on a bit." Sally ordered a beer from a passing waiter.
"Thanks for meeting me Hugh. Brings back memories this place. The old days, work, drink, pass out, repeat."
"Weekends the same minus the work," said Hugh as they clinked glasses to memories of old times.
A waiter came by, asked if they were going to eat, before Hugh could answer Sally said she wouldn't be staying long. That and the Q3 forecast call set alarm bells ringing; it was too soon for a Q3 forecast call.
"What's going on Sal?" Sally looked away, wrapped the table with her knuckles.
"They told me to do this in the office. I told them if it had to be me then it would be my way." She turned to Hugh and dropped the bomb, "I've got to let you go Hugh."

Hugh's world tilted on its axis, sending him further and faster down his one-way street.

"Sal please tell me I misheard; I'm being fired?"

"Head office gave me the promotion, then told me I had to let you go. I argued against it. They plan on hiring two rookies for your salary and giving each the same target as you. Double the revenue for the same cost. Just math."

"Math has really got it in for me today. You can give them whatever target you want, they have no relationships, no sales skills."

"That's why they're cheap. What they do know is the technology, current and future, they're young, its what customers want to see, makes them feel they're doing business with a progressive company. Management can be older, back office too, but not on the front line."

"And you're management while I'm surplus to requirements. I'm the right side of 45."

"There is no right side of 45 if you're over 40. Its simply bad timing is all. There was a time when the lack of balls in my pants meant I'd be in your seat. Now it puts me in this seat."

"Sal, I get that, have no problem with it, either one of us makes a good VP but fired, I did not see that coming."

"Times up on the white man's privilege, it's the world we live in now." Sally signaled for another round.

"You know me, I'm not that white man you're talking about, there's a lot of guys like me, we aren't the big bad white oppressor everyone is painting us to be."

"The thing is, you may never have been first in line but you sure as hell have never been last."

"Sure feels like it now."

"That's only relative to the pretty good position you've had until now, and it's still pretty good. Can you imagine what it would feel like for achievement to mean that your kids get a basic education, or your family has the health care it needs, that cleaning jobs and fast-food restaurants don't represent your only career opportunities? The losing hand you feel you got right now beats 8 out of 10 hands a lot of people get dealt to play the game of life day in day out."

Their drinks arrived, Hugh downed his JD, laughed grimly before saying, "You make it sound like you've had no benefits, only us white men, all of us just holding you back, while you've endured nothing but suffering."

"Hugh that's not what I meant," said Sally as she stood to leave.

"Let me guess it was the math talking."

"I've got a tab running, eat something, take a day out, when you come in we can talk about your transition."

"And you can..."

"No. Don't say another word Hugh. I'm going now." Sally did Hugh the small favor of leaving before the JD took control of Hugh's side of the conversation.

Chapter Seventeen

Sally Albright sat in her car not going anywhere, not feeling good about what had just transpired with Hugh. The senior management team of precisely six white men all over 55 years old, had begrudgingly promoted her and then made her first act of management firing a friend. They were the real enemy to equality, Hugh was just a casualty no one cared about, tarred with the brush of others success and condemned for it.

Chapter Eighteen

Hugh soaked up some of the JD with a burger and fries and then undid the burger's good work by drinking more JD. The JD served the purpose of keeping his thoughts fluid, not letting anything linger too long in his mind. He knew his new reality was a bitch-bastard that would be waiting for him tomorrow whether he woke with a hangover or not. He opted for a hangover.

Too many JD's later Hugh watched a couple of women enter the Old Tavern. They took a booth on the wall adjacent to Hugh, where it was easy for him to discretely observe them. There was nothing remarkable about the couple; two people happy in each other's company, holding hands, sharing a meal, conversation, the intimacy of a quick kiss in a restaurant. Two people who looked in love. Two lesbians. And Hugh's journey down his one-way street reached its destination: a dead end road where Hate lived. Hugh didn't know which house, but he had the address.

Something stirred deep inside Hugh Mann. Something ugly.

Chapter Nineteen

Hugh got home too late to tell Laura about the meeting with Sally, whose advice he followed by taking the next day off to come to terms with the situation. Over a late breakfast, a hangover and Laura for company, he told her he was being let go by the company.

"Can they do that; let you go just like that after all the years you've given them?"

"In business loyalty tends to follow the money and right now I'm a negative 2for."

"What's a 2for?"

"Sally says they can hire two rookies for my salary, give them each near enough my target, thereby getting 2 for the price of one. Plus, they're younger, smarter, I'm an old dog with no new tricks."

"I did see you struggling with a revolving door when we were out last week." Hugh didn't have any time to be confused because Laura immediately burst out laughing at her own joke. He loved watching her laugh, loved how the happy side of the road was her default position, thanked the heavens Amber had the same characteristic. She came round to him, wrapped her arms around him, said, "They're all wrong, you'll show them." She took a step back, looked at him earnestly, "And I guess today's a good day for you to put up the shelves in the garage." She smiled wickedly as his face dropped. "I'm joking, go out, take some time to clear your head, the shelves can wait, what's another day on the past 6 months."

"Thought I might get the racer out, go for a ride."

"Good idea."

"And you're not worried about me getting another job, about money coming in?"

"Maybe a little but I know you'll get another job, with your experience and contacts, you'll get a lot of offers."

Chapter Twenty

Alvin Schwartz was a big lumpy man, standing nearly two meters in his socks. His was the appearance of chiseled boulders left to weather on the steppes of Russia for a thousand years. He worked in the warehouse for a big home improvement store and always went to work in his overalls, wearing his hard hat and workman's gloves. Alvin Schwartz had a secret; five beautifully manicured painted nails on his left hand and the most lustrous shoulder length auburn hair imaginable. If pushed, Alvin would describe himself as non-binary, someone whose gender identity is not exclusively male or female. For Alvin the label was for the benefit of others, he didn't like something that described him in terms of what he wasn't. He didn't want a label, he just wanted to be. He understood why people wanted other gender identifiers to be recognized, to broaden the norm to all-inclusive as opposed to the prevailing 1/0 binary exclusive. But he dreamed of a time when identifiers weren't necessary, beyond personal wishes, because it simply wouldn't matter anymore.

Alvin lived a life of quiet solitude, expressing himself in poems that no one read, and inner monologues narrating the industry of the ants in the extraordinary ant farm housed in his spare bedroom. A recent rent increase had forced a change that he was apprehensively looking forward to. Alvin had taken a weekend job as a waiter to cover the extra rent money needed. It was at a restaurant where he could dress and be how he wanted to be. Hence, the apprehension.

Alvin was sitting on a pallet in the far corner of the warehouse, his usual spot for eating lunch because it meant he could eat alone with his gloves off. A teenage girl approached, looking from a scrap of paper she held to the article numbers on the storage shelves. Spying Alvin, she walked straight over.

"Excuse me, could you help me...Wow!" She had seen Alvin's nails. She squatted to be level with Alvin, stuck her hand out and said, "Hi, I'm Amber, may I see your nails?"

Alvin put down his half-eaten sandwich and let the girl look at the nails on his left hand. Each nail had a highly detailed ant painted on it. They were in different poses in different outfits, one had a spade, one a pneumatic drill, another lifted weights, one wore swimming trunks, and one wore a crown. The ants and their outfits were multi-colored, while the background on all was a high gloss cream. Alvin painted them himself using a magnifying glass and a steady right hand.

"This could be the coolest thing I have ever seen." Alvin was experiencing a new feeling, that of someone who was seeing beyond his lumpen features, seeing something beautiful about him, something of him that had nothing to do with accepted norms of classical beauty.

"The real ants are far more impressive," said Alvin.

"You have these ants, like in a comic strip or something," said Amber, still admiring each nail.

"No, the real ones look like normal everyday ants, but they do extraordinary things."

"Oh, I know all about ants, we had to do a project on them for biology." Alvin had noticed a white pin badge the girl was wearing.

"What's that pin for, I've never seen a plain white one before?"

"Well, I wanted to put 'no labels' on it but then that would have been a label, so this is it until I find a better solution."

Alvin Schwartz felt as though he'd found a kindred spirit and somehow it removed his apprehension about his new job at the restaurant. He put his sandwich down and asked the girl what she was looking for.

"A frame to go around a poster that looks exactly like this pin." Alvin helped her find the frame and for the rest of the week was a happier person as a result of this chance encounter.

Chapter Twenty-One

The week had not been kind to Hugh, unless friends and former colleagues sidestepping the hole he'd fallen into was considered kindness. Three lunches, six coffee catchups, nine meetings in all that could be summed up in six words: too old, too expensive, too bad. Laura remained optimistic, told Hugh it was too soon to reach any conclusions.

It was Friday evening and Hugh was determined to put work thoughts out of his head for the weekend, starting tonight, pizza night. He was 2 glasses into a bottle of red, the perfect buzz on an empty stomach, Amber and Mich were upstairs, Laura, having made the dough and sauce, supped on her first glass while chatting with her Mom on the phone.

Hugh dropped a pizza which started the ruination of their last ever pizza night. He'd never dropped a pizza before but then he'd never seen his daughter holding another girl's hand as they skipped down the stairs. Timing. The bitch-bastard that had him as man out of time for his job, now had him passing the stairs holding hot pizza as Amber and Mich, their laughter preceding them, came down the stairs holding hands. They let go of each other's hands before they knew Hugh had seen, too late, the pizza was already airborne.

Hugh said nothing, played it cool, apart from the pizza splattered all over the floor. Post pizza clear-up he was determined not to make any comments, frankly not trusting himself to say anything that wouldn't offend someone. Laura hadn't seen anything and no doubt if she had, would have said there was nothing to see. Hugh sought refuge in red wine. The more he drank the more he got upset with himself because he could see how nervous he was making the girls feel, because he knew he was the problem, and in his heart of hearts he didn't believe he was wrong.

Rarely has more alcohol on top of too much already ever been a good solution to anything, but Hugh gave it a go. The result was a brutally cringe inducing attempt by Hugh to demonstrate his mastery of the gender spectrum.

"Cisgender is where it all starts and I...I am cisgen which means I'm an ally and thus a bender," said Hugh.

"Dad, stop. Please."

"It's OK Amber, I have studied, and I know, for example, gender fluid means it's raining, no wait, sorry, it means something is leaking."

"OK mister, your dance with the red wine is finished for tonight. Let's get you upstairs, I'm sure Amber and Mich will see clearing up a small price to pay for putting an end to your very special lecture."

"Anything you want Mom."

Mich offered a pained smile.

Hugh woke with a hangover for the second time in five days.

"Please tell me I didn't say gender fluid means it's raining."

Laura needed a while to finish laughing before enlightening Hugh on the full extent of his performance the night before.

"You know why though, right?"

"Too much red wine," said Laura.

"No, well yes, but there was too much red wine because I saw Amber and Mich holding hands, I think they're an item."

"I know."

"She told you?"

"No. I think she wanted to tell us both after the Parade. We know how that went."

"So we just accept it?" said Hugh.

"Yes, I think we do. It is the choice of our daughter," said Laura making her way to the bathroom.

Laura returned robed from the bathroom, "And there's nothing wrong with her choice Hugh." It wasn't a question. Laura went downstairs to make breakfast. Hugh hid under the covers. It was no good, his thoughts found him, whispered their simple words; boy, girl, pink, blue, marriage, making babies, making grandchildren. Simple words for a simpler world.

Chapter Twenty-Two

Laura did everything she could to convince Hugh going to Proud for dinner was not a good idea. Even Amber, who had been so excited to go, was fine to give it a pass.

"Mich can't make it anyway, we can go another time, you know, when you're...better," said Amber.

"Better? I'm not sick. Look we all know I am not finding it easy to adjust my views, but I don't think avoiding the issue is going to help, and if I'm going to understand the queer community, it will be better with all of you there. So, please tell Mich to join us if she can, and I promise not to embarrass anyone."

Amber really wanted to go and didn't need any more persuading, she went upstairs to update Mich. Laura remained unconvinced.

"You saw your daughter holding hands with her girlfriend for a split second and the only way you could deal with it was to get drunk and spout rubbish about gender definitions."

"I was caught unawares, tonight I'll be prepared and no more than two glasses of wine, three tops."

"I just think it would be easier if you took some time to process the fact our daughter is not conforming to the norms you, me as well, expected. I don't know what her label is, maybe she doesn't and that's OK. Nothing, for any of us, needs to be rushed, we need to arrive at a good place, as a family on the same page. And going to a queer restaurant after last night's antics definitely qualifies as rushing."

"I'll tell you how I've been processing Madam Psychiatrist but it's going to cost you a cappuccino."

Laura set up the machine to make them two cappuccinos which they now sat in the garden drinking.

"We have this thing about rites of passage into adulthood and I was thinking it doesn't stop there. It also happens from adulthood into older adulthood. I think the first indicator is when you recognize you're starting to sound like your own parents. You know a cliche about how music was better when you were younger, it all sounds the same now. It's true but it has nothing to do with the quality of the music, its only timing, the younger generations must have their own music, their own fashions. The topics were the same, it was us people that were shifting as we moved along the age groups. This gender topic is so unlike anything before it, ze/zir, they/them, ve/ver, non-binary, gender fluid. Can you imagine explaining this to our Dad's?"

"Why bring our Dad's into it, you are more than enough," said Laura as she spooned some cappuccino froth into her mouth. Hugh smiled ruefully.

"Fair point. This isn't about seeing round the bend, it's like suddenly there's this mountain in front of me blocking out the sun, I have no idea how to climb it, but until I do, I'm not going to see daylight again."

"And going to the restaurant tonight is about helping you climb the mountain?" said Laura.

"I don't agree we have the time you think we do. Feels like the opposite to me."

"Fine, we'll go, just don't mess it up."

Chapter Twenty-Three

Alvin was not having a good night. He had never been in a public place as himself and he liked it that way. The restaurant had a relaxed uniform policy; bare arms were OK, shorts were OK but no hot pants, which didn't matter because servers had to wear a rainbow half-apron, and no heels. Alvin wore a kaftan cinched at the waist by the apron, Reebok hi-tops were hidden by the kaftan. The ensemble below Alvin's head might as well have been invisible because for the first time in his adult life Alvin Schwartz had let his hair down in public. It was magnificent. The more people looked the more self-conscious Alvin felt. If only he didn't immediately feel judged he would have seen people only gazed with admiration. Instead, Alvin worried his make-up only served to highlight his ugliness, an ugliness that was only in his head and nowhere else. He was making his way to the bathroom to remove his make-up when someone called his name.

It was the girl who he helped find the frame, Amber. She was waving him over.
"Hey Alvin, so you work here too?" said Amber.
"First night."
"Cool kaftan," said Mich.
"Show them your fingernails," said Amber.
Alvin showed his ant-painted nails, which Mich and Laura thought were as amazing as Amber had. Hugh grunted a 'very nice' then feigned studying the menu. Hugh had been studying the menu ever since they arrived 15 minutes ago. The food was standard steakhouse fare and nothing that needed studying, except that it was a way for Hugh to avoid focusing on anything else in his immediate surroundings.

As the maître d' showed them to their table Hugh realized with a sinking feeling how wise Laura had been to suggest they postpone their visit to Proud. The restaurant and its inhabitants were like a mini-Parade for Hugh, the decor was colorful and extravagant, as were the people, there was a distinct lack of button-down oxford shirts and pressed jeans, apart from the ones Hugh was wearing. And that was Hugh's problem, he was the odd one out. He knew they had come to a queer restaurant but still, how could it be so different, why did he feel that he was amongst a different species? Gender fluid couldn't be more accurate. He couldn't tell men from women, couldn't tell if someone had been a woman and was now a man and vice versa. He didn't know why it mattered to him, just that it did. There were men, who were clearly men, but they wore eyeliner. What did that make them? Because men didn't wear eyeliner in Hugh's world. There were so many variations. No, wrong word. There were so many deviations from what was normal, Hugh felt like a 16-bit computer trying to compute algorithms designed for a quantum computer. Hugh actually laughed to himself, a quantum computer used qubits, qubits that could do something called quantum superposition, which meant quantum states could be added together and always create another valid quantum state. Hugh felt the irony of his analogy in two ways, (1) Always creating valid states, like valid gender identities, (2) It was quite a high-end analogy, not something an old duffer like him should be thinking up, if the job market was any indicator.

"Sir, what can I get you...Sir?" said Alvin.

"Huh," said Hugh looking up, thinking, *'and now Quasimodo's cousin, who's taking our order, has more in common with my daughter than me.'* Hugh didn't realize how wrong and mistaken this thought was. The insult to Alvin was obviously wrong and the idea that Alvin had more in common with Amber was wildly misjudged. There was a path where Alvin and Amber could be friends, based on their shared feelings towards identity, call it Amber's developing white flag view but that was only one facet of Amber, 16 year old teenager with so much life to live. Twenty-nine year old Alvin, with his poems and ant farm, needed the love and comfort of the wider queer community, if he would ever let them in. Amber was a Mann, shared DNA, family memories, she was as much her father's daughter as her mother's. And like her mother she didn't stay angry with anyone for long, her Dad could be grumpy, a bit boring, like most parents, but she never doubted he loved her. It was for a simple reason that Amber, until now, had felt the unequivocal love of her Dad; the way he looked at her Mom. She had made him explain it to her once. She noticed that he would often look at Mom and smile to himself, saying nothing.

"Why do you do that Dad?" asked 14 year old Amber.

"What's that sweetie?"

"Smile at Mom like that when she's not looking?"

They were doing a spot of family gardening, which meant Mom doing most of the work, Dad mowing the lawn and Amber on weed duty.

Hugh gave his daughter a smile like the one he had just made as he watched his wife, wearing a head scarf, sleeveless shirt, old Capri paints and flip flops, wipe her brow, blow a strand of hair from her face, looking as beautiful as he'd ever seen her.

"You notice things don't you." He poured them each a drink from the pitcher of iced water on the garden table.

"I'll tell you why if you promise never to tell your Mom. Promise?"

"Cross my heart," said Amber, making a cross sign over her heart.

"Treasure. There are these little things your Mom does that are my treasures. Little moments that give my heart a squeeze all the time."

"How many are there?"

"Hundreds."

"Nah, name three."

"Ok. One, that she can look so good in gardening clothes, two, the way she greets us in the morning, three, the way she talks to you." Amber wasn't fully satisfied.

"And do you have any treasures from me?"

"More. I've only known your mother as an adult, I've known you since you were a diaper pooping rugrat to the smelly teenager you are now." Amber managed a good punch to Hugh's arm, another trait from her Mom.

"Tell me some."

"I can't do that, they wouldn't be treasures if I told you." Seeing the look of disappointment on his daughter's face, Hugh decided it was time to share his wisdom on relationships.

"You're a teenager, I think you're ready for the Rules to Relationships." Amber rolled her eyes.

"Not a ten point list from one of your many self-help books."

"A three point list of pure gold from yours truly but I'm wondering if you can really handle such wisdom."

"Dad, just tell me."

"Rule 1, find someone who makes you laugh and that you can laugh with, Rule 2, find someone whose company you can enjoy on Monday nights."

"And why only Monday nights?"

"It's the most boring night of the week, if you can do Monday's the rest will take care of themselves. Rule 3, find someone you can be quiet with, which is not as easy as it sounds. Comfortable in silence with someone is a real sign a relationship could go the distance."

"And what about maybe finding the person attractive?"

Hugh brushed Amber's fringe away from her eyes, "If you've found someone that works for Rules 1 to 3, chances are you're with the most beautiful person YOU will ever meet."

While Hugh enjoyed seeing so much of Laura in Amber he quite often missed what she had from him. Like the way she was already observing him observing Laura before she asked him why. How she really thought about his three relationship rules, how she sometimes knew when he smiled to himself at something she did, thinking she hadn't seen. How his daughter started filling her own treasure chest with priceless mundane moments of their family life. How one of her greatest treasures was seeing how much her Dad enjoyed her Mom in almost everything she did. Hugh would never know that all Amber would ever want from a relationship is what she saw in her Dad's eyes when he looked at her Mom.

The Hugh Mann that could give his teenage daughter relationship advice that would last a lifetime, was decidedly absent from the restaurant that night. Instead, a man lost at sea, looking into the present with eyes from the past, didn't see the glory of Proud, a place where color was everywhere and nowhere, a place where there was no reference to old norms of identity, just identity as whatever a person wanted it to mean. Everything that Hugh found wrong with Proud was crystallized in Alvin, their waiter. Alvin, who impressed his daughter and Mich with his painted nails, who laughed with Laura as he tossed his impossibly beautiful hair. Alvin, who simply looked utterly ridiculous to Hugh.

Alvin lingered because Amber and her family were like a lifeboat for him, helping him realize he could stay afloat in this place as himself. Maybe people staring at him was all in is head. Amber's Mom was lovely. She sensed his nervousness and while her husband took an age to choose from the menu, told him the disaster of her first waitressing summer job when she was a student, and when her husband still hadn't made a choice, ordered for him.

Alvin left with their order as an impromptu pseudo-Karaoke broke out to the latest track spun by the Saturday night DJ. The girls half danced in their seats, laughing at their own uselessness until Laura showed them what stiffness really looked like.

"Come on honey, bust a move, that's what the cool kids say, right Amber?"

"Mom, cool kids have never said bust a move."

Hugh was saved by Alvin returning with their drinks. Once Alvin had served the drinks he said, "I'll be right back with your food and here," he took a nail polish from his apron and gave it to Amber, "This is the base I use, try it, you can paint or stick whatever you want on top."

"Thanks Alvin, we'll come by your store next week, show you our masterpieces," said Amber.

"I'd like that, message me and I'll bring extra sandwiches."

"Cool, tag me," said Mich doing something on her cell, Alvin did likewise and in about 3 seconds Alvin and the girls were connected.

Hugh observed all of this silently while inside his common sense exploded in a fit of righteous indignation. As Alvin was about to leave Hugh said, "Alvin is it..?"

"Yes, can I get you anything sir," said Alvin happy to make contact with Amber's Dad.

"Why..."

"Hugh, your question can keep until Alvin brings the food," said Laura diplomatically cutting him off, anticipating Hugh was going to be anything but diplomatic.

"Sure thing," said Alvin taking his leave.

"Hugh, were you about to break your promise not to embarrass anyone?" said Laura in mock admonishment.

The irony of Hugh ignoring Laura's question was that he fully intended to break his promise. Maybe it was the explosions going off in his head that made him deaf.

"I'm going to use the men's room before the food arrives."

"Hurry back or you'll miss the show," said Laura as the next pseudo-Karaoke got underway.

The men's room was down a passage that went past the kitchen entrance. Hugh waited until Alvin came out of the kitchen.

"Hey Alvin, what's your game?"

Alvin spun round, no easy feat as he was balancing three loaded plates, to find Hugh glaring at him with hate-filled eyes.

"Sir, game, there's no game."

"Yeah there is," said Hugh stepping towards Alvin.

"The game is freak-man befriends normal family." Hugh emphasized each word with a poke to Alvin's chest, for the final word he added a flourish by flicking Alvin's hair. Alvin threw a hand up trying to stop Hugh touching his hair, resulting in him throwing food all over himself, plates smashing as cutlery clattered to the floor. The commotion drew the attention of the whole restaurant as the music stopped. The only person unaware of the attention was Hugh. But everyone in that restaurant recognized Hugh, they knew what prejudice looked like, they had all seen it, many had felt it in the blows and kicks from the 'Hugh Mann's' that had been kind enough to offer special commentary on their personal life choices. Hugh didn't see Laura hurriedly shuffle the girls out of the restaurant, giving the Matre'd everything she had in her wallet as she passed. He definitely didn't see the shock on Amber and Mich's faces as they left holding each other's hands tightly.

Staff members escorted Hugh out of the restaurant. He found Laura and the girls waiting in the car. The silence on the drive home was deafening.

Chapter Twenty-Four

The restaurant manager took it upon herself to apologize to Alvin for Hugh's behavior. She meant it too. Not because she felt any ownership for the brutish thuggery of Hugh's behavior, simply because she was angry the hate existed in the first place and saddened that it had found its way into her restaurant. She gave Alvin the rest of the night off.

Alvin cleaned himself up as best he could and rushed home. When Alvin realized the twenty minute walk had already taken thirty minutes he knew he had made a mistake; down-town on a Saturday night was no place for Alvin, with his hair down and make-up still on, he hadn't even changed out of the kaftan. It wasn't only Hugh's actions; it was the contrariness of Hugh to his family that had him so confused. It would have been easier for Alvin if the whole family had been similar, but that he felt such an affinity to Amber who had that man as her father, it wasn't making much sense for Alvin. He began retracing his steps, looked at his cell to route a way home when he heard them.

"Hey faggot, I got a juicy one for you."

"That makes you sound like a faggot dickhead." Laughter from many voices followed the brief exchange. The street was one removed from the main drag. It was deserted of people but lights were on in flats above shops. Alvin turned to face six mini–Hugh Mann's. Early to mid-twenties, preppy-style, smart enough to know better, drunk enough not to care.

"Your kind should stay in the queer district," said dickhead 1

"Yeah bad enough you even got that place," said dickhead 2

"I don't want any trouble, I just want to get home," said Alvin.

"No problem *ma'am*. No, actually there is a problem because we want to give you trouble, the kind of trouble that means you will never make the mistake of bringing your ugly faggot ass to this part of town again," said dickhead 1, dickheads 2-5 providing the laughter soundtrack.

A calmness settled over Alvin. He knew how this poem ended but at least he was himself. He thought of Amber and Mich, they had seen him as he was and liked him. He smiled and flicked his hair.

The fight was short and brutal.

Chapter Twenty-Five

The following morning Hugh got the silent treatment from Laura. He knew she'd let fly with both barrels once Amber was out of the house. He had no defense for his actions at the restaurant, he barely understood them himself. Laura went for a morning jog, leaving Hugh to take Amber to soccer practice. Maybe Laura thought it was a good idea to push them together, give them a chance to talk. Hugh wasn't sure talking or acting were either of his strong suits at the moment.

The silence from the night before seemed to have lingered in the car. Hugh had never felt so awkward around his own daughter before, never been in a situation where he was so obviously in the wrong.

"Amber, look, I'm sorry..."

"Dad, you keep saying that, but nothing is changing." Hugh didn't have an answer, she was right.

They drove on in silence, Amber certain she could hear the cogs in her Dad's head grinding away as he searched for something to say. He stopped by a coffee shop.

"I'm going to get a coffee, do you want anything?"

"I'm good."

Hugh was getting out the car when Amber said, "I get that you're struggling with the whole LGBTQ+ topic, I wish you weren't but that doesn't bother me as much as you not seeing me anymore. I'm a part of this group you have a problem with, even if you took it out on Alvin last night, it's really about how you feel towards me."

Hugh hated this moment so much. He felt himself once again at the dead-end of his one-way street, he was at the door of the place where Hate lived, looking through it and seeing his daughter. He wanted to run away and bury his head in the sand, while praying time could slip back 6 years, so he could correct whatever went wrong to make Amber this way. And that was Hugh through the doorway of Hate, into the house where Big Bad lived. It wasn't the feeling of aggressive anger he had towards Alvin, it was as Amber said, a choice he made not to see her for who she was but rather what he wanted her to be.

    Amber saw her Dad look scared, like something terrifying was coming for him. It's not a look a child should ever see on a parent. He mumbled something about getting a coffee and left her in the car. If he hadn't looked so scared she would have been mad at him for having said nothing in response to her comment about not being seen by him. Instead, she felt sorry for him. She checked the time on her cell, decided being late for practice was worth it if she and her Dad could find a way forward. She was getting out of the car when her cell beeped, a message from Mich, *Have you seen the news?* Amber was going to respond when she got to the coffee shop, needing to cross the road first. Mich sent a link which Amber clicked in auto mode. A picture filled her screen with a headline underneath. Amber stopped, as her world tilted, a shift she could not imagine ever resetting. Until that moment Amber had been a young person on the threshold of the grown-up world desperately wishing for round tables where everyone had an equal place. Now the harsh reality of straight edges, sharp corners and hard surfaces stared back at her from her phone. She looked up and saw the architect of this hateful ugliness coming towards her.

    Exiting the coffee shop, Hugh was momentarily surprised to see Amber stopped in the middle of the road looking at him in a way he had never seen before, a way he would never forget. Then everything went into super-slow motion, everything except the truck hurtling towards Amber. Hugh screamed, Amber looked blankly at him, brakes screeched, then Hugh's world went silent save for a dull thud, like a sack of potato's dropped from a first-floor window, a solid, life-ending kind of thud.

Chapter Twenty-Six

LAURA

Hunger woke Laura from a restless sleep, no doubt heavily influenced by sitting against a tree as a place to sleep. There was no reliving of perfect picnic moments or imagined future happiness, just an uncomfortable darkness. She was getting annoyed at the lake, its beautiful reflection of the sky and wooded banks seeming so disrespectful to her ugly sorrow. She was looking for a stone to throw at the lakes' perfect surface when she heard footsteps approaching.

"Come on tiger, let's get you home and fed, throwing stones is rarely a good solution to anything," said Jean offering Laura her hand.

"How did you know I wanted to throw a stone?"

"I know the face you make before the stones fly, even if they're only words."

They were in Laura's kitchen transferring Jean's sandwiches to plates when Laura forcefully pushed her plate away and said, "Sometimes I think family is another word for fighting."

"It most definitely is," said her mother.

"And also laughing, loving, crying, joy, sorrow, happiness, sadness, longing, it's all family."

"I know Mom, but this isn't a Hallmark moment, it's real life and some families have more of one thing than the others. The weeks before the accident it's like the only soundtrack we had at home was disharmony. Hugh and Amber were getting further and further apart, and I couldn't bring them together, only choose a side which was a no-win situation. It was soul destroying."

"A sea is always a sea, whether it is calm or stormy but in the moment you are experiencing the storm it feels like only the storm is real because that's your present." Jean looked at her daughter and, to use her sea analogy, realized the lifebuoy she was throwing was not landing near the woman overboard.

"Did you ever see your father cry?"

"Dad, never. He was a graduate with honors from the crying is for wimps' school of thought," said Laura.

"I believe there would be less fighting and wars in this world if men knew how to cry, instead of bottling up the tears and turning to fists and guns, a good cry would let pressure out of the emotions and allow problems to be re-approached with a clear head and not a hot-head."

"Mom is there a point besides generic man-bashing?"

"I didn't say all men, don't mean all men..." she took a sip of coffee.

"...just those with balls," said Jean.

"Mom!"

"You were 16, steamed up about something, probably your Saturday night curfew and you stormed out the house. It was nothing really, you needed a bit more freedom and your Dad wanted to protect you from everything, he thought the best way was to keep you close as much as possible. He also got one of my analogies, you know, about the butterfly needing to fight its way out of the cocoon to make sure fluid went into its wings so they were strong enough for the butterfly to fly. I remember feeling quite proud of that analogy. He didn't even look up, just said, 'it's still a butterfly and they get squished easily,' and then he carried on banging something with a hammer."

"A hammer, really Mom?"

"I made that bit up, but the rest is true. It's also true that after you stormed out with dramatic door slamming, I found your Dad in the garage a little later tidying up stuff that didn't need tidying. He slapped away the tears when he heard me coming. Before I could say anything he turned and looked at me with these red eyes, wet cheeks and said, 'I don't have words big enough to tell her how much I love her. I know it's my problem that I worry, but she is our beautiful butterfly."

"Mom, I wouldn't have thought it was possible to make me feel more shitty but you managed."

Jean came round to Laura's side of the kitchen island taking her daughters' hands, squeezing them so tight it was painful, her wedding ring digging into the flesh of Laura's hands. Laura tried to pull away, but Jean only squeezed harder.

"This is what family is about, bonds of unity through all circumstances. In this world that offers so much, that all the bright young things want to go and have their experiences in, there is nowhere other than here with you, with this shitty situation that I would rather be." She gave Laura's hands a last squeeze before letting go.

Rubbing her hands, encouraging the circulation to get going, images of her 16 year old self and her father flashing in her mind, Laura saw her Mom staring at her, a sad smile on her face as her tears flowed freely.

"Did you choose a side?" Jean asked.

"Yes. Before you ask, to explain I'd have to go into Amber's room."

They sat either side of the kitchen island eating in silence, Laura staring into a past she would never forget and an immediate future she desperately wanted to avoid. Jean didn't want to make life any more difficult for her daughter than it already was, but she reckoned it better for Laura if she was with her when she went into Amber's room, and better still if there was a purpose besides the bitter-sweet memories held within the walls of her daughters' bedroom.

Jean cleared their plates without Laura seeming to notice the sandwiches were finished.

"Mom did Amber ever speak to you about identity?"

"There was one time she asked me what I thought about gay rights. I told her what your father and I always told you, equality doesn't have borders, equality for some and not others can never be equality. You know what she said?"

"Right on Nana with a high-five," said Laura smiling.

"Exactly. I also told her the time and place of my youth was very different from hers, and it was easier to talk about live and let live when much of what was different, the let live groups, wasn't near to us. Then the cheeky monkey puts on a slow drawl accent and says, *'So you're really jus' a knuckle-draggin' redneck.'* I was about to be mightily offended until I saw the big grin on her face. I used you as our defense, she said she could see first-hand how our attitude to all members of the wider community had developed in her own Mom."

"And what did she say to that?"

Jean needed a moment to find a way to push her words past the image of the memory, her voice thick, she said, "Nothing, she just came up and gave me a big hug, sometimes I think I can still feel it...," Jean tore off a piece of kitchen roll to dab away her tears, "...Her face was right here by my shoulder and she whispered, *'You did good Nana.'"* Laura gave her Mom a tight-lipped smile before taking her own piece of kitchen roll. She went into the lounge returning with a bottle of single malt and two glasses, pouring two fingers into each glass.

The whiskey burned its way down Laura's throat and with it her short-term fear of entering Amber's room.

They stood facing the flag poster and the plain white reverse poster next to it, Laura doing her best to maintain tunnel vision on the posters.

"Mich gave her the LGBTQ+ poster flag for her birthday. As soon as she put up the poster flag, she put up the white one too."

"So, you're saying she was a white supremacist?" said Jean.

"What...no Mom," then Laura saw the smile on her Mom's face and they both laughed. For a moment Laura was lost in admiration for her Mom; only she could make her laugh at this moment, and with a joke about white supremacists.

"Good one Mom," said Laura high-fiving her Mom in honor of Amber's way of recognizing anything funny.

"To be clear, your granddaughter was not a white supremacist, but identity was her big thing. I think Mich and her might have been together but for Amber it wasn't about being gay or not gay, and with all those flags, for some reason she needed this blank poster. See that torn corner there?" said Laura pointing to the top right corner of the blank poster.

"It looks like she took the poster down too fast and ripped the corner a little," said Jean.

"I think she wasn't happy with the blank poster, but I don't know what she wanted to replace it with," said Laura.

"Did you and Amber speak much on this?"

"We had a few conversations, but it was just starting, she was taking the first steps to finding herself, I only wanted her to know I was there for her, that our home was a safe place. I think she was hoping the Parade would be like an opening for whatever it was that she wanted to say."

"Was it?"

"Yes, but she wasn't the only one looking for an opening to say something, though I think Amber had a plan and Hugh, well he had an explosion."

"So, you took Amber's side?"

"In that final week Mom, I'm not sure what I did. Hugh had his reasons, he was flailing around blindfolded in the dark, but he had his reasons, and it seemed like he was about to get the blindfold off and find the light switch, then the accident happened."

"If you knew what was going on with Hugh, why don't you give Mich a call, meet her for a coffee, see if you can get some insight on what Amber was thinking."

"Because seeing her without Amber would be like sticking needles in my eyes, needles that find their way to my heart."

Jean held Laura as the tears and sobs worked through her daughter.

Part IV: HOW? - THE ASTROPHYSICIST

Chapter Twenty-Seven

Gerald gave Hugh the rucksack which contained bottled water, sandwiches, a camping light and some odd-looking biscuits. They had walked a little way from Gerald's office to where a narrow path led into the shadows of the tall trees which covered the mountain.

"I think I hear your guide arriving." There was a rustling from up the path, something was approaching fast, from the cover of the trees burst a flash of golden fur as a jubilant looking golden retriever bounded towards Gerald. The dog sped around him in ever decreasing circles until it stopped, happily panting and rubbing its flanks against Gerald's legs, finally sitting and looking expectantly up at him.

"Not me girl, he's got the treats," said Gerald pointing to Hugh. The dog did a double-take from Gerald to Hugh and then launched into the same process, running around Hugh, rubbing against his legs before sitting in front of him.

"Let me guess, the funny biscuits in the rucksack," said Hugh.

"Better keep them close to hand if you want to keep Charlie happy. Keep her in treats and she'll keep you from getting lost."

Hugh gave Charlie a treat, before pocketing a handful in his trousers. Charlie then backed away from Hugh barking excitedly, stopping at the path, waiting for Hugh to follow. Gerald came and stood close to Hugh.

"Remember the honesty of animals, the mirror of self-reflection doesn't work without honesty and watch Charlie closely, she knows what she's doing." Gerald clapped Hugh on the shoulders, "I hope you find what you're looking for before what you're running from catches up with you."

Chapter Twenty-Eight

AMBER

As Amber followed Mia from the beach through the tall, dense sand grass, she took the chance to ask questions.

"How come you're my Helper, it's not like I know you?"

"Would a drowning woman care who helped her?" said Mia.

"I'm in danger then?"

"You're in danger of asking too many questions too soon." Mia abruptly turned to face Amber, held her hands and squeezed them gently. The sand grass towering over them as sunlight struggled to penetrate the gloom.

"Stop worrying about things you think you need to know, it's the surest way to miss what's most important."

Like a curtain pulled away to reveal an artist's masterpiece they exited the forest of sand grass into a garden of breathtaking beauty. Rainbow colors assaulted Amber's eyes as Mia lead her along a paved path which snaked through the carnival of flora. As they went further inland the sea breeze faded, giving way to a sticky heat accompanied by a warm mist, making Amber feel like she was taking a shower with her clothes on. As they rounded a bend there was a bench set back from the path. Mia took a seat and waited for Amber to join her. Amber couldn't understand why a bench would be here, opposite nothing more than a clump of damp leafy plants when all around was a feast for the eye in this garden sanctuary.

"This seems an odd place for a bench when the pretty stuff is everywhere else."

"Can you imagine a beauty so great that it has to blossom on its own, although transform would be a better word than blossom?" said Mia.

"I can't imagine anything more beautiful than this garden."

Mia pointed at one of the plants.

"Can you see that?"

"I see a lot of leaves," said Amber.

"Look closer, see the not-leaf."

The more Amber looked the more leaves she saw, where there was an abundance of color elsewhere in the garden, here was only green and shadow darkness. A breeze ruffled the leaves and Amber saw what Mia was pointing to; a cocoon hanging from the underside of a leaf. Looking like a leaf folded around itself, the cocoon was the size of Amber's thumb.

"People love the idea of hairy, slug-like caterpillars transforming into beautiful butterflies, but not many really know what goes on inside the cocoon," said Mia as she approached the leaf to inspect the cocoon. Amber joined her.

"The caterpillar releases enzymes that literally digest its own body, its mainly liquid in there which nourishes cells called imaginal disks, from which our fragile beauty grows. Some of the memories from when the butterfly was a caterpillar come through this liquid transformation. While nature's programming is responsible for the transformation, that takes nothing away from the effort required by the caterpillar. She has to make sure she has enough energy for the transformation to be possible. The lives of people are a lot less organized than a caterpillar's, people arrive on the Sea of Eternity from the many situations that lives take and then Helpers, like me, take them from whatever point they are on of their souls' journey." Mia returned to the bench and waited for Amber to join her.

"This whole place is a cocoon for you and your soul. The Sea of Eternity, the beach and this garden are here for you to transform. Like the liquid that transforms the caterpillar, your physical transformation happened in the Sea Of Eternity, your memories are with you but there's so much more to your soul, so much more to happen for your transformation to be complete."

Amber felt like she was waking from a dream but instead of the dream slipping away as the reality of her surroundings took hold the dream persisted in her consciousness; she wasn't waking from the dream, she was waking into the dream, the dream was reality, the dream was truth. And as Amber Mann awoke into the truth of being her soul, as she felt the solidity of this truth its foundations were attacked by boulders that came crashing down in the form of questions, doubt and fear.

"If I was transformed in the Sea of Eternity, even a little, how come I look exactly the same?"

Mia returned her gaze with a smile and simply said, "We tend to fill in the gaps of perception and knowledge with things that we do know. Right now, how you look is like an assumption in math, for now your appearance is the 1 that balances the equation, until you work some more things out and no longer need the assumption. You're in your cocoon, when you're ready to come out, then you'll see what your soul really looks like. Inside the caterpillars cocoon it might look like a gooey mess but the knowledge to fly is already there, it's just a question of time."

This made sense to Amber, if her soul was different to her body, she could understand not shocking the system any more than necessary.

"You said it's a question of time, is there a time limit for this transformation to happen?"

"If you think eternity is a time limit."

"You're saying I'm going to live forever?"

"Souls are eternal. Transformation is not the end, it's just the beginning, as it is for the butterfly, there is a whole life to be lived for an eternal soul."

"Where are all the other souls?"

"Let's go to Sparky's and have some ice-cream." Mia was up and disappearing round a bend in the path before Amber could quiz her further on the ignored question about other souls.

Chapter Twenty-Nine

HUGH

Hugh lost track of time as Charlie led him ever deeper into the mountain forest. The way became gradually steeper until Hugh was virtually climbing, wishing desperately that he had the advantage of the four legs of his guide. The whole time they were in the shade of the forest, with just enough light to allow Hugh to follow Charlie. They were never far from a stream from which Charlie regularly drank. At one point Charlie led Hugh to a place where he could sit and drink from the stream himself. While Hugh took a moment to rest, Charlie sat next to him, licked Hugh's face just once and then lay down resting her head in his lap. It was a peaceful idyllic moment interrupted by Charlie jumping up and growling. Hugh was no expert on dogs, but he knew she sensed danger, though he could neither hear nor see whatever was worrying Charlie.

"What is it girl?" By way of response Charlie bounded off into the forest, leaving Hugh alone in the clearing. It didn't take long for all sounds from Charlie to disappear, leaving Hugh alone in a dark forest with birds chirping high above. Then the birds stopped their song, the forest stilled, an absence of sound and movement. Hugh heard a deep growl followed by something moving quickly through the trees. Branches were ripped from trees as the thing moved towards Hugh. Another growl as it started moving faster. There was no question of fight or flight, the only option was flight, except Hugh was paralyzed with fear. Suddenly Charlie was in the clearing, knocking Hugh to the ground, barking urgently in his face. She ran off, away from whatever was coming for Hugh. Paralysis spell broken, Hugh grabbed the rucksack and sped after Charlie. Chasing Charlie, Hugh had never run so far so fast before in his life. As he took a moment to catch his breath and a drink of water, he realized they had run deeper into the forest, the trees now so dense, the path was coming to a natural end. He thought they would have to turn back, the very thought of which caused his hands to shake, spilling water from the bottle over his face.

Charlie turned on the path and as Hugh followed her around the turn light assaulted him, stabbing at him through the dense foliage. He shielded his eyes letting them adjust to the combination of shadow and light, then followed where he had last seen Charlie.

Hugh couldn't see Charlie, but he could hear her barking beyond the trees. As the light beyond the last line of trees beckoned, Hugh turned and looked back into the darkness of the forest. He knew what he had escaped, and he knew Big Bad had only just begun the hunt.

He came through the last of the forest onto a clear open path, maybe 10 feet wide. Charlie was jumping excitedly, simultaneously sideways and backwards up the path, encouraging Hugh to follow her. Hugh had followed her this far; he wasn't going to stop now. The path hugged the mountainside, a sheer drop on the other side, Hugh knew they were high but only because they were above cloud level and all he could see was a sea of clouds stretching away in all directions. The sun, which was beyond the bend of the path, bathed the clouds in a warm marmalade fuzziness. Ahead the path widened and ended at the entrance to a wooden hut. The hut was built onto the side of the mountain, it's gray weather-distressed wood replicating the mountain's stone color. A slanted roof protected against snow falls and provided cover over a bench and table on the cloud-side outer wall. Two steps lead up to the front door. Charlie sat at the bottom and barked once. The door opened and a woman, late 50's, bright eyes in an open face framed by unkempt hair that Hugh couldn't imagine looking better in any other style, gave Charlie a treat, who immediately disappeared into the hut. The woman started walking towards Hugh, hand outstretched in greeting long before she got to him.

"I'm Lennie Rosenthal and you must be Hugh, Gerald told me you were coming, bringing some big questions with you..."

"Yes..."

"But are you willing to learn? That's my question Hugh. Knowledge doesn't lay in the answers, you know that don't you?"

"Yes..."

"It's in the finding." Lennie put an arm around Hugh's shoulders, like they were old friends.

"Now I have to show you my observatory and my garden, we'll have tea there later. You won't like it. The tea, yes but not the garden." She led him into the hut which was so dark Hugh could barely make out the rustic furniture populating the living area which had a small area sectioned off for cooking. A short hall off the back of the main room had a toilet and what Lennie told Hugh would be his room, on one side, the other had Lennie's larger room. The hall ended at a door that was exactly opposite the front door. They went out down two steps and walked around the curve of the mountain onto an open plateau. To the right of the plateau was Lennie's observatory, a white domed building sitting proudly on a promontory that looked like the edge of the world. The white walls of the observatory intensified the already brilliant sunlight, bleaching all color from a patch of wild grass roughly the size of a tennis court between the observatory and a tall hedge behind which, Hugh assumed, must be Lennie's garden. He could hear Charlie barking excitedly on the other side of the hedge. Beyond the grass, the hedge and the observatory the mountain fell away to what Hugh now thought of as the cloudscape; a sea of misty cloud stretching as far as he could see. The setting sun infusing the cloudscape with a fiery glow.

A steel staircase leads them up to a wide balcony that fronted the upper level of the observatory. A table with a pitcher of iced water and glasses were set in the middle of the open space.

"Shall we," said Lennie as she showed Hugh to a seat and poured the water.

"Not much of a talker are you...", she didn't wait for an answer.

"Never mind, I've enough words for two, maybe more." She paused to drink.

"Gerald said you could help me find...", before Hugh could finish Lennie cut across him.

"What have you lost? You can't find something that isn't lost. On the other hand, you can find something that you weren't looking for?"

"Gerald said he and his acquaintances could help me find the soul of my daughter. Though I'm not so sure if he meant he could really help me find her soul or help me come to terms with her loss."

"But you believe finding her soul is possible, why?" said Lennie.

"I had a connection with her soul. I know it was something real, not something to help me process my grief."

Lennie was quite a moment before saying, "Well, you better tell me all about it then."

When Hugh had finished recounting his vision after the accident, Lennie walked to the railing, joining her, Hugh felt as though he was floating on the clouds.

"I can help you find an answer but only if you're willing to see what can't be seen," said Lennie.

"I'm searching for my dead daughter's soul, so I think that's a yes," said Hugh.

"Are you good with languages?"

"English and a bit of Spanish, languages were never really my thing," said Hugh.

Turning to walk towards the main building, Lennie said, "Well get ready for a crash course in the language of the Universe."

Chapter Thirty

A door on the balcony level took them into the main building. Ambient lighting lit a spiral metal staircase. As they descended Hugh judged the space to be large from the way their footsteps echoed, he couldn't be sure as everything beyond the staircase was in darkness. The staircase took them directly onto a raised circular platform about 10 feet across. At the front of the platform was a control panel full of switches, dials, a keyboard and screen. Hugh's eyes had adjusted to the gloom, and he could make out the general shape of the observatory. Ahead of them was a circular space about the size of half a football field. The walls were straight for about 60 of their 100 feet height before curving to form the domed ceiling. Immediately behind them was a straight wall that bisected the room, which Hugh estimated meant a quarter of the observatory space must be behind the wall, though he couldn't see a way to get into the room from where they were.

Lennie took up position by the control panel and told Hugh to stand to her left and look to the corner where the inner rear wall met the outer curved wall, about the 7 o'clock position assuming Lennie was staring straight ahead to 12 o'clock.

"Are you ready for The Greatest Story Never Told?" asked Lennie. Before Hugh could answer the darkness was pierced by an exploding dot of white light about halfway up the joint of the inner and outer wall.

"That's the First Spark at time zero, the beginning of our Universe," said Lennie.

"You mean the Big Bang," said Hugh.

"Yes, in common parlance but Big Bang doesn't capture the essence of giving birth to the Universe, First

Spark is better. When we have tea ask me why but now concentrate, we literally have billions of years to cover."

Lennie's light show spread across the wall of the cavernous observatory showing the expanding universe. From the corner where Hugh observed the First Spark the Universe spread in 8 segments ending in the adjacent corner, at what would be the 4 o'clock position. Each segment showed the rapidly expanding Universe at a given time and temperature. There were 4 segments leading up to and including a segment showing the Universe at 1 second old, then came 3 minutes, 300,000 years, 1 billion years and finally 15 billion years. Temperatures went from 10 to the power of 32 degrees Kelvin to a mere 3 degrees Kelvin, which is still a mind bogglingly cold -454 degrees Fahrenheit. Apart from the small labels of time and temperature at the top of each segment it was a glorious image of stars, galaxies and nebulae, clusters of beautiful blue-white brilliance that were quite meaningless to anyone who wasn't an expert in related subjects.

"Our observable Universe, with a little help from all manner of telescopes and mathematics. It's the canvas on which the real art is painted," said Lennie as she flicked switches and turned dials on her control panel. Squiggles of different shapes and colors appeared large all over the Universe and then reduced in size to be barely visible.

"What you are seeing are subatomic, elemental and quantum particles. Muons, gluons, quarks, bosons, ions, neutrinos, to name a few. There's a beautiful symmetry in that to better understand the vastness of our Universe, of everything in it, we must study things that are so small, that a strand of human hair would seem like Mount Everest next to a quantum particle."

Hugh felt that while he could follow what amounted to a very impressive presentation, showing things of unimaginably large and small scale, once outside the observatory an ant would be small and a mountain big, close would be anything less than 1 hours' drive away and far would be anything longer than a 3 hour flight. The majesty and mystery of everything Lennie was showing him, while valuable for scientific endeavor was of little relevance to the average person, and he was beginning to fear Lennie wanted to offer an alternative answer, one that would ask him to accept finding Amber's soul in a specific place would not be possible.

Lennie pressed more buttons, each press resulting in a single vivid red letter appearing spaced equidistant at the top of the Universe. The red letters in order were G, H, D. Hugh thought he actually knew what the letters meant and was eager to show that he had something to bring to the party.

"God, Heaven, Devil. G, H and D," said Hugh.

"A reasonable guess," said Lennie.

"So not right?" asked Hugh.

"It's a puzzle of sorts and perhaps the answer is more interesting to you than everything else I've shown you. I'll tell you this much, G is broken, H is the reason and D is helping fix things."

Hugh was perplexed and worried that he would need to develop some knowledge of astrophysics if his time spent with Lennie was going to be of any benefit.

"You needn't worry about this puzzle, I'll explain it tomorrow. Let's have some tea in the garden and I'll show you your real puzzle," said Lennie as she started to go towards the stairs. With the main chamber now relatively well-lit Hugh could see a door in the rear wall next to where the First Spark was fizzing away on the wall.

"Why don't we use that door?" said Hugh.

"It doesn't lead anywhere," said Lennie.

"A door that goes nowhere in this place, that doesn't seem right?"

"That's surprisingly accurate and trust me, you can't handle Nowhere," said Lennie as she turned and went up the stairs.

Hugh was alone with the Universe. With its 15 billion year history spread all around him, showing the majesty of galaxies, swirling nebula's and exploding stars, he was drawn to the First Spark, and he noticed it wasn't fully in the Universe room. A part of the First Spark was hidden behind the wall and in what Hugh now knew was the Nowhere room. Hugh heard a door close, looked up and saw that Lennie had left the Universe room. It took Hugh but an instant to decide he was going Nowhere. Hugh stood in front of the door leading to the Nowhere room, the First Spark fizzing away beside him, he grasped door handle and found it locked, not even the slightest movement, no matter how hard he turned the handle. Hugh accepted he wasn't going Nowhere today and went to meet Lennie in the garden for tea.

Chapter Thirty-One

They entered the garden through a wooden gate built into the tall hedge that defined the borders of the garden. The observatory balcony was located in a way to give an endless uninterrupted view across the cloudscape and little else. Hence, Hugh had not even tried to see into the garden. If he had perhaps its breathtaking beauty upon entering would not have come as such a shock to him. A lush emerald green lawn carpeted an area about the size of a tennis court. Beds full of exotic flowers and plants bordered the lawn on three sides, leaving the cliff-side open to the cloudscape. They were standing on a 15 foot wide graveled semi-circle area opposite the cloudscape at the other end of the garden. A fire-pit surrounded by roughhewn logs for seats and makeshift tables was in the center of the graveled area. There was a distant sound of running water, though Hugh could not see the source. The garden was more than a visual experience, it communicated an intense feeling to Hugh, as though all his senses combined to create a sense beyond anything he had ever experienced before, he wanted it to last forever, but a split second was all he got. Lennie was leading Hugh across the lawn to the far side of the garden before he could even attempt to process what he was ill-equipped to understand. As they approached the cliff-edge the sound of running water increased. Like the observatory, Hugh felt as though he was standing on the edge of the world. Water gushed from a precipice no more than 10 feet below them, disappearing below the sea of clouds.

"You must have passed the river when you came from Gerald's hut," said Lennie.

"Charlie seemed to follow it to your place. What's it called?"

"The river has its purpose; it doesn't need a name. It nourishes the mountain and takes what needs to be taken to the sea."

"Like all rivers leading to the sea," said Hugh.

"Quite right. All things going to the sea."

"I didn't say things..."

"...I guess you'll be wanting to know about your puzzle now," said Lennie, ignoring Hugh's last comment.

They were sitting on the logs by the fire-pit, Hugh admiring the lawn, which up close was more sumptuous than any lawn he had ever seen, a flawless rectangle of green-bladed perfection.

"My garden is infested with moles. Whenever I get the lawn to this wondrous state without fail moles will visit under cover of darkness and destroy the pristine beauty of my garden. You have to solve the puzzle of the moles."

Hugh could see no evidence of moles present or past, the lawn was as described, pristine. He knew enough about gardening to recognize a uniform lawn; there were no different colors, no uneven mounds, no signs of new soil, this lawn was a single unit, no patches joined up, one perfect whole.

"I cannot see that you ever had anything disturbing the presentation of your lawn," said Hugh.

Lennie abruptly turned to face Hugh.

"Were you not impressed with my Universe demonstration?" she said pointing to the observatory for emphasis.

"Yes..." said Hugh somewhat startled by Lennie's aggressive tone.

"And if someone shows you such wonders, tells you they can help you find the soul of your dead daughter, tells you they have a mole problem, why would you be so arrogant as to look at their garden for three seconds and then say you see no evidence of the problem they have just told you they have?"

"I simply meant I can't see any..."

"You simply spoke without thinking." Lennie stared fiercely at Hugh, daring him to speak. Hugh thought better of saying another word.

Lennie had one more word to say before stomping off. Tapping, not too softly, Hugh's temple with her fingers, "Thiin..kiing!"

She left Hugh standing in the middle of the lawn and exited through a side gate past the flowerbeds on the far side of the garden. Looking at the perfect lawn, Hugh felt his comment had been reasonable, in fact to say anything else would have been silly. A person staring at a calm blue sea would comment on the tranquility of the observed ocean and not unseen waves that might be possible at another time or unseen dangerous sea life lurking below the surface. He felt unfairly reprimanded but atop this mountain he knew he was at the mercy of his hosts' hospitality, and moles or not, if Lennie could help him in his quest for Amber's soul, he would play along with her puzzle.

As Hugh was reconciling with playing along with whatever Lennie required from him, she re-entered the garden carrying what looked like a rolled sleeping bag.

Lennie gave Hugh the sleeping bag and a mat to go under it.

"You'll need these, it gets cold and damp at night. There's a shed outside the gate I just used. In it you'll find everything you need to deal with the moles. Meet me for breakfast on the balcony tomorrow morning."

"I thought I had a room in the hut," said Hugh.

"You do but you won't be using it tonight." Lennie left, going towards the observatory, not waiting for any further comment from Hugh. He was still staring at where she came from when she was again in front of him.

"I don't like un-thinking." She stared deeply into his eyes, then her gaze wandered over the garden before returning onto Hugh.

"Do you understand..." she tapped the side of his head again, "...un-thinking. It's never good and won't help you find your daughter's soul." She walked away a little from Hugh, tamped on the ground with her foot, Hugh assumed flattening an imperceptible mound, then returned, standing so close their noses almost touched.

"You can have any opinion you want so long as you have given it enough of your own critical thinking. Your own, that's very important." With one last tap on the side of his head, she left him in the middle of the garden holding the sleeping bag and the mat.

Hugh found what he needed to make a fire by the shed Lennie had mentioned. He also noted a large padlock on the shed door, with no key in sight. Sitting by the fire, there was a moment when the fading light and the firelight were aligned in their luminosity and it seemed the entire garden was lit for a few precious seconds by the heart of the sun, everything in the garden was a burnt orange that rolled from the garden out onto the infinite expanse of the cloudscape. For a moment Hugh felt peace and unity with his surroundings. Then the sun set, and darkness came. Being awake in the dark was not good for Hugh. Ironically, after all the stars Lennie had shown Hugh in the observatory, the night sky was devoid of any discernible stars. The fire was going out and the darkness was so complete Hugh wasn't sure he could find his way to the shed to get more supplies to keep the fire going. He didn't mind going to sleep, he simply dreaded the time it took him to fall asleep. The time when all thoughts lead to Amber.

Except tonight his dreams had a different destination, Laura. Though his soul would be no less tortured come morning just because his dreams were of what he had lost instead of his guilt.

Chapter Thirty-Two

Much like in Lennie's garden, Hugh is in darkness. A small voice inside Hugh's head reminds him he is dreaming but it's not loud enough to challenge the fear of this loneliness, it's not comforting enough to prevent the pain Hugh feels twisting his insides as the darkness becomes more than darkness, a black hole to nowhere into which Hugh feels himself falling. He desperately wants to get up, but he can't move, he tries to turn away from the hole but feels a force keeping him in place, keeping him face down on Lennie's lawn. Hugh doesn't know if he's dreaming or not now, but it feels real, and he is terrified.

He is about to be swallowed by the black hole when a dot of light appears. Hugh is falling towards the growing brightness, an orange light similar to the one earlier in Lennie's garden. The light overwhelms the darkness and suddenly Hugh is standing in his childhood bedroom, standing by the window as sunlight streams in. He closes his eyes enjoying the warmth on his face, the dancing red-orange colors on the back of his eyelids. It's a Saturday morning, he knows this because of how he feels. For 11 year old Hugh Mann Saturdays were about excitement and adventures, carefree time when the school week was over and there was still another day of weekend before Monday returned. On this Saturday morning looking out over fields to the distant forest, with the warm sun on his face, Hugh felt like he was seeing the whole world. So, when he closed his eyes to better enjoy the moment, Hugh sang. He sang a child's made up song to the Universe, he sang about love for all living things, that he was happy to be alive and grateful to whoever made everything; in that moment the young Hugh Mann felt connected to everything, so much more than he could see with his eyes open.

The darkness returned and Hugh was falling again, except this time he felt an anxious anticipation. The dot of light appeared and once again grew to a brilliant orange light that engulfed the darkness as Hugh fell into it and found himself standing in front of a coffee machine. It was his second day in a new job and while he could remember most of his induction training from the day before, how to get an extra shot in his coffee was not part of the training.

"Some of us have jobs to do," said an irritated voice from behind him.

"I'm sorry, I'm new...," said Hugh turning to see the disappearing form of a woman who stopped momentarily at the entrance to the office kitchen to warn a colleague about the Bozo hogging the coffee machine.

"I was trying to get an extra shot," Hugh half shouted to the departing form of one of his new colleagues.

Hugh's dream time shifted to lunch time the same day. He was leaving the building to grab a sandwich when a woman approached holding out a coffee.

"You're new, I was rude, this is my apology," said the woman as she offered Hugh a take-out coffee.

"Thanks. I'm Hugh, you are?"

"Laura..." She smiled and in his dream Hugh was lost in the memories of so many moments where that smile was all that mattered to him. The love that was in their life together blossomed in an instant in his dream as a complete feeling, like an uber-feeling with all the emotions contained within. He knew there was a better way to express what he was feeling, but like a child on tip-toes desperate to get the good cookies from the top shelf, it remained beyond his grasp and uber-feeling was as good as his mental cookies were going to get. Whatever the label, the feeling overwhelmed him. The sobs came. Gently sobs, at first silently accompanying the happy memories until 'memories' takes on its full meaning of something past, something not to be experienced again and with that finality come the heavy, can't-breathe-sobs, small waves of pain, foreshadowing the inevitable tidal waves.

In the darkness Hugh Mann cried for lives lost, cried because of the feelings that men spend their lives suppressing, cried until the sanctuary of sleep washed over him and took him dreamless to the morning light.

Hugh awoke exhausted.

The lawn was damp yet refreshing and...different. There were four fresh small mounds of earth randomly dug in the garden. Molehills. It made Hugh forget about his dreams and go in search of Lennie, because if the problem of the moles was real then by solving it Hugh could really get some help from Lennie in his search for Amber.

Chapter Thirty-Three

They had breakfast on the balcony. Although the garden wasn't visible from the balcony, Lennie didn't seem to need to see it to know the mole holes were there.

"Told you so. Now you can see your puzzle," said Lennie.

"About the shed, it's locked and I guess you have the key."

Lennie took a key from her pocket and gave it to Hugh.

"You'll find the tools to repair the lawn and whatever you might need to address the problem of the moles. Make sure you understand the nature of the problem before you decide on the appropriate course of action," said Lennie. Hugh was fairly certain a shovel could be used to fix the holes and the moles but decided against sharing this with Lennie.

"About the crying," said Lennie.

"Was it that loud?" asked Hugh.

"I thought it was an interesting approach to dealing with the moles but then I realized it was not a dreadful version of the Pied Piper's fluting but rather a person, you, in a lot of pain. So, tell me, what causes a man to cry so much in the middle of the night?"

Hugh stared at his half empty glass of water, barely able to understand for himself the emotions he had felt. He watched a drop run down the inside of the glass, weaving a solitary path until it merged seamlessly with the rest of the water in the glass. He thought of his crying as the solitary drop of water then remembered the uber-feeling he had had before his emotions overwhelmed him, he realized the whole body of water in the glass was like this uber-feeling and he knew to explain himself to Lennie he needed to talk about the whole. The whole of what Laura means to him.

"I dreamed of my wife and our life together and the memories upset me."

"So why aren't you with her? Why are you on a mountain with me, with plans to go further traipsing over this mountain to speak with more strangers when you could be with this woman who obviously means so much to you," said Lennie.

"Because we are broken and it's my fault."

"Tragedy is a part of the human experience. Not a part anyone wants to experience but the complexities of our existence make it impossible to entirely remove tragedy from our lives. There are parents in a hospital somewhere devastated that their baby was stillborn, a mother in an undeveloped country cries for the food and water she knows her children won't get, a phone rings with news of a family member that will never walk through the front door again, and so much more on scales that make individual deaths seem trivial," said Lennie.

"Death is never trivial," said Hugh.

"Of course not, though the way some people live their lives makes me wonder if they really understand that death is never trivial. Still, that is a topic for another time. I want you to understand that being broken, as you put it, is not unusual, it is a part of the human condition that cannot be avoided, if you are lucky it will happen in a normal sequence."

"How can there be a normal sequence for being broken?" asked Hugh.

"The nature of the human spirit is at least as complex as everything I showed you yesterday in my Universe presentation. On this idea of being broken, let me tell you what a standard sequence might look like," said Lennie as she drained her water glass before continuing.

"As a young adult, say teens to early 20's, you might touch the borders of 'broken' with the death of a grandparent it might be another 30 years before you break fully into the land of 'broken' when you experience the death of a parent, say 5 more years when your other parent dies and now you have resident status in the land of 'broken'. You understand mortality, that you are next in line and confirmation arrives in the form of the beautiful gift of a grandchild. When you hold your grandchild for the first time, closing your eyes losing yourself in that magical newborn smell, with the thrill of the promise of the life to be lived, in that moment the part of you that has taken up residence in the land of 'broken' knows how much of your life has passed, of lives already lost and that you are nearer to the end than the beginning. It's bittersweet, but if we are lucky journey's end will be reached after many steps, baby to child to adult to parent to grandparent, broken is an aspect of life but it is not all there is."

"That is not my life though is it. I have taken a short-cut to this land of 'broken' you speak of and there is nothing bittersweet about it. It is foul and utterly terrible."

"Tragedy. That's where we started. A part of life for which everyone has empathy, and implicit happiness while tragedy continues to avoid them," said Lennie as she stood to leave.

"Come on, let me explain something a little more concrete to you, the Big G and H and D."

Hugh put his hand on Lennie's forearm, indicating she should sit again.

"Laura and I were in our first year of dating, we had a cabin in the woods for a long weekend. On the first morning after something more than breakfast in bed she jumped out of bed and grabbed a wrapped present from her bag and gave it to me. It was a T shirt printed with, 'Sorry, I'm new' on the front. After a morning of love-making my face was a picture to be given this T shirt. It had a meaning connected to the first time we met. The thing is, you had to hear Laura laugh. It would just burst out of her and when it was her joke she didn't, probably couldn't, wait for you to get the joke, while you were still processing she would be laughing, and it was always happy. I know that sounds silly, of course laughter is always happy. But with Laura hearing her laughter was like having your favorite meal from childhood at the perfect moment, it was the feeling it gave me. She wasn't innocently happy, oblivious to sorrows in the world, far from it. There's a saying about people who cry easily, that they're born close to water. Laura was born close to water but she wasn't soft, just very empathetic. Being someone who is by the same analogy born nowhere near water, for the longest time I thought her tears were a suffering, a pain that had to be stopped. I got to understand her ways over time."

"You love your wife, you're telling me about the things you fell in love with," said Lennie.

"To say you love someone is the movie title but it's not the same as watching the movie. I simply enjoyed her all the time, everything about her, every detail of every frame of our movie. Then Amber was born. A friend told me when he held his child for the first time at that very instant, right there in the birthing room, everything changed for him, his whole world became different when he felt the connection to his child."

"And you had the same feeling when you held Amber for the first time. I do understand your loss but if I'm to help there's knowledge I need to impart to you..." said Lennie pointing at Hugh, "...and there's the problem of the moles you must solve before I can give some guidance on the matter of souls," she finished, somewhat impatiently and stood up.

As though she hadn't spoken, Hugh continued, and Lennie resignedly re-took her seat.

"I felt no such thing when I held Amber for the first time. But when I saw Laura holding Amber for the first time, then my world changed."

"Because you saw your newly made family for the first time," said Lennie.

"It was more than that," said Hugh as he could feel connections deep inside of himself being made.

"It was not an easy birth. Laura was in labor for 47 hours, at the end of which she was exhausted, torn, bloody and in pain. Amber was immediately taken to a station in the birthing room for her vitals to be checked and measured. She was swaddled and I was allowed to hold her momentarily while the nurses made Laura a little more comfortable. She was still being cleaned up when they gave Amber to her. It was the greatest thing I have ever seen. Everything is raw in that moment, the physical conditions and the emotions. A mother meeting her child for the first time is a magical moment. When that mother is your partner, that child your daughter, what you feel is beyond what you see," said Hugh as his voice trailed off into a whisper.

"What does that mean, what you feel is beyond what you see?" said Lennie.

Hugh thought back to the uber-feeling he felt last night in the garden.

"You asked me what makes a man cry in the middle of the night, why I'm here with you and not with Laura. For you to understand what I've lost, you needed to know what I had first. Last night in the garden I had a feeling in my dream that was like the moment I saw Laura hold Amber for the first time, a feeling where all emotions coalesce into one uber-feeling, an emotion so intense I wouldn't know how to label it."

Lennie took Hugh's hand in her own, "Understanding powerful forces is something I've dedicated my life to, maybe some of what I've learned can help you."

Chapter Thirty-Four

    Once again inside the observatory, the vastness of the Universe spread across the curving surface, 15 billion years from time zero Big Bang to the exit into what Hugh now knew to be called the Nowhere room, which he was determined to get more details on from Lennie. As before, the Universe was divided into four segments with all manner of atomic, subatomic and quantum particles detailed and equidistant apart were the big red letters, G, H, D.
    "You thought G stood for God and in a way, you are right, but the god of this Universe is Gravity. The principle is the same, a way to explain and understand, bring insight to that which at first seems unknowable. Gravity, all things with mass or energy, be they planets, stars or galaxies are brought toward one another, gravitate as it were. On Earth gravity gives weight to physical objects and on a larger scale the gravitational pull of the moon causes the ocean tides. Newton's law of universal gravitation is serviceable for most applications, but Einstein really knocked it out of the park with his general theory of relativity."
    Hugh yawned. Loudly. It was not subtle. Lennie took the hint with a chuckle.
    "Don't worry I have a point to make and it doesn't involve any need for physics lessons. As I was saying, gravity binds the Universe, keeps the moon spinning round the Earth. Conventional wisdom says gravity would slow things down, so this expanding Universe you have before you, should ultimately start to contract. That's where the H comes in," said Lennie as she pressed a button on her console to make the H pulse a few times.
    "Not H for heaven but perhaps a sainted scientist, Edwin Hubble or to be precise, the telescope named after

him, which sent back the images which have formed the basis for the theory that the expansion of the Universe might be accelerating. I sense your excitement building," said Lennie as she observed Hugh stifle another yawn.

"The D is for dark energy. The Universe, after roughly 7 to 8 billion years of slow retardation, has been accelerating. So dark energy is posited to explain the acceleration, its mass sufficient to explain the acceleration. The clever bit is that while we can't detect it, we can use Einstein's general theory of relativity to explain it. Observations suggest the known Universe is 68% dark energy. To complete the recipe another 27% is dark matter and the rest, which includes you me, Earth our Sun and Moon and everything we can see in the Universe, make up the last 5%."

"I really don't see the relevance or any way that this is helpful," said Hugh.

"You're searching for the soul of your daughter, a soul, something for which the idea is entrenched in how much of humanity thinks, but for which there exists no tangible proof and I've just explained to you that 95% of the Universe is unknown. 95% Hugh Mann. The scientific community has more fundamental questions than answers, and you really don't see any parallels?"

"There could be a place in the Universe where souls exist, in the 95% we don't fully understand, that's what you're saying," said Hugh.

"I'm assuming souls exist within us and I'm saying there could be a way for this to be possible. But before we go into possibilities, it's time for you to deal with the moles."

From the gorgeous cosmic imagery of Lennie's Universe Hugh went to the tool shed to get a shovel to deal with holes and moles.

Chapter Thirty-Five

AMBER

Amber quickly caught up with Mia as she walked along the path, which once again meandered through glorious forest gardens.

"You didn't answer my question about the other souls."

"Just 'be' little one. All your questions will be answered and many that you don't even YET know, but not a single question will be answered before the right time. The time now is for you to just be and enjoy the walk."

Although frustrated at what she considered to be Mia's pseudo Zen wisdom, Amber had little choice but to follow her quietly along the path. The further inland they went the denser the forest became, until they were in a dusky twilight as the canopy from the tall trees blocked the sunlight.

In stark contrast to the vibrancy of the forest garden, the dark forest had a dreary colorlessness that seemed to drain Amber's energy, she was getting slower and colder until she stopped, shivering alone in the dark. Amber was scared but didn't know of what. The dark didn't normally bother her but the knot in her stomach said otherwise. When Amber realized she couldn't see Mia her breathing quickened and she squeezed her eyes shut. Bad move. *She was on a road looking at her phone, looking up, seeing her Dad shouting at her, what did he shout? She couldn't hear over the sound of screeching brakes.*

"Amber, hurry up, you're almost there," called Mia.

Opening her eyes returned Amber to the dark forest, up ahead Mia was standing where a beacon of light shone through the edge of the forest.

Sparky's was a diner with very little spark. A teal painted wooden hut sat in the middle of a dusty open space about the size of a gas station without the pumps, partly in the shadow of a mountain that had remained invisible to Amber until they exited the forest. Whatever was behind Sparky's was in the mountain's shadow, while the apron of dirt in the front basked in bright sunshine coming in over the forest. Benefiting from this sunshine was a pool, the sort found at low-price motels for cooling off in and drinking cheap cocktails while sitting in dirty-white plastic chairs.

"Take a seat by the pool, I'll get us something to drink," said Mia as she went inside the diner.

Sitting by the pool Amber was making a re-assessment of her first impressions of Sparky's. While it lacked a sheen of shininess, everything was clean and decidedly solid. There were no plastic chairs, rather two solid wooden chairs and a matching table.

She sat by the pool and kicked her feet in the cool water, mesmerized by the sunlight playing on the rippling water giving the effect of rents of pure light throughout the pool. Before she knew what she was doing Amber was floating in the pool, eyes closed, cooled by the water and warmed by the sun, she drifted into a dream.

Floating on waves of heat before falling upwards in a never-ending corridor of colors. Something like the northern lights but not expansive, this was a concentrated corridor of warm colorful light. The corridor of light gently deposited her into the Sea of Eternity where she automatically started swimming through the calm sea, the moment feeling utterly blissful until she felt something scratch her. She stopped, treading water as she looked to see what else was in the water with her. Nothing was under or floating in the water near her. She had clearly felt something but could see no mark on her body either. She continued to swim, searching for her perfect moment. Once again the Sea of Eternity warmed and comforted her, closing her eyes she could feel the intense warmth of the color-corridor. Keeping her eyes closed while she swam further, Amber returned to the color-corridor. There was something different, a ragged tear ran down the length of the color corridor, a tear in which there was only emptiness, a black void of...Amber screamed as a hand shot out of the tear, snatching at her face. Panicked, twisting left and right, searching for an enemy that had come from darkness. Vigorously rubbing the water from her eyes, Amber recognized where she was; standing in the pool by Mia's hut, Sparky's Diner. Something wasn't right though. Standing. She was standing in a pool where the water would normally be up to her chin, here it was brushing against a chest she barely recognized.

"Come on out, I've got a towel and the best fruit smoothie you will ever drink," said Mia, standing by the pool holding two large glasses each filled with an explosion of thick foamy color.

Amber gingerly got out of the pool as Mia put a towel around her shoulders and led her back to one of the chairs.

"Who am I?" said Amber, looking at her hands as though she had never seen them before.

"The soul is not a body in the way you know a body to be," said Mia.

"This looks like a body, just not my body." Amber was no longer a 16 year old girl, she was woman in her mid-20's, there was a resemblance to her younger self, but the instant aging was freaking her out.

"Your soul's transformation is influenced by your experiences from before you were here in the Place Between. How you are now is a reaction to something from your past."

Amber remembered how well she felt in the corridor of light, the fear she felt when the hand attacked her, and finally the disappointment she felt for how her Dad was towards her and the person he had shown himself to be. Her Dad was a hateful bigot. She knew with absolute certainty that she was who she was now because she didn't want to be the young girl pushed around by Hugh Mann.

Amber looked at the bluey-green paint gracefully fading all over Sparky's Diner and said, "Can I change my name too?"

Mia had not been exaggerating when she said the smoothie would be the best ever, the explosion of color delivered a tangy sweet citrus flavor unlike anything Amber had ever had. As she slurped her last dregs she asked,

"What's in this?"

"Just fruit the way it should taste. Do you want to know why my place is called Sparky's?"

"Sure."

Mia threw a small clicker remote to Amber, it looked like a garage opener.

"Press the button on the left and watch the front door."

With little fanfare fairy lights sparkled around the door.

"Not very impressive I'll grant you. Can you see the other words on the sign?"

Amber squinted and could make out 'Diorama' in small letters underneath Sparky's Diner.

"Sparky's Diner Diorama?"

"Exactly right and the light show around the door is the Big Bang going off and when we go inside that will be like the Universe, almost 15 billion years expanding from the seating area through the kitchen to the back door."

Amber was starting to wonder if it really was only fruit in the smoothie.

"You don't need to worry, I'm not going to talk to you about the Universe, galaxies, black holes and what not.

We'll have some ice-cream and I'll tell you how souls are made from emotions."

Amber picked up Mia's empty smoothie glass and gave it a sniff before saying, "People die at different ages, have different emotional experiences." Amber walked to the edge of the pool, looked at her dark reflection, as she thought about her Dad and the hand reaching out for her in the dream.

"Most people don't live fairy-tale lives, probably no one, some children have short painful lives, never knowing love and they're dead at 3 years old. How could the emotional experiences from such a life help make a soul, how could..."

"Stop," Mia was standing next to Amber, arm around her shaking shoulders as hot tears rolled down her face and fell into the pool.

"Not everyone has the life they want," sobbed Amber.

"You're trying to see the stars while looking through the wrong end of the telescope. It's normal for a young soul newly arrived in the Place Between. I'm here to help you, get you looking through the right end of the telescope. To start, all I want you to understand is The Places, OK?"

Amber nodded her head like a small child who knows that's what the adult expects while not really knowing why she was nodding in agreement. Recognizing the look, Mia smiled and said, "The Place Before is where you lived with your family, The Place Between is where you are now, where your soul came via the Sea of Eternity when you died. The Place Beyond is where transformed souls go."

Amber didn't look like a teenager anymore but still seemed to think like one as she wiped her eyes and said, "I'm hungry."

"Well, that is good to hear. On the menu we have ice-cream for starters, quantum reality as a main course, all tied together with a piece of string for dessert," said Mia as she dangled what had been her rope bracelet but was now a length of rope with one of her rings tied to the end. The ring gently swayed, twisting back and forth. Somehow it managed to glint in the darkening evening shadows as Amber pondered the knot wrapped tightly around its golden surface.

Chapter Thirty-Six

HUGH

As before, the shed was locked, Hugh had a key, which no doubt would fit the lock, except now the padlock had been replaced by a combination lock. Hugh couldn't understand why Lennie would give him a key to the padlock if she was then going to replace the lock anyway. Was this a part of the puzzle? He examined the lock for a hidden keyhole and finding none went in search of Lennie. It was nearing midday, the heat was high. In the corner shade a table was set with a chair and a pitcher of iced water. It was but a moment for Hugh to be sitting in the chair enjoying a refreshing glass of water. The shade was cool, the waterfall added nature's soundtrack and Hugh felt peaceful, in a moment out of time. Until he saw the molehills. The few seconds' respite was crushed by thoughts of Amber, the help he needed and these blasted molehills that were somehow between him and getting that help from Lennie. His dark mood was interrupted by the sound of distant barking getting closer and louder. Suddenly Charlie burst through the hedge, bounded through the flowerbed, scattering petals, mud and shrubs everywhere, skidding to a halt in the middle of the lawn. She seemed to run in a circle and jump simultaneously, barking joyously as she did. Her barks seemed to be directed at the molehills. She stopped all movement and stared alertly at one of the molehills. Hugh could see the smallest movement of mud on the molehill at which Charlie was staring. Hugh found himself getting excited, was Charlie his secret weapon against the moles? Hadn't Gerald told him to watch Charlie closely? Charlie darted forward, her excitement causing her to totally misjudge the distance to the molehill. She hit it at quite some speed and ended up in a sitting position, front legs splayed either side of the molehill, her head covered in mud, a much bigger mess in the garden and no sign of any moles. Charlie proved to not be a quick or a good learner. She charged to two of the remaining three molehills in an identical fashion to the first, the only difference was her end position, which was a variation of on her backside, each time covered in more mud than the last. For the fourth molehill she took a stealth approach. Hugh could see the mud moving on the molehill, the mole had to be there. He was gripping the table with whitened knuckles, whispering to himself, "Good girl Charlie, you can do this." By all accounts Charlie could. She took what seemed an age to get close to the molehill. Hugh could see Charlie sniff while the mud was still moving. And then Charlie barked, went up on her hind legs and pounced, of all things, like a huge cat, a cat with absolutely no hunting skills whatsoever. With a deep sigh, Hugh let go of the table, sat back in the chair and drank his water, while he watched Charlie, bum in the air, tail wagging, head in the molehill, barking away with the crazy idea that this was the way to catch a mole. He couldn't help but smile as he watched her wagging tail. Then up popped her head, smothered in mud save for her eyes and pink tongue lolling from her jaws. She saw Hugh straight away and bounded over to him. Charlie put her front paws on his leg and licked him before he could move, thus sharing her mud with him. She barked and nudged a water bowl just behind the table. Hugh poured her some water, which she splashed as much as she drank. She then looked up as though she was seeing the molehills for the first time and proceeded to attack them with the same ineffective gusto as before. All Hugh could do was smile and laugh. Between holes two and three Charlie came to Hugh and wouldn't stop barking at him until he joined her in the garden. They ended up playing a sort of chase game around the molehills.

Hugh was muddy, sweaty and very happy; it felt like the most fun he had had in a long time.

Hugh and Charlie both needed a drink. The pitcher was almost empty, so Hugh gave Charlie the last of the water and took the pitcher to the observatory balcony for a top up. As he approached the observatory he noticed a set of stairs he hadn't seen before, mainly because it was a narrow steel spiral staircase painted white, so from straight on they were virtually invisible against the white observatory walls. Assuming it to be a short-cut to the balcony, Hugh went up them. At the top he found a small section of the balcony that was walled off from the area he had been on with Lennie. There was nothing but the tap to fill the jug, which he did. As he turned back to return to the garden Hugh realized from this part of the balcony the garden could be seen. He rested on the wall to the side of the staircase and admired the beauty of the garden, the color of the flowers was magnificent, the waterfall could be heard and the perfect lawn was a total mess, a beautiful mess with a mud-covered dog running around, barking madly, between obliterated molehills doing nothing but making the mess a whole lot worse.

Smiling from ear to ear, Hugh ran down the stairs to join Charlie in the garden and continue in the fun. In his smile was the knowledge that he had the solution to the puzzle of the molehills.

Chapter Thirty-Seven

AMBER

Inside Sparky's was much like any other diner, with red leatherette banquettes either side of pale green Formica tabletops, lots of shiny chrome, and a jukebox adding a distinctly retro vibe. There was a counter, the sort for pies or ice-creams which Mia led Amber past as they went to a booth at the opposite end of the diner.

Sitting opposite Mia, Amber noticed where there would normally be the napkin and ketchup holder, there was instead a children's night-light which had lots of little stars, circles and swirls cut into the cover that shielded the globe shaped lamp inside. Mia pulled the night-light to the center of the table before saying,

"Welcome to the Universe." She pressed another button on her little remote control and the lights in the diner went out. Amber heard Mia fiddling with the night-light before a click heralded a faint whirring and the night-light started slowly turning on its base.

The walls, floor, ceiling and surfaces between were covered in a crude multi-colored light show of the Universe. Amber remembered something similar from her childhood. While the one from her childhood had accompanying soothing music to help her fall asleep, this one had Mia narrating a story that went back to her childhood.

"When you were a newborn baby the potential for your physical development was fully present in you, it simply needed nourishment and time to develop and grow. It is no different with your soul, it's a physical thing that needs time and nourishment to grow. It's just not physical..." Mia lightly pinched Amber's left forearm.

"Ouch."

"...in the way you understand physical. Up to now, that is."

"I'm still no closer to understanding how souls can be made from emotions," said Amber.

"OK, time for some ice-cream. Before I put the lights on I want you to answer one question for me. When you were a newborn baby in the hospital with your parents, and you literally hadn't seen anything, did the moon exist?"

"Huh?"

Mia laughed as she said, "That's not an uncommon answer. What I want you to understand is just because you haven't seen something doesn't mean it does not exist or will not exist, like the moon or the older version of baby Amber or the soul version of baby Amber."

Mia switched off the night-lamp and put the diner's lights back on.

"Come with me to the ice-cream counter," said Mia as she led Amber to the counter at the other end of the diner. Mia went behind the counter, bending down to plug something in before standing up behind a brightly lit frozen ice-cream serving station. Creamy, glossy ice-cream sparkled under brights lights, all shades of brown, vanilla, orange, red, green and even blue. A festival of flavors was on offer from forest fruits to tropical specialties to classic chocolate, strawberry, rocky road or maraschino cherry, to name a few.

"I like to use ice-cream to help explain how souls are made from emotions, because if there's one food that is associated with emotions it's ice-cream, the gold standard for comfort food."

Mia passed Amber a small cone.

"That's you."

"This empty ice-cream cone is me?"

"It represents the you behind the eyes that see, it's the you that's wondering just how crazy I am, it's the you that's wondering which flavor to choose, it's the you that used to respond to all the inputs from your body when you had one. It's all that's left of you and it is all of you, all you need to become your magnificent soul."

"Strawberry," said Amber handing her cone back to Mia.

Mia couldn't help laughing, she had helped many souls and never had one responded to her 'you' speech by simply asking for strawberry ice-cream. As her laughter subsided Mia realized the road Amber was taking would not be an easy one.

"OK, a ball of strawberry it is," said Mia taking a serving scoop from the wet tub.

Mia held the serving scoop with the ball of strawberry ice-cream close to the cone but did not put it in.

"The cone isn't complete. It needs the flavor of experience to become something more, to start the journey towards becoming your soul."

Mia placed the strawberry ice-cream in the cone and gave it to Amber. As Amber tasted the creamy lusciousness an outpouring of joy rippled through her body. Her eyes were closed as she stood inside Sparky's, looking human but her form shimmered ever so slightly as Amber's soul continued its journey of awakening.

After a moment Amber opened her eyes. She felt well but not enlightened, she felt like a patsy for a street magician's trick; it might look like magic, but everyone knew it was a deception.

"As delicious as that was, it tells me nothing about how a soul can be made of emotions," said Amber as she swallowed the last of the cone and the ice-cream.

"Your brain was the physical playground where your consciousness grew, the I that is you. It is where experiences were felt and interpreted. What happened in your brain wasn't a deception, it wasn't merely the organizing of firing synapses and neurons, of electrical impulses in the human computer of your mind. It all breaks down to that which we are made of, the most fundamental building blocks in the entire Universe."

"Which are?" said Amber.

"Which I will tell you about after you've eaten this," said Mia as she handed Amber another cone, this one a light brown ball streaked through with a creamy white ice cream.

"Eyes closed," prompted Mia as Amber took a bite into a fantastically delicious chocolate ice-cream, she hardly finished the first mouthful when she took another bite and...gagged as the taste of fried onions overwhelmed the chocolaty deliciousness. The experience was horrible, and Amber wanted to throw down the ice-cream cone and leave Sparky's, leave Mia, and yet she couldn't even open her eyes. Mia's voice floated to her like the scent of fresh baked bread on a warm breeze,

"Don't resist, let the flavor develop, move forward into the experience, feel the color and intensity of the emotion."

There was a moment of absolute emptiness, as though Amber stood in a black void and then the emotion hit her like a tidal wave, except she was not separate to the feeling, something to be buffeted and blown about, she *was* the feeling. Amber felt herself rushing through the void, vibrant colors of pure energy, elation and euphoria were the starting point for the ever increasing joy she was feeling. The emotion, which was all of these things and more, was forming into something, wrapping around itself, taking a shape as it was becoming something even more powerful. The colors intensified; Amber felt on the verge of...birth into flight. The feeling went as quickly as it came, leaving Amber panting, holding a half-eaten ice-cream in Sparky's Diner.

Chapter Thirty-Eight

HUGH

Hugh played with Charlie in the garden, the two of them combining to be superbly ineffective catchers of moles. Having Hugh to help her put Charlie in a frenzy of doggy happiness. She barked excitedly for Hugh to join her at each hole she stood over, her rear-end in the air, tail furiously wagging, head between her paws on the edge of the hole.

"What is it girl is there a mole in this one?"

Charlie maintained her position, gave one bark, moved her eyes to show Hugh he was expected to enter the hole. Hugh put his arm into the damp hole. He was in as far as the armpit and all he could feel was wet earth. The process was repeated many times at each hole, their lack of success only served to encourage Charlie to run to another hole as though it was the first one she had ever seen. Hugh was a mess of sweat and mud when he finally flopped down in the middle of the garden, exhausted and the happiest he had been since the accident. Charlie approached, did a few on the spot circles before laying down next to him and instantly falling asleep. Hugh put a hand on Charlie's flank, rested his head on the other arm and joined her in the land of nod.

Hugh dreamed he was playing with Charlie and the mole holes. As he lingered between consciousness and sleeping, he recognized the theme of his dream, could still feel the regular rise and fall of Charlie's flank beneath his hand, and assumed he was remembering what he had last done before the oblivion of sleep took hold. He was right, darkness engulfed him as he fell into a deep sleep. And then he was wrong. The darkness was not sleep's unconscious oblivion, it was a mole-hole big enough for Hugh to sit in, eyes wide open with nothing to see. He could feel damp cold earth against his back as he wondered why no light was coming into the cavern from the entrance hole above. He looked up and all he could see was the tiniest pin-prick of light, like a solitary star in a pitch black sky, not bright enough to offer the comfort of any light.

A scraping sound told Hugh he was not alone. Something was standing up. Hugh heard a low guttural breathing followed by the dull thud of approaching footsteps. The thing stopped and sat in front of Hugh; the sounds suggested sitting but he still couldn't see anything. He wanted to stand, to have the option to run, he didn't know where to, but it would be away from whatever was in front of him. He couldn't move, he felt like a weight-lifter, so far beyond his limits, straining to go up, when the weight was crushing him ever downwards.

"You know what you did." The voice, ugly with accusation, fetid breath burning his eyes. Hugh squeezed his eyes shut. A clawed hand grabbed his face, Hugh heard his skin tear, felt the warm flow of blood on his cheeks.

"You can't unsee shame." Hugh squeezed his eyes tighter shut, doing his best to see and feel nothing. Hugh sensed the creatures other hand before his face, he felt the tip of a claw against his forehead, the prick of skin breaking, the pain of a white-hot needle piercing his mind, finding a room Hugh thought was hidden, picking a lock Hugh thought couldn't be picked, opening a door that was never meant to be opened, and two clawed-hands threw Hugh into a memory he desperately wanted to forget.

"You will never squeeze your eyes closed tight enough to unsee what you did."

Hugh was on the street outside the coffee shop. Amber was crossing towards him, she smiled affectionately when she saw him. In that moment he loved her as much as he ever had. He was at fault for the discussions, the arguments and the fights about gender, about LGBTQ+, and yet she was coming to him to make peace. Then she stopped to look at her phone, something she saw horrified her, and when she looked up at him it was with a look that was far more terrifying than anything in the cave of his dreams could ever be. Amber was frozen, repulsed by him, unable to move a centimeter closer to him, Hugh took a step forward on the sidewalk and he saw her flinch, although he was nowhere near her. Something not in the picture was coming, he needed to tell Amber, he shouted her name but in the blink of an eye the scene had changed to some kind of swimming pool. Amber was underwater swimming in a tunnel of multicolored light, it made Hugh think of lava lamps. He was outside the lava lamp area, in murkier water. Amber seemed peaceful, not actually swimming but "floating" under water. He registered something different about her, was she bigger? More likely a trick of his underwater vision. He swam hard towards her, his leading hand breaking through into her area of colored light, and in so doing rousing her. She thrashed in the water, terrified of something. She couldn't see him and then for an eternal second, she did. Instantly she turned and swam away, the fading with her receding form. Hugh couldn't catch her, this dream, like all his dreams since Amber's death, was not his friend.

It was morning when he awoke, the garden abuzz with life and Charlie licking his face in greeting. She was ready to start round 2 with the mole-hills. Again, Hugh felt more exhausted than when we had fallen asleep. He patted Charlie as he replayed his dream-memory. What had Amber seen on her phone? He knew it was Big Bad that had come to him in his dream, unlocked the memory he didn't want to see. At least now he had re-visited how Amber had looked at him, and in the second part of his dream was given confirmation that his desperate need to find Amber was only equaled but her need not to be found. By him.

So, Hugh, preferring to avoid searching for the truth, locked the memory away again and went to find Lennie. He had a solution to the problem of the molehills, and he knew more than ever that he needed her help to find Amber.

Chapter Thirty-Nine

AMBER

"What just happened?"

"That was your soul hitting first gear for about half a second."

They were sitting in a different booth, this one had two jars of different sized marbles where the napkins and ketchups would normally be.

"You said something about fundamental building blocks of the Universe."

Mia reached over for the jar with the larger size marbles. She unscrewed the lid, flipped it over and poured some of the marbles into the upturned lid.

"Do you know what an atom is?"

"It's the smallest part of a chemical element," said Amber.

Mia gave Amber a little round of applause.

"Very good. It's the smallest part of ordinary matter that makes up pure elements, like aluminum, copper, gold, iron, mercury or silver."

She held up one of the marbles.

"If this were an atom, it would take a billion of them stacked on top of each other to be the same height as you."

She quickly opened and emptied out the jar with the smaller marbles in the same fashion.

"If we go subatomic, inside the atom we end up at quarks and electrons."

Mia held up a small and large marble.

"So, we've got a billion of these big ones making up the height of an average person and then we've got a billion of these small ones making up just one of these big ones." Mia smiled. Amber scowled.

"Stuff is small, I get it and it's a billion times a billion, I can do math too."

"Yes you can, but can you do time?" said Mia as she got up and returned to the table with night-lamp. Amber joined her. Mia used her remote to turn the lights off in the diner before turning on the night-light. Once again, the diner was bathed in the crude Universe light show.

"Here we are inside the Universe, sciences, religions, sun gods, sea gods, forest gods, no gods, fingers crossed, and many more ways that people choose to understand the world they live in, all of them are languages of interpretation. Some offer more practically powerful explanations, others more spiritually powerful and some do both, but whatever language you choose to interpret the world, the Universe does not change, it's just how you choose to see it."

"Why do you keep saying world and Universe?"

"By Universe I mean the thing that contains all the matter humankind has some knowledge of, the thing that started with a spark and is roughly 14.5 billion years old. By world, I mean all that any individual experiences in their lives. Make sense?"

"So world means the places I go, people I meet, things I do?"

"And your mental life, the thoughts you have, that's a big part of what you experience."

"Got it. Languages of interpretation. And how does this help me understand souls are made up of emotions?"

"Follow me on two points and one question. Point 1, tiny particles make up all the stuff in the Universe, a Universe of which we have knowledge of roughly 5%. Point 2, you had a little experience of your soul a short while ago, so you can have whatever language of interpretation you want, but the reality of eating some chocolate and onion flavored ice-cream to stimulate the emotions of your soul is something you need to interpret somehow. To help you with that interpretation, here's my question." Mia didn't immediately ask a question, rather she went and stood by the entrance to the diner. When Amber was by her side she said, "The fairy lights around this door represent the first spark, that started the Universe, you can say Creator or God, whatever floats your boat." Mia pointed to the door, "First spark, time zero," she hooked a thumb over her shoulder, "...starts 14.5 billion years of Universe, in this case, Sparky's Diner." Mia opened the door and stepped outside with Amber close behind.

"Question, if the first spark, is time zero, represented by the door we have just stepped through, where and when are we now?"

Chapter Forty

HUGH

Hugh found Lennie sitting at her little table on the observatory balcony overlooking the never-ending cloudscape, a simple breakfast of bread, cheeses, jams and a fresh pot of coffee prepared for two.

"I thought we'd have breakfast on the balcony, the view really is to die for," said Lennie as she went to the balcony railing to look out over the cloudscape. Joining her, Hugh felt energized as he stared out over the fantasy-like sea of endless clouds imbued with veins of orange from the sun shrouded beneath. There was the distant tinkling of water, which he imagined sparkling like diamonds as it chased a path down the mountain.

Seated at the table, around mouthfuls of bread layered with creamy cheese and slurps of coffee, Hugh proceeded to explain his solution to the mole problem, and quickly realized the distance between the sense of an idea and a practical explanation is as great as any between the galaxies Lennie had shown him yesterday.

"Your Universe presentation is beautiful chaos, black holes, exploding super novae, the Milky Way and other galaxies. There might be rules for the theories that help you understand the greater whole but the Universe itself is beyond rules because there is so much that is unknown, at best you can learn to read it, make rules for what you observe, but always with the knowledge the rules might not hold for future events and they apply only to a minuscule amount of the Universe. Your garden is sculpted, structured beauty, but though beautiful, it is not a place for order. It is also about beautiful chaos; the molehills represent that chaos." Hugh sat back feeling like he swung for a home run and had only managed a punt for first base.

Lennie poured them more coffee.

"Flowery words that don't say too much. I heard no solution to the problem of the molehills in my garden, whether you see them as a metaphor for universal chaos or not."

"Quite." said Hugh, who was starting to think making it to second base would be an achievement let alone a home run, before he blurted out, "Charlie is the consciousness and the chaos."

Lennie stopped mid-stir of the 4 sugars she had spooned into her coffee, mouthed a silent repetition of what Hugh had said then finished stirring her coffee. Hugh said not a word more when Lennie finished a lip-smacking last bite of jelly and bread followed by a sip of coffee.

"Chaos or not, you certainly have me confused, are you now blaming Charlie for the molehills?"

"Emotions."

"Is there anything else?" asked Lennie.

Hugh didn't answer because in his mind he had returned to an imagined giant hole beneath a molehill, a dog barked excitedly above and Big Bad sat in darkness across from him, patiently waiting for the inevitable reckoning. Hugh was in the memory of a memory, when, with a clarity he had never felt before, he understood all emotions were relevant, all had their place and with that insight he did what every good coward does, he ran away as fast as he could. Hugh let go of the memory of his dream and returned to the present with Lennie.

"I played with Charlie as she tried and failed to catch the moles. I fell asleep and dreamed I was in a cavernous molehill, above the hole Charlie was barking happily. In the hole I was facing my inner demons..."

"...and did you like it with your demons?" said Lennie, in a not particularly kind way.

"No, it's why they're called demons. But I did realize they have a role to play, like all emotions. Charlie above and me below, like emotions in the Universe of your garden, we were all a necessary part of the garden."

"How necessary?"

"Because there is no solution to the molehills, at least not in terms of fixing them, they are an inevitable part of the garden. Charlie and I were complimenting them, our emotions brought something greater to the garden and it was centered around the molehills." Hugh sat still as Lennie stared intently at him, he didn't fully understand what he had just said but it felt right. There it was again, a clarity of thought that was entirely new to Hugh, it felt like he was looking through a powerful pair of binoculars, everything was up close and in ultra-HD, the only problem being he had no idea what the clear picture was of.

Lennie gave Hugh a curt nod before saying, "It's time to take you to the Nowhere Room," as she gave him a blue rucksack, "bring this."

Chapter Forty-One

The side entrance door to the observatory was the same bright white as the wall it was set in, the reflected sunlight making Hugh's eyes water. So, when Lennie opened the door to reveal a room of darkness, Hugh could not understand why no light was penetrating the dark, not even a centimeter of light went beyond the threshold. It was an absence of light so extreme Hugh couldn't be sure there was a floor, it looked more like empty space.

Lennie walked in and disappeared from sight. After a moment Hugh followed. When Lennie closed the door Hugh instinctively widened his stance to prevent himself from falling over. The darkness was so complete Hugh could not see his hand in front of his face, he felt as though he were in a void in outer space.

"Follow me Hugh Mann."

"How can I if I can't see you?"

"Better," said Lennie, taking his hand as she led him further into the room.

"This is the Nowhere Room. Before we can go into the observatory I have a question for you, can you tell me exactly what time it is?"

Hugh couldn't see his watch, but he knew they had breakfast at just after 9am.

"It's about 10am."

"Wrong."

"I can't see my watch and plus minus 15 minutes, 10am is accurate."

"Your watch can't give you the answer I want," said Lennie as she stopped walking and let go of Hugh's hand.

"What do you see?"

"Nothing..." As the word left his mouth, Hugh saw he was wrong. A small point of light was directly ahead of him. About the size of a dime with hardly any luminescence, it hung in the air about 2 meters high.

"I see the suggestion of light, a dot in the air in front of me."

"*A suggestion of light,* I like that. You've earned yourself a clue. We are in the Nowhere Room, on the other side of a door you can't see is the main observatory chamber. Now can you tell me what time it is?"

Having no intention of getting caught in a Lennie riddle, Hugh walked to the suggestion of light, extended his arm so that the suggestion of light might allow him to read his watch. He stretched in a way that his index finger was pointing at, and close to touching the suggestion of light. Forgetting all about his watch, Hugh was mesmerized by the image of his finger nearly touching the suggestion of light and the infinite blackness between, a long forgotten image of a painting on a ceiling...*The Creation of*...and in an instant he knew what the suggestion of light was, and the time in the Nowhere Room.

"This sad dot of light is the tiniest piece of what you called the First Spark in your Universe presentation. As we are in a room before the main observatory where the Universe presentation begins, we are before time started, therefore there is no time," said Hugh.

By way of answer Lennie said nothing, simply opened the door and walked into the expanding Universe. As Hugh followed her across the floor of the main chamber, the Universe presentation came to glorious colorful life spreading across the walls and domed ceiling.

"I hope you didn't forget the rucksack."

Hugh stopped in his tracks. He had. He rushed back into the Nowhere Room, leaving the blossoming Universe for the void of nothingness. Two steps inside the Nowhere Room and he couldn't see a thing. Hugh turned to the door, light from the Universe stopped at the door. To Hugh it seemed the light went out of the Nowhere Room into the Universe, a one way journey that started with the minuscule *suggestion of light*. Standing in the darkness of the Nowhere Room, looking out into the light of the Universe, Hugh felt his heart explode. It was the only way he could describe the tsunami of emotion that washed over him. He was laughing, crying and then as still as a mountain, feeling at once like the tiniest mote of dust in the Universe and equally a part of a whole so much greater than the Universe, it gave him a sense of well-being that had a name, it flashed in letters of fire in his mind, beautiful, unreadable.

Hugh let out a breath he hadn't realized he was holding and almost immediately started gasping for air. He didn't want to leave this feeling, but he couldn't contain it, he was being overwhelmed and in danger of passing out. Hugh grabbed the rucksack and ran out of the Nowhere Room.

They were sitting in the middle of the observatory floor, the Universe shining magnificently all around them.

"Do you know what just happened to me in that dark room?"

"Yes. There's a lantern in the rucksack, place it between us."

"Can you tell me, because it felt like I was going to die."

"You were. But that power from which you felt danger is the same power that sustains you. It was your soul responding to the language it understands; The First Spark, and what is about to be explained to you. Now light the lantern," said Lennie, pointing to a side-pocket on the rucksack holding a book of matches. Once Hugh had the matches in his hands Lennie turned-off the Universe presentation with a remote. The darkness was absolute until the match sparked to life. The candle flickered before the dance of wax to wick to flame to smoke began.

"You're searching for the soul of your dead daughter, who you saw on a door on a sea in the sky as she died in your arms. You want to know where in the incomprehensible vastness of the Universe might this sea be."

Lennie was lost in the shadows, only her voice reached Hugh as he stared mesmerized into the flame.

"You're searching for 'Where?', when your search should be starting with 'How is such a sea possible?'. What does the candle tell you?"

"It's many things," said Hugh. As he spoke it felt as though pathways of understanding were opening in his mind, and while Lennie had given him a sense of the almost incomprehensible scale of the Universe, it became irrelevant as Hugh understood his personal oneness with the Universe.

"The candle is wax that melts, wick that burns, flame that binds and smoke that dissipates. In turn all this stuff breaks down to your quantum level and is out there in the vastness of space," said Hugh.

"Very good. The next step is to see yourself as the candle, to recognize how the physical material is changed by the elemental flame, how the smoke seems to disappear from the world before our eyes. In death there is a spark of energy that releases the particles that make up your soul.

Hugh felt like Lennie was leading him to a place of great understanding, at the same time he was incredulous and more than a little doubtful.

"Why has this release of the soul never been seen or recorded in any substantive way?" said Hugh.

"The quantum level is not observable by the human eye even with our most powerful microscopes. Scientists have created specialized equipment to contain and work with quantum particles, where observations are inferred from measurements made by detectors. The equipment, known as 'colliders', are massive and not designed to examine quantum activity in humans."

"Observations are inferred, what does that mean? Either something is seen, or it is not seen," said Hugh.

"Scientists are interested in charge and momentum of particles, the detectors in their equipment measure how the particles move inside magnetic fields. You have to remember this is the quantum level, that's a decimal point followed by 16 zeroes and then come the numbers. Quantum particles persist for fractions of a second and travel at light speeds. The scientific investigation of any and all things quantum does not lend itself well to the expiration of human lives. It's simply not feasible to measure the human soul leaving a body when a person dies."

"So, I should take on faith everything you are telling me? I'd expect that from a Priest not a scientist."

"Faith and science are 2 sides of the same coin, the coin being hope. They are languages of interpretation. Individuals choose how they want to interpret the world they live in."

"I would rather something more concrete, you're a scientist, this is your laboratory, and you speak of hope. It doesn't seem robust enough for a scientist."

Lennie gave a little laugh before saying, "I can't give you concrete but maybe wet will suffice. Have you ever heard of the 3 Cup Experiment?"

"No, and please don't tell me it's another puzzle I need to solve."

"I'm going to demonstrate why all systems of belief, be they scientific, religious or let's say, alternative, have equal merit, if not equal power to explain. How they are all languages of hope."

Lennie took the rucksack from Hugh and retrieved three plastic cups and a bottle of water. She lined the cups up between them and filled each half full of water. Lennie blew the candle out, so they were once again sitting in darkness.

"Take this and press the green button," said Lennie, handing Hugh her remote control. Once Hugh had pressed the green button the Universe came to life around them.

"Now for the purposes of our experiment you are the unknown architect of the Universe. People are trying to understand you, and how you did your architecting." Lennie pushed the cup on Hugh's left towards him.

"This cup contains all scientific knowledge to date." She pushed the middle cup towards Hugh.

"This cup contains all of the main religions." She pushed the last cup towards Hugh.

"This cup contains the Unicorn Theory of creation, which says two giant celestial unicorns were playing in the primordial soup of the pre-Universe, and when their horns clashed it made the spark we know as the Big Bang, and the rest is history."

"You're joking right?" said Hugh.

"I'm doing an experiment. Please don't interrupt unless you have something useful to contribute."

"Sorry," said Hugh feeling the sting of Lennie's reprimand.

"We have 3 cups representing Science, Religion and Unicorns. The wetness of the water in each cup represents reality."

"By reality you mean the actual Universe."

"Yes, I mean the wetness of the water represents the reality of the Universe."

"Now comes the practical part of the experiment and I will need you to volunteer to take the readings." She took a pad and pen from the rucksack and gave them to Hugh.

"Are you ready?"

"As I'll ever..." Before Hugh could finish Lennie threw the contents of the scientific cup in his face. As he spluttered and wiped water from his eyes she continued as though nothing had happened.

"Please note down how wet you found the water from the Science cup to be."

"What...," and Hugh had the contents of the Religion cup dripping from his face.

"Please note down how wet you found the water from the Religion cup to be."

"This is not an experi..." Hugh was quickly wiping the contents of the Unicorn cup from his face.

Struggling to hide a smile, Lennie passed Hugh a towel from the rucksack.

"I could have asked you to put your fingers in each cup."

"You don't say," said Hugh as he mopped at the puddles of water surrounding him.

"But I find water in face to be more effective. So, was there a difference in the wetness of any of the systems of belief?"

"Of course not," said Hugh.

Lennie stood with her arms shoulder width apart, palms up and turned on the spot, "The reality of the Universe pre-exists any and all theories known to humans, undoubtedly math offers more insight than unicorns but neither change anything that matters, pun intended, in our Universe."

"How does this help me find Amber's soul?"

"From the candle you have an idea how her soul might have gone to a different place. If you want to find her it seems you would have to make a similar journey."

"But that's exactly my point, I saw her from the road, wherever she is, I saw her, I don't need to die to get to her. I just know I need to talk to her, to explain things."

"I didn't say you have to die, and I didn't say you don't have to die. I told you how a soul could leave a human body, how it could be made of quantum particles and exist in another dimension. What you do with that information is up to you."

Lennie sat back down and looked expectantly at Hugh. Hugh understood the look, he'd seen it many times at school from fresh faced teachers, hoping they were getting through to him and his classmates, penetrating past the only thought that really matters to school kids; when is the bell going to ring? At school Hugh was sadly bell focused, but now he felt he could be a better student.

"Before all the quantum explanation and water in the face you mentioned the language of the soul and my soul responding to it."

Lennie looked pleased with her student as she said, "Can I have the remote back?"

Once Lennie had the remote, she returned them to darkness and started to speak.

"Back in the Nowhere Room you saw the suggestion of light, The First Spark that started the Universe."

Lennie clicked the remote and the First Spark fizzed to life in the corner of the observatory.

"First Spark, Big Bang, God, Creator, call it what you want, what it did was give the building blocks that make up our Universe."

Another click on the remote and the walls of the observatory were filled with muons, gluons, quarks, bosons, ions, neutrinos and all manner of quantum particles. Only a few at first and then their squiggly numbers rapidly replicated until they covered the entire observatory wall's surfaces so densely that Hugh and Lennie were once again in darkness.

"They are everywhere making up everything."

Another click on the remote. Hugh, expecting the Universe presentation, was surprised as an electric blue outline drew itself across the walls. Starting at the first spark it sketched first a single outline and then tendrils of the same electric blue speedily painted in the details. Not until it was complete did Hugh know what he was looking at.

"The human brain," said Lennie.

Another click and brain image was filled with quantum particles.

"Of course, quantum particles are the building blocks of our physical selves, but they are so much more."

The particles started to pulse, a kaleidoscope of colors, as they pulsed some of the particles moved together creating more intense pulsations.

"Emotions are made of quantum particles. Souls are made of emotions. One step up from the raw building blocks of quantum particles, is where you find our human souls."

"Souls...are...emotions," Hugh uttered the words in slow motion before flipping to high speed, "...but how would that even work, we don't all have the same emotional experiences, we die at different ages and a thousand other questions."

Lennie laughed a little before saying, "Most people don't ask detailed questions about the soul, the idea being enough. You have your reasons for asking, but I'm just here to teach you how a soul is possible."

"Then at least tell me why I felt I was going to die before."

"Do you think a human can handle being a soul before its time? If the book of becoming a soul had a thousand pages, you were turning to the first page and it took your breath away, almost fatally. There is nothing more powerful than a human soul."

Chapter Forty-Two

They were once again on the balcony, sitting at the table with the remains of their breakfast.

"I feel like I'm constantly waking from a dream where great things are revealed to me, but the more awake I become the more the revelations slip away from my knowing them."

"The acquisition of knowledge is more than reading facts, it's understanding facts and bringing them together as a greater whole than the individual facts." Lennie stopped to drink her water, put her glass down and stared calmly at Hugh. He was expecting more of her wisdom on knowledge but it was clear for the time being, Lennie was a closed book. Hugh was fit to bust; he had said he felt like he was on the edge of new insights and instead of help from Lennie all he got was some coffee-table wisdom on knowledge. His outburst was stopped before it started by Charlie bounding onto the balcony, knocking the table sideways, causing cups to tip, coffee to spill, as she searched for breakfast crumbs. Her search over, she put her front paws on Hugh's lap as she gave him a slobbery greeting. And finally, Hugh Mann saw the dots Lennie wanted him to join, his binoculars were getting close to focusing on something he could understand.

"The key to the molehill puzzle was emotions, all emotions. Everything you showed me in the observatory about the Universe, the astronomical scale of everything actually comes down to the infinitely small matter of particles." Hugh hit a bump in the road. Lennie continued to stare, offering neither encouragement nor discouragement.

"Two facts...two facts..."

"What is the knowledge from your facts Hugh Mann?"

Fire burned behind Hugh's eyes, forming letters that turned to smoke before he could read them, an endless cycle of flaming letters and vanishing smoke. He felt the tears flow as the word in flames warmed him at his core.

"Souls are made of emotions and emotions are made from quantum particles, particles that existed from before time began," said Hugh from a place that didn't feel like himself.

Lennie smiled and took his hands in hers, "That's enough Hugh, you can work with that." She looked at Hugh with an affection that was as warm as any he had ever seen.

Hugh was happy, he had solved Lennie's puzzles and had started to understand the true nature of a soul. But there was a hole in the whole of what he was learning; what was the word in fiery letters that flared and burned so brightly? The word that made him cry even though he couldn't read it.

Chapter Forty-Three

LAURA

A combination of having had nothing but her Mom's sandwiches to eat, another whiskey for dinner and mental exhaustion, resulted in Laura falling into the welcoming arms of sleep just before 8pm. She dreamed of the lake, much like her late morning visit earlier that day, she was sitting by the tree watching calm water beneath a big sky. She saw movement in the lake, a person swimming away from her to the middle of the lake. She ran to the shore convinced she had to get the swimmers' attention. The swimmer was too far away to hear her. To Laura it seemed her words went up into the big sky, while the swimmer, whom she could no longer see, must have dived beneath the surface, away from her words. She thought of the words she was searching for, unwritten words in a place between, like invisible sounds floating above the surface of the lake.

Laura's dream shifted to memories of Hugh and a game of monopoly with her parents early in their relationship. Hugh's strategy of buying all the cheap properties and as many utilities as possible, because he wanted everyone to be able to afford his accommodation and provide good services, had prompted her father to seriously ask Laura if she thought Hugh was a good prospect as a life partner, when she wasn't getting his point he simply said, *will he contribute to the household income or give it all away?* When Laura refused to take her Dad seriously he found a roundabout way to quiz Hugh about his future plans and was none too pleased with Hugh's general glass is half full, fingers crossed approach to the future.

Like a butterfly flitting between flowers, her dream went from one happy memory of Hugh to the next, kindness, laughter, generosity and safety were all flowers for the butterfly to visit, but every now and then its wings were caught by a thorn, every prick causing an involuntary kick from Laura as she slept deeply. Her Hugh-butterfly was flying towards the most beautiful rose Laura had ever seen when a gust of wind blew it of course, its beautiful wings shredded by thorns upon which it remained trapped.

Part V: WHAT? - THE JIGSAW MAKER

Chapter Forty-Four

Hugh was once again in the mountain forest, rucksack on his back, Charlie happily trotting ahead. Lennie had sensed his confusion as they were saying goodbye. He told her it felt like he had parts of the instructional manual for some magical machine, but he couldn't understand all the pages he had or if any were missing. It was her answer, which was in two parts, that he was now pondering, and it was the distraction of his pondering that allowed him to get lost in the forest of Big Bad.

"I can tell you that the manual for what you call a magical machine has 3 sections, How, What, Why. You have the pages for How because you know How material matter can change and you know souls are matter and you know How emotions energize souls."

"I don't think I know how emotions energize souls."

Lennie had looked at him a while before saying, "Perhaps not but I think you felt it when you saw the word in flames you could not read." Hugh couldn't deny the feeling was overwhelming, was beyond anything he had ever experienced, it made no sense, but he could only say that he felt like exploding in one moment of unbounded joy.

"Do you believe in Santa Claus?"

"Not since I was 6."

"A lot of children around that age start to wonder how reindeer's fly, how a sack can hold enough presents for so many children, how Santa visits all the houses, how he fits down chimney's, especially of the houses that don't have chimneys. Do you know how many of those questioning children worry about the answers to those questions when they're playing with their new toys? You're looking for a soul Hugh Mann, some people will say it's a question of

faith, as a scientist I would tell you it's like trying to see why nature doesn't like straight lines or why water fills spaces completely."

Hugh smiled at the analogy. He understood Lennie wanted him to enjoy the gift of the new knowledge and let the rest of the manual come together.

He realized the forest was quiet, he couldn't see or hear Charlie. It was too quiet.

"Charlie?"

No response. The quiet was broken by the softest of growls followed by the snapping wings of birds taking flight.

'Close your eyes, shut them tight and see what you did.'

Hugh frantically looked around but saw only the empty forest path.

'Do you remember his name?'

"Charlie! Where are you girl?"

A cacophony of angry birds and breaking branches shattered the silence as something heavy moved fast in Hugh's direction.

'Let me come whisper of a fond memory, tell a tale of actions and consequences.'

Whatever was coming would soon be with him. Hugh was as rooted to the spot as any of the tall trees around him. A flash of golden fur about his legs and Charlie's was pulling at his trousers, urging him to follow her. The spell was broken, and Hugh fled behind Charlie, and as he ran after her he could sense the unseen monster slowing.

But Big Bad didn't stop.

Chapter Forty-Five

Hugh didn't have to follow Charlie for long before they left the shade of the forest and stood above a valley of picture-postcard perfection. They were atop a hill of red, orange, yellow and lavender mountain wildflowers which sloped down to a midnight blue lake. Hugh assumed it was a lake, no movement troubled its surface, not a ripple disturbed the reflected glory of the mountains surrounding the valley. The lake was as wide as a football field and as long as two, running across the valley. On the far shore of the lake was a hut similar to Gerald and Lennie's. On the other side of the hut the valley rose again, another carpet of wildflowers leading to a path that disappeared between mountains.

Simply looking at the valley calmed Hugh, pushed away whispers from the darkness of the forest. He was about to sit and linger in the moment, was halfway down when a movement stopped him. In the shade behind the hut a man was sitting at a battered fold-out wooden table whittling at something too small for Hugh to see. There was an open stony bank area between the hut and the lake, but the man and his table were camouflaged in the shadows. Charlie was down the hill in a flash, carving a dark furrow in the field of color. She shot from the cover of the wildflowers, leaped and splashed landed into the lake. Hugh had only reached the bottom of the hill when Charlie was giving the man an excited wet greeting on the other side of the lake.

Approaching the man Hugh could see he was wearing nothing but a tired pair of dirty pink boarder swim shorts. Whatever he was whittling had disappeared into the pockets of his shorts. Hugh stood in front of the table like a freshman waiting to sign-up for a club. The man made a show of squinting up at Hugh who was back-lit by the sun, before standing and extending a hand. Something around the man's neck caught the sunlight, sending a stabbing flash into Hugh's eyes, such that as he reached to take the man's hand, he shielded his eyes with the other hand and fell backwards.

From handshake to hand-up, the man pulled Hugh to his feet, "Now that's a greeting I won't forget. Name's Beli and you can call me Beli."

Moving quickly past the puzzling name introduction Hugh said, "I'm Hugh..." Beli waved him silent.

"Gerald sent your details along the postal system, such as we have one on the mountain. Pull up a chair and I'll catch you up on what's going to go down here in the valley, if you want to avoid going down the mountain again."

"Why would I go down the mountain?"

"Do you like honey?" said Beli as though Hugh had said nothing.

"Sure." Beli went into the hut and returned quickly with two dumpy short-stemmed goblets each filled with a thick amber liquid. He walked past Hugh and stood by the edge of the lake waiting for Hugh to join him.

"What you're holding there is a goblet of mead, ale made from honey." Beli raised his glass before toasting, "To finding fortune in yesterday's tomorrow."

The heavy glasses made a solid clunk in keeping with the powerful kick delivered by the mead. Hugh had something to say about the toast, but the mead knocked it out of him.

"That's strong stuff."

Beli clapped him on the back as they returned to the table.

"Mainly honey, you'll be drinking it for breakfast tomorrow," said Beli as he laughed.

Sitting at the table Hugh could see the objects responsible for blinding him earlier were dog tags.

"You were in the army?"

"I was."

"Gerald said you were a Priest."

"Before the army," said Beli as he took a folding carving knife and a small piece of wood from his pocket.

"And now I'm a jigsaw maker." He inspected the object of his whittling, nicked it in a few places before throwing it to Hugh, who caught it in one hand, impressing Beli by not spilling any mead from the goblet in the other hand.

"You know what that is?"

"A jigsaw piece. Incomplete."

"How do you know it's incomplete?"

"It has no picture on it."

Beli looked at Hugh for a long while, a smile slowly creeping up his face. Before it got too far, he finished his mead and said, "So what did you learn from Lennie?"

"About the Universe, matter and how souls can be in us until we die and then released, these quantum particles I mean, and they travel to wherever souls go. And emotions, they are the language of souls."

"Some, but not all of those sound like Lennie's words. Which is OK, to make something your own you need your own words otherwise you're likely just repeating without understanding." Beli was quiet a moment, nodded to himself, as though confirming the result of an internal conversation, left the table and returned with a jug full of mead which he used to charge their goblets.

Beli raised his goblet for another toast. Hugh wasn't sure if Beli's internal ruminations concerned anything more than the consumption of more mead. The toast answered his question.

"To what comes next." After downing a good slug of mead Beli continued, "Lennie taught you How a soul can travel. I'll teach you about What goes on when a soul arrives."

Hugh waited while Beli drank some more and stared at the mirror-lake. With Beli as still as the lake, Hugh pushed for what he thought was the obvious information Beli had not given.

"Where. When souls arrive where?"

"You're on a time limit. And you've got puzzles to complete." Beli put his hands flatly together, in a classic praying position but instead of up, he pointed them at Hugh.

"Puzzles completed, you go up the mountain," he pointed up with his right hand, "Fail the puzzles and you go down the mountain, get a different kind of help from Gerald," he pointed to the ground with his left hand.

"Why is there a time limit? Lennie told me about the Universe being billions of years old, about before time started, that souls are eternal and yet I have a time limit."

"Because something lasts forever doesn't mean you have forever to deal with it. Be careful of faulty thinking Hugh Mann. I think 3 days spent halfway up the mountain with me and then we know if you go up or down."

Hugh was completely lost, in place on a mountain with a strange man in swim shorts, lost in time he was being told was rapidly running out.

"This makes no sense, eternity is time without end, souls are meant to be eternal, and you say I have three days."

"Souls have things to do, places to go, they don't float around without purpose. You have eternity to deal with your own soul but a whole lot less time to deal with your daughter's."

The news was a kick in the gut for Hugh, it didn't spur him on, it paralyzed him, left him on the floor in a dark room, not as alone as he wanted to be, *Close your eyes and see what you did.*

Chapter Forty-Six

AMBER

They were sitting by the pool in the heavy wooden chairs. Amber stared at Sparky's run down teal exterior and the string of fairy lights flashing around the entrance.

"If those lights are time zero and that door is the entrance to the Universe, then we are before time, outside the Universe."

Mia didn't say anything for a while, letting some of the pieces fall into place for Amber, she would add the missing pieces when the child started to understand the really important questions.

Amber thought about matter and particles, the fantastical scales of the small stuff that made up everything in the vast Universe and something clicked into place.

"There was stuff out here, where we are now, before the Universe was created, particles I guess," said Amber.

"While scientists study light that is millions of years old, look as far out into the Universe as they can, or as far into the molecular nature of matter as they can, the most amazing unknown is so much closer and equally a question as big as any humankind is trying to answer."

Mia reached over and with a single finger gently tapped Amber on the temple.

"Consciousness. The I that is you. There are particles from out here, from before time started, that have not yet been discovered inside the Universe. Particles that make neutrinos and electrons look big. Particles that flash around in the most powerful computer in the Universe, hungry for input so they can fuel their growth."

"Where is this computer?" said Amber.

"I just showed you, it's your brain, the playground where your soul grows."

Amber felt like shutters to the dark room of her mind were opening, light was revealing answers she had always known but never needed before this moment.

"The cone was meant to be like the particle and the ice-cream was the emotion, the fuel."

"Excellent," said Mia clapping with delight.

"No, not excellent." Amber was blindsided by a rage she hadn't felt coming.

"How can it be excellent when some people have shitty lives. All this talk of magical particles while inside your Sparky's Universe it's a mess of prejudice, hatred and intolerance. There's nothing excellent about that."

"Have you ever drunk gasoline?"

"Huh? No, of course not." The unexpected question stalled Amber's anger.

"Good and I wouldn't recommend it. Though as fuel in a car it's excellent. It stays in the tank waiting for the driver to drive the car wherever she wants to go. Which is exactly like the particles in your brain which are fueled by emotions. I know inside there," Mia pointed to Sparky's, "...seems like ugly chaos, but from the inside the design can't be understood. It's like being in a room inside a fantastic building, if you never leave the room you will never know anything about the rest of the building."

"But now I have left, and I still feel the unfairness of it all."

"You are in the process of leaving, and dealing with what you see as the unfairness of it all requires only one thing."

Amber was looking at Sparky's waiting for Mia to say the one thing. When she didn't, Amber turned to Mia to see her holding out her piece of rope with the ring attached to it.

"Time to teach you about eternity."

Chapter Forty-Seven

HUGH

"Do you understand the purpose of a jigsaw?"

"It's a picture puzzle, you have to put the pieces together."

They were on the other side of Beli's hut; the valley opened out before them and rose to the base of the surrounding mountains. Directly ahead was a panoramic view of the cloudscape between the mountains, a well-trodden path meandered across the field of wildflowers up to the cloudscape precipice.

"So, you understand what a puzzle is but not its purpose. Every jigsaw has the same purpose, no matter how many pieces, no matter what the picture, completion. My friend Liam taught me that simple, yet not so obvious fact using a cut up comic strip," said Beli.

"Speaking of completion, you completely ignored me when I asked you where souls go."

"Oh, very good, I see what you did there. And I won't answer your question until you complete my puzzle. It's a simple wooden jigsaw, complete it, I'll answer your questions and send you on your way up the mountain, but first we have dinner, drink some mead and go watch the clouds."

Dinner was hot buttered crumpets and mead.

"Priesthood to the Army to making jigsaws half-way up a mountain, there must be a good story linking that lot up," said Hugh.

"There's a story, can't say whether it's any good or not. I became a priest and went to war."

"Huh," was all Hugh could manage but Beli seemed to not notice.

"I'll grant you that's not so common, but it will make more sense once you know about Liam," said Beli as he poured them more mead.

"Whose Liam?" said Hugh.

"Liam Frager was my best friend. Best buds in school growing up in a no-name town in the middle who-cares-where. There was some factory work but if you were on the shop floor it seemed like you were always one software release away from being out of work. You could play your way out with a college scholarship, take your chances at the factory or in the army."

"But you didn't take any of those options," said Hugh.

"Like so many in that town, I dreamed of a wealthy distant relative that would turn up one day and rescue us from our future. It wasn't the poverty, though that was no fun, the worst was the pointlessness of it all, the lack of options, simply going nowhere slowly. But I was lucky. Mom had a brother, a Priest who said there was always a place for me at his seminary if I wanted it. What I wanted was to believe that there was someone who had a plan and gave a damn. So, choosing the Priesthood was a way out and a search for answers. Liam chose the army."

"And your Uncle couldn't get a place for Liam?"

Liam was broken before he went to war. Becoming a Priest wouldn't have saved him. The night before he was due to ship out we were going on a bender, but I couldn't find him anywhere. I came home to freshen up and go wait for him in the bar, and there he was in my bedroom reading the comic books we shared as kids. He was crying as he read them. I sat next to him on the bed, thinking my inner-priest might know what to say, but I didn't." Beli took a long draw on his mead, it seemed to Hugh like it helped him visit the memories of his friend.

"New recruits being scared the night before shipping out doesn't seem so unusual," said Hugh.

"I thought the same, told him so. He must have read something funny in the comic, because he laughed like we used to when we were kids. Then he put the comic aside and turned to me with his red rimmed eyes, wet cheeks and said, *'Beli I got to go, I know I'm not soldier material but nothing over there scares me as much as what I might do if I stay here a day longer.'* And I knew he was fighting the same demons I was, mine were making me run off to be a Priest, and his were making him run off to fight a war he didn't understand. We weren't bad kids, didn't have police records, didn't do drugs but we both felt the switches inside that could be flipped to make us do something bad."

"I don't get it. I mean I understand the lack of prospects but what does *something bad* mean?" said Hugh.

"I sometimes think being good in a dead-end place is more dangerous than being a dead-beat. Because Liam and I didn't drink too much, didn't do drugs, didn't do crime, the futility of our situation was playing at maximum volume in our young heads, the kind of volume that can make you do crazy things. We never went to where the crazy lived in our heads to find out. I became a Priest and Liam went to war." Beli went to pour more mead, found the jug empty and went inside to refill.

It took Beli a while to return, his heavy landing on the bench suggesting not all the mead went into refilling the jug.

"We buried Liam a month later. Out on maneuvers in his first week he went to help an injured local kid. The kid wasn't injured, and the sniper didn't miss his shot. Liam spent three weeks in a coma before he died. That last night we spent together, in the time when you've had enough drink to talk the rubbish that really makes sense, but not so much that it's only rubbish, Liam asked me to find the meaning. He didn't say to life but that's what it was, the purpose, the *why are we here?* He told me life was like the comic book pictures, separate moments of action that only work, only say something meaningful when you see them altogether. He said it wouldn't be easy and not where I expected. I asked him how he could be so sure. And he told me, *'Because look at the shitty lives we got, look what we gotta do to get something.'* He grabbed my arm and squeezed it real hard, *'You know what I gotta do, right?'* He was telling me he had to die. He knew he had to get out, the army, where he wouldn't survive was the only option and he was fine with it. It was why he read the comic books with tears in his eyes."

"So that's why you became a Priest to go to war," said Hugh.

"I only started at the seminary after Liam was buried. With what happened to Liam, I was glad to be safe in the seminary. But the more I understood about being a Priest, the more I realized how much religion is for the living. You can have however many commandments you want, be good, forgive, forget, heaven, hell, doesn't matter, it comes down to two things; people want a personal spiritual comforter, and they want it in the community of others who want the same thing. Life after death, eternity, the soul, it's all for the tomorrow that never comes. It gets close when people they care for die, closer still when they get the feeling the grim reaper is looking them up in his address book, but I guarantee you most people have spent more time thinking about and praying for a free parking space when they go shopping than they have about their soul, eternity and whatever might actually happen when they die." Beli took a deep draw on his mead, burped, then said, "Most people."

"Did you find the meaning Liam asked you to?"

Beli charged their tankards before saying, "Ms. Sawyers cat had to die first."

"What? Whose Ms. Sawyer and why did her cat have to die?"

"I'll tell you all about Ms. Sawyer and her cat, but if you want to know about the meaning Liam asked me to find you'll need to tell me about your own puzzle."

"The only puzzle I have is yours," said Hugh.

Beli stared at Hugh way past the point of acceptably comfortable before raising his tankard to jovially toast, "To the lost Hugh Mann." Beli drained his mug, drinking as though his life depended on it.

"Ms. Sawyer was a 94 year old spinster who had just lost the only thing she cared about in the world, Leon, her fat cat who had made it to 19 years before preceding her into the beyond."

He spoke fast, drank faster, as though the drinking fed the speaking, the liquid a necessary lubrication to free memories stuck safely in the past. Safe for who wondered Hugh? He didn't have time to dwell on anyone's safety as Beli was silently staring into the bottom of his empty tankard. Once refilled, he raced away with his story like a wind-up toy when first released.

"I would visit her once a week, sit with her, pray with her. In the early months, I would listen to her, but it wasn't long before I was doing all the talking, maybe she was listening, maybe not. It was like the cat kept her tethered to life, gave her purpose and routine. When Leon was gone she had nothing to live for, that's what she said."

"Surely there was something more than feeding her cat in her life," said Hugh.

"Not if you asked Ms. Sawyer. She had no family, any friends were already dead. After 6 months arrangements were made to put her in a home, her house sale would cover the costs, it wasn't expected to be a long stay. She hadn't been very lucid on my last few visits, it was one of the main reasons she was going to the home. On my last visit to her home, she was energized for the whole visit, like I'd never seen her before. She moved around the kitchen to make coffee and set out cookies. When the table was set, she sat down and started to reminisce about events and places visited throughout her life. It turned out Ms. Sawyer had visited a lot of places, her passport was on the table with all these stamps in it, all over Europe, Australia, China, India, South Africa. Leon came into her life only when she stopped traveling. The conversation was light, happy, she sort of moved as the stories went from one place to another, it's important to understand this because all of sudden she became very focused, very still, as she took my hands in hers and looked directly at me.

'I've nothing left to live for but there are plenty more journeys to make. Do you know anything about my next journey?'

"I said I didn't."

'That's what Liam said you'd say. He said to tell you to keep looking for the picture, see it all together, like a jigsaw.'

"I was stunned, I couldn't speak and then I was desperate to hear more but whatever was giving her this energy was already fading, I could see her reverting to the older Ms. Sawyer, who had no more words to say, nothing left to live for. I was holding her hands now, pleading with her for more details on how she could be giving me a message from Liam, and for one final moment she found some words,

'I had a dream last night, Liam was there by the clouds and the water.'

"Ms. Sawyer passed away that night. One month later I shipped out to where Liam's old unit was stationed to be an army chaplain. What Ms. Sawyer had said felt like a switch had been flipped inside me, there was this communication from beyond, it meant everything, and I was a Priest, caring for souls was my job and here a soul had reached out from the beyond. When I told my superiors they thought it was nice for me, advised me to keep it for myself, use it as a source of inspiration but not to talk about it to anyone. I didn't understand them, I thought maybe they didn't believe me, but wouldn't fellow Priest's believe me? Maybe they were jealous they didn't have their own similar experience. In the end it didn't matter because the switch had been flipped in me, I had had the contact from the beyond, I had to act," said Beli.

"What did you do?"

"I told anyone who would listen, and quickly discovered my fellow Priests were right. As wonderful as this experience was for me, it was only for me, like you can't drink a glass of water to quench another person's thirst, you can't have an experience for someone else, you can't have faith for someone else."

"So why join the army as a Chaplain? And how does that get you here?" said Hugh.

"The army bit is easy, I needed to be where Liam was last, it felt like the only place I could go next. How come I'm here? You've got a jigsaw to complete before we talk about that," said Beli as he drained the last of his mead before stumbling off to bed. Hugh drank the last of his own mead, took three attempts to stand and then made an inelegant stumble to his own room.

Chapter Forty-Eight

Hugh's room was almost identical to the one he had at Lennie's hut, comfortably sparse, with a rustic wooden bed, matching nightstand, a basin with cold water to wash in the morning and a chair, against which his rucksack rested. The only significant difference was a small mirror on the nightstand. It wasn't much use, as a crack ran diagonally across its entire length. He sat on the bed looking at the mirror, the crack perfectly slicing his reflection in two.

'The two Hugh's' he thought, as a sad ironic smile crookedly stared back at him. He put the mirror back on the nightstand wondering if there really were two Hugh's, the misinterpreted man struggling to maintain his place in a world that had run away from him, before he even realized he needed to run to keep up. Or was the word misinterpreted misplaced, and he was simply a man struggling in a world that had revised its value of him, deeming his algorithmic dollar value not worth much?

Hugh stripped to his boxers, splashed water on his face from the basin and let the cold water run-off. The mirror above the basin, unlike the one in Lennie's room, had no cracks, it seemed almost artificially clear as though his reflection was in ultra-high definition. He didn't like that and quickly retreated to the bed, where he flopped down, wanting nothing more than a dreamless sleep to quickly pass by so he could complete the jigsaw, get Beli's help and be on his way.

Chapter Forty-Nine

Hugh didn't remember going to bed. He remembered mead, lots of mead, which the drool around his mouth confirmed. He remembered a room almost identical in Lennie's hut; a cot, wooden chair and a mirror above an enamel sink. He stumbled his way to the sink and splashed cold water on his face. Hugh didn't know if it was the water in his eyes playing tricks, but he was certain he saw someone else reflected in the mirror, someone standing behind him, quickly turning revealed the bare empty room. Turning back, all he saw was a perfect reflection of his haggard self. *'Close your eyes and see what you did'* hissed the voice from the shadows. Hugh smacked the water from his eyes and ran from the room to find Beli. Larger than life Beli, who would give him mead and a jigsaw to complete. Hugh had a clear and simple goal; to complete a jigsaw to get Beli's help. Voices from the shadows would have to do more than whisper if they wanted to stop Hugh Mann.

Beli was having breakfast in the garden, crumpets and unbelievably, mead again.

"Sit down Hugh, eat some breakfast and enjoy your breakfast mead," said Beli as he passed Hugh a hot buttered crumpet and poured mead into his mug.

Hugh chomped on a crumpet while the reality of the full tankard of mead had him questioning the wisdom of drinking it for breakfast.

"Breakfast mead must be not quite as potent as dinner mead then?"

"In a way, you could say that."

Satisfied, Hugh drank deeply from his tankard and immediately spluttered as the powerful ale made its way to a mostly empty stomach.

"Breakfast mead. It's just mead at breakfast," said Beli slapping the table to emphasize the point amid his laughter. Hugh couldn't help but find Beli's laughter infectious as he ate more crumpets to soak up the mead sloshing around inside him.

After clearing away the breakfast things Beli took Hugh to the lakeside of the Hut. On the battered old wooden table was an equally distressed wooden box, about the size of a large chopping board, twice as deep and looking like it had spent many a year as a makeshift chopping board. The lid was hinged the way a checkers game board would be. Beli unlatched the hook and flipped open the box, immediately small jigsaw pieces spewed forth, covering an entire third of the table. Hugh picked up a few pieces, felt their rough surfaces and realized the picture had been hand painted. The picture. Hugh had a nagging feeling concerning the picture, but Beli interrupted his thoughts before the source of the nag could be reached.

"Nothing too difficult, complete a thousand piece jigsaw and then I'll tell you what needs to be told. Shouldn't take you beyond tea-time if you make a good start." Beli had almost rounded the corner of the hut when Hugh reached the source of his nagging feeling.

"Picture. There's no picture to show me how the pieces should go together."

Beli smiled at Hugh like a parent might a child who has just asked *'how do mirrors work?'*

"You'll work it out." He was gone before Hugh could protest.

Although frustrated, Hugh was also energized. He had a challenge, it was in front of him and while not having a picture might slow him down, it wouldn't stop him. He pulled the table out of the shade of the hut, took a seat and made a start where everyone starts jigsaws; corners and edges.

By lunchtime Hugh was very frustrated. He had all the edge pieces in two piles, one dark for the bottom half, the other light for the top half, assuming the lighter blue pieces were the sky seemed a safe assumption. However, not only was it slow going systematically fitting pieces together with nothing to guide him except the shape of the interlocking tabs and blanks, the real source of his frustration were the circa 850 pieces sitting proud on one side of the table, a squat mountain of duplicity, silently waiting to mislead, deceive and worst of all, delay.

When Beli arrived with lunch, unsurprisingly mead and crumpets, Hugh had completed roughly half of the edging. He observed Hugh hunched over the table, out of the shade facing the hut. Up to now Hugh had worked faster than most, but he was still stumbling around in the dark with no idea where to find the light.

"I somehow expected you would be quicker," said Beli around a mouthful of crumpet.

"I expected a picture to guide me."

"Fair point."

Hugh, happy for a break, gladly accepted a goblet of mead from Beli. The midday sun was blazing, and he couldn't imagine a more perfect liquid to quench his thirst, not that Beli was likely to have anything besides mead anyway.

"I need to see the picture to complete the puzzle."

"Indeed you do. Crumpet?"

"Are you going to show it to me?"

"Of course. You just need to see it. I'll leave the crumpets here."

Beli left Hugh staring after him, wondering if they had been having the same conversation.

After lunch it didn't take Hugh long to complete the edging and not much longer still to end up with his face pressed in the mini-mountain of non-edge pieces, screaming in silent frustration at the futility of trying to quickly complete a 1000 piece jigsaw with no picture. Screaming over, he stood up, hands on hips, blew off the jigsaw pieces stuck to his face, took a few deep breaths, retrieved pieces that had fallen on the floor and resumed his task. He found a few clumps of pieces that fit together but no more than the law of averages would allow. To make progress he needed to see a clear picture. Instead, all he had was a multitude of dark pieces. At first he thought of Lennie's Universe presentation as a solution to having so many dark pieces, but that didn't work with the blue sky pieces at the top and green and brown ones at the bottom. A loud splash interrupted his lack of progress, turning he saw Charlie swimming across the lake towards him. It wasn't long before she was bouncing around giving him a muddy-wet greeting. Greeting over he returned to the jigsaw only to have Charlie almost pull his legs out from under him. She barked, jumped backwards, bum in the air tail wagging. Hugh knew the look; Charlie was in molehill play mode.

"You know what girl, a swim in the lake might be just what I need." Hugh stripped off and chased Charlie into the lake. He swam to the middle and then floated, staring at nothing but the blue sky. The gently rocking motion of the water soon had Hugh half-dozing as he was warmed by the sun and cooled by the water. He was in a space between, neither awake or asleep, neither sinking or swimming, he could hear the birds in the trees and Charlie bounding through the field chasing butterflies.

Chapter Fifty

AMBER

Mia and Amber were sitting at a booth close to the rear entrance of Sparky's. On the table between them was the length of rope with the ring secured to one end.

"Life is unfair. Some people live in palaces while others live dirt poor and die in ditches. Some are war criminals committing heinous crimes, others are their victims, innocently caught in the cross-fire of situations they had nothing to do with. Others leave an average house to live an average day, decades of life ahead of them and they get run over by a bus or a truck. You get the picture, and it's why we need this rope," said Mia, as she picked it up and untied the knot securing the ring.

"From your end of the telescope the world is unfair. When you get to the Place Between, everything that has happened to you is fuel for your soul. The ingredient that binds this place together, makes everything work, is time, eternity to be precise."

Mia held the ring horizontally in front of Amber.

"Let's say this is a person's 85 year life span, and then someone like you, dies about here." Mia laid the rope on the table and put one end through the gold ring, keeping it near to the end.

"The ring is you, 16 years old, hit by a truck and now here with me in Sparky's Diner."

"Let me guess, over time I'll forget, I'll forgive, maybe people who really suffered will meet their tormentors and it's all forgive and forget. I don't buy it. Being patient doesn't seem anything like a good solution to all the injustice and simple unfairness in the world," said Amber.

Mia didn't say anything. She took the ends of the rope between her palms and rubbed them, as one might a stick when trying to light a fire. After a few moments she showed Amber that the rope was joined in a loop. Amber took the rope looking for a join, but the rope was a seamless loop with the gold band on it.

"85 years becomes an eternal loop of time, and you are on it for as long as you want and need to be."

"To forget," said Amber.

"No. Outside Sparky's is the mountain you will climb. At the top is a place where you will spend time while your soul grows and heals. Which simply means where you will learn how to use the fuel of your emotions to transform into your soul. For someone like you the way to the top of the mountain will seem like a casual stroll. For some of the others I mentioned, it will be tortuous. It is not about cosmic revenge, have some pain because in life you were a pain-giver. For anyone to become their soul they must honestly look into the mirror of self-reflection, and for almost everyone this is a painful experience. Whether it's a hot desert that takes years to cross or a sea of fire navigated on a raft or a dark forest filled with horrors hiding in the shadows, everyone must get to the top of the mountain. For some it could be a windy walk in the rain. Don't be distracted by the paths others have to walk, just understand that for all of us, the destination is the same."

"So, what is at the top of the mountain?"

"It's called Freedom Club. There are many different Freedom Clubs at the top of many mountains in the Place Between. A soul's path always leads to the right Freedom Club."

"So, is there like some uber-architect responsible for all this?" said Amber.

Mia took the rope and placed it over Amber's head, "There's a Plan. You'll understand more when you get to the Freedom Club."

At least that is what Mia hoped for Amber, but she knew the dangers that lay ahead for any new soul. Not everyone was ready to be their soul, and in eternity there was plenty of time to hide.

Mia surprised Amber by standing quickly and saying, "It's time to get you on your way up the mountain."

Amber stepped through the back door of Sparky's into a cloudy cool morning. Most of the mountain was hidden behind a low ring of clouds.

"Take these," said Mia giving Amber two marbles, one each of the different sizes. As Amber pocketed the marbles Mia pinned a lapel badge to her shirt. It was ice-cream in a cone, all white.

"It's your job to fill in the colors." Before Amber could ask what she meant, Mia was hugging her tightly then saying, "Straight ahead to the tree-line and you'll see the path."

Mia was already opening the door to Sparky's when Amber said, "Will I see you again?"

"I hope so," said Mia before disappearing inside Sparky's Diner.

Chapter Fifty-One

HUGH

Hugh awoke with a feeling he could barely recognize. He felt rested. He had floated to the edge of the lake and was gently awoken as his body nudged the shoreline.

He saw Charlie running around midst the flowers on the far side of the lake. It was getting to the point that simply seeing Charlie, whether at rest or play, would bring a smile to his face. In this moment seeing Charlie from across the lake brought not just a smile to his face but a giddiness to his whole being, because he not only saw Charlie but also the picture that was the source of the image for his jigsaw. As he triumphantly sat down to complete the jigsaw, knowing it wouldn't take him long now that he knew it was the lake, field of flowers and the forest in the distance, he noticed Charlie sitting bolt upright staring at him from across the lake. She gave one bark then continued to sit and stare at Hugh, who had no time for games with Charlie, pieces were falling into place. Hugh felt something like happiness. Almost.

Progress with the jigsaw was swift for about a hundred pieces and then things ground to a halt. Whatever Hugh observed of the lake, the hill full of wildflowers and the forest behind did not align with the fragments of picture painted onto the jigsaw pieces. Frustrated he slumped back in his chair, across the lake Charlie sat and stared, barked twice and continued to watch him. Hugh heard sounds from the other side of the hut and quickly left hoping to find Beli.

Beli was chilling on the porch whittling away at another blank jigsaw piece when Hugh found him.
"Your jigsaw doesn't work."

"Jigsaws are simple things, it's difficult for them not to work."

"But Amber, she's somewhere that I can reach, I know it for sure."

"Well, yes, that's why you're on this journey."

"I know. I know. When I was with Lenni I had a dream." Hugh pauses. "Maybe nightmare is more accurate. We were underwater, together. There was a barrier between us, I pushed against it, broke through, we almost touched, I saw her and she saw me."

"And what did she do?"

"Didn't you hear me, Amber and I were somehow in the same place, connected with something between us but I know if she...I know I could have fully broken through, got to her."

"If she had what Hugh?"

Hugh turned away from Beli, strong winds beyond the mountains made the cloudscape a turbulent sea of fire in the afternoon sun. The clouds made shapes, pretending to be things they were not, a beautiful falsehood of fire and wind. Hugh realized the falsehood was his own, the clouds were just clouds, he chose to see the falsehoods.

"If she had stayed."

Hugh continued watching the drama of the cloudscape, trying not to see giants pushing and shoving, battling for space as the sun's rays burned them from within, trying not to see his daughter turning and swimming away from him. Hiding the earlier dream from Beli, the one that ended with Amber asking, *Why Dad, why did you do it?*

As though he sensed Hugh was keeping something back, Beli said, "You have to see the picture clearly, and when you see the picture clearly and yourself in the picture, only then will you be able to complete it."

Beli's words floated from the cloudscape through the mountain pass along the path in the field of flowers and shook Hugh from his paralyzing reverie.

"Finish your puzzle Hugh."

Standing once again in front of the puzzle, Beli's advice made little sense to Hugh. Of course he had to see the picture clearly, and he could see everything in front of him clearly, but it remained stubbornly inconsistent with the jigsaw pieces. He was certain the picture was of the lake and surrounding area, but there were inconsistencies between what he observed and the reality of Beli's painted picture, as though a filter shifted the picture in a way he couldn't quite understand. The thought of a filter made him think of the wall between him and Amber when he saw her in the sea. He knew it was more than a dream, maybe it was seeing into another place, as he believed he had when he saw Amber in the clouds at the time of the accident, but wherever he was seeing, the picture was clear. For Hugh it was no dream. Charlie's frantic barking snapped him into the present. She was agitated, half-way up the hill still on the other side of the lake, barking at an unseen danger, moving in circles. Suddenly she sped down the hill, skidding to a stop at the water's edge, her barking becoming so frenzied Hugh was swimming across to her before he realized he was in the water.

As he reached the other side Charlie backed away.
"What is it girl? Come here, let me help you."
In response Charlie moved further up the hill, barking wildly, eyes fixed on Hugh.
"Are you scared of me?" Charlie immediately stopped barking, sat and stared at Hugh with her beautiful big brown eyes.
"Good to know you're not scared of me girl." He was letting himself fall into a sitting position as he got close

enough to Charlie when she sprung up and ran to the top of the hill barking once again until he finally joined her.

Hugh flopped down at the top of the hill on the edge of the forest, exhaustion seeping deep into his bones, a result of the hard swim and anxiety over whatever had been disturbing Charlie, who was now playfully trotting around Hugh, licking his face on every half circle before lying next to him, head on his lap looking out across the lake. Nestling in his lap she was a picture of contentment, which only seemed to increase when he stroked her behind the ear. He was struggling to reconcile her crazed barking with the Charlie resting peacefully in his lap. He shuddered as the smile on his face fought with the tears in his heart as he saw a girl turn and swim away from him, as he saw the table with puzzle he couldn't complete on the other side of the lake, as he saw the lake...AS HE SAW THE LAKE.

"Charlie you clever girl."

From the vantage point of the hill Hugh could see how the lake reflected the hill and the forest while it was also a part of the reflection, a reflected image that was inverted. Hugh had his clear picture and for a moment, a smile on his face and in his heart, as he raced Charlie down the hill.

It was late in the afternoon as Hugh rushed down the home straight of completing the jigsaw. Beli was providing a distracting soundtrack which Hugh was miserably failing to ignore, unlike Charlie, who was snoozing and drying off in the sun.

"Its significant Amber swam away from you. Time's running out, you need to be going up the mountain tomorrow or it will be too late."

"Too late for what? No don't tell me, I've got maybe 20 more pieces, then I'm done, I could leave today."

20 pieces later Hugh was crawling in the dirt, a worried man. The jigsaw was complete, a perfect picture of

the valley reflected in the lake. If there was such a thing as a master jigsaw-maker then Beli was it. The picture had an ethereal quality, where the essence of the air itself seemed to be captured in the spaces between the earthly subjects. The skill was in the way the picture had been cut into 1000 pieces and then repainted to reveal virtually no joins when the jigsaw pieces were placed together.

"There's nothing here and I know I picked them all up. Are you sure all the pieces were in the box?"

"100%. Unlike your puzzle which is only 99.9% complete." Beli's amusement was matched by Hugh's anger.

Hugh extricated himself from under the table and stomped off to the lake, needing a moment to calm down, knowing full well he needed Beli on-side if he was going to get to the bottom of the missing piece. Hands on hips with clenched jaws, his reflection stretched away from him across the lake. Hugh wanted to scream that his reflection was a lie, it told no truth, it didn't feel what he felt, it was a cheap flawed image, lacking depth, unlike his real self by the side of the lake, stony sand scrunched underfoot, teeth grinding, fists clenched as his heart silently cried for his daughter to turn back and swim towards him.

Hugh hadn't realized it had started to rain until he saw his reflection become blurry, then Beli had an arm around his shoulders.

"That'll be the tears." Hugh smushed the tears off his face, saw the sun was still shining as Beli lead him back to the jigsaw.

There it was, rather there it wasn't, the space for the missing piece right in the center of the puzzle. 1 piece from 1000 meant Beli's 99.9% was accurate.

"There's a lot that can be learned from what can't be seen," said Beli.

"Like can I learn that you'll call it even, tell me what I need to know and send me on my way?"

"The rules of your challenge will not change but you can learn along the way. Tell me what you see?"

"I see the hole where the missing piece should be."

"And isn't that something. There's a picture, quite a good picture if I say so myself, it's 99.9% complete and all you see is the missing 0.1%."

"Can you blame me? You keep telling me I'm running out of time, for what I don't know, and the only thing standing between me and moving on is that one stupid piece of your puzzle."

Hugh was panting as Beli was smiling kindly back at him.

"Do you really think one piece of a jigsaw is what's standing between you and completion?" said Beli as he once again put an arm around Hugh and gently led him to the front of the hut.

"Wait here."

Following numerous thumps, thuds, clinks and clangs as Beli bustled about inside the hut, Hugh was a short while later following Beli's large form along the path leading to the cloudscape. Beli's was somewhat obscured by a tatty picnic rucksack strapped to his back, undoubtedly the source of much of the thudding and zipping, as Hugh imagined Beli trying to achieve the world record for how many crumpets and bottles of mead could be stuffed into a rucksack.

"Do you like board games?"

Hugh was seized by a fear that Beli was taking him to the cloudscape for a game of monopoly.

"Sure, rainy days with the family, a good way to kill time," said Hugh.

"Roll a die, move forward, move back, take a card, get some money, pay a fine, buy property, be first, be last, get the most, get the least. Rules. Play by the rules and win the game."

"Yep. That about covers it," said Hugh.

They were through the field of wildflowers and making their way along the stony path between the mountains which framed the view of the cloudscape.

"The rules of the games we play are a reflection of the rules we have in life. The problem is that we get used to looking for only one type of answer, I need to move so many spaces, I need to roll a 6, I need to acquire, I need to visit, I need the treasure."

The path was opening out onto a luscious grassy knoll. Wildflowers provided a natural border on either side, ahead the cloudscape was just broaching the grass as the path crested, leading them fully onto their magical picnic blanket.

"Sometimes the game is not what you think it is, the answer not as you expect. Like the picture for your jigsaw, it was always in front of you but the rules you were applying to jigsaws stopped you from looking at the reflection in the lake. I told you to look for the clear picture and to see yourself in the clear picture, that was your clue. Only when you thought Charlie was in trouble did you come out of yourself, away from the rules of board games and find your way to seeing the clear picture."

Beli stopped in the middle of the emerald green grass. As Hugh came alongside, the sight of the cloudscape extending to the horizon and beyond gave him an intense sense of infinity, of space without borders of time without end, that he stumbled only saved from falling over by a strong arm from Beli steadying him.

"It's magnificent, almost otherworldly," said Hugh.

"Don't label it, just enjoy it," said Beli as he sat cross-legged in front of the rucksack unpacking bottles of mead and crumpets wrapped in tin foil.

Chapter Fifty-Two

They sat on the edge of the mountain, legs dangling into the nothingness of the cloudscape, their feet not visible. The sun set the clouds aflame, the wind gave them a sense of agency, a carpet of clouds on fire as far as the eye could see. To Hugh it felt as though he was sitting on the edge of the world, there was the faintest sound of running water, he imagined a waterfall somewhere way below the cloudscape. The majesty of the flaming carpet of clouds was brought into incongruous relief by the big man in pink boarder shorts belching loudly between glugs of mead and mouthfuls of crumpet. Though Hugh had to admit Beli's mead only added to the beauty of the moment, and he had somehow managed to pack the crumpets in a way to keep them warm without getting soggy. Taking another crumpet from the large pile in their silver foil wrapping, he chuckled at the realization he could marvel at un-soggy crumpets almost as much as the glorious cloudscape. Almost.

Beli had torn a corner off the silver foil, rolled it into a loose ball which he now threw at Hugh's head. Having got Hugh's attention, he belched once more then said,

"You asked me how I ended up here making jigsaws after I went to Liam's old unit as a chaplain. After Ms. Sawyer gave me Liam's message, after I told my fellow Priests and anyone who would listen, I felt alone, in a new place with no one to talk to."

"But you hadn't gone anywhere," said Hugh.

"Not physically. But I knew this message from Liam was from somewhere else, somewhere beyond where all the living people were. And when you say it out loud like I just have to you, it sounds mad, even to people of faith. They like the mystery and love the hope of life after death but don't want any crazy to go with it."

"Although Liam had died you thought going to the place he was last alive might be a way to connect with him. You're telling me to go to where Amber died?"

"No. Drink your mead and listen. It felt like I had been given a magical machine that could cure all pains and illnesses but no manual, the keys to the kingdom but no instructions on where to find the kingdom. That's what spiritual experiences can feel like, they change you, lift you up and then leave you alone, let you sink back down to earth, different but still in the same place," said Beli.

Hugh was getting impatient. He couldn't deny Beli's story was interesting, similar even to his experiences with connecting to Amber but his need for answers was overriding any latitude he was prepared to give Beli for storytelling.

"So, you become an army chaplain, travel to a desert war zone in the hope of connecting with your dead best friend?"

The sharpness of Hugh's tone as he searched for a short-cut to the point of Beli's story stopped Beli from speaking further. He stood up and Hugh thought his rudeness had brought an abrupt end to proceedings as Beli went to the rucksack. Instead of picking up and slinging the rucksack over a shoulder, Beli retrieved a tennis ball and a black marker pen from inside it. Sitting back down, swapping the tennis ball and marker for his bottle of mead, from which he drinks deeply, Beli said, "Where was I? Desert, Liam, seeking a connection to somewhere beyond, is that about it?"

"Yes," said Hugh, looking at the tennis ball and pen expectantly as Beli completely ignored they were even there.

"The irony of being out in the desert where Liam's life ended was that I had never felt further away from my friend. No one knew him, except as, '...*the poor kid who got himself shot in his first week...*'. And there was no connection to Liam. I spent the days holding a morning service, praying with units before they went out on details, and holding the hands of the wounded and dying that returned," said Beli.

"Were the casualties really so high," asked Hugh.

"How many hands of dying soldiers do you need to hold before you decide the number is high?" said Beli.

Hugh had no answer. He only had to think of Amber's death to know that one death was too much.

"Praying to a silent god, comforting the injured and dying, then staring into the desert for the ghost of my best friend. Anything to help those soldiers was time well spent. As the light would fade from their eyes there was always a moment when they pleaded fearfully for answers, why did it have to end this way, where were they going, will it be a better place, so many different ways to say, 'what does it all mean?' I had no answer. I did of course give them answers, said what I thought they needed to hear, but every day I spent in the desert the less I believed anything I said. Sitting on a sand dune staring into the majesty of the empty desert made me crazy angry with God. Why the silence? Why not drop a sign, some updated stone tablets in the middle of the desert, give a little confirmation, guidance, anything?" said Beli.

"God works in mysterious ways, man should not presume to understand the mind of God, you were a Priest, this silence should not have been a surprise to you," said Hugh.

"It wasn't, but I was coming to a different perspective on the silence. The beauty of the silence is that nothing is said, and all answers are possible. In that lack of detail is the essence of hope, which is so helpful for so many people. The problem for me, was my hope meeting the harsh realities of war, where too many real-world unhappy endings were trampling all over hope day after day. After a particularly brutal and bloody afternoon in the infirmary I was early to the desert to watch the sunset and lose myself in conversation with my newfound favorite companion, Jack Daniels. Jack always delivered on his promise, accelerated oblivion until the next day, unlike Liam, who just never showed up. Except this evening, he did. Sort of," said Beli. Hugh was hooked on Beli's story, wanted to know what happened, how did Liam appear in the desert. But Beli had stopped talking. Instead, he was drawing on the tennis ball with the marker pen. He made 2 dots on the ball at what would be the North and South pole positions.

"What happened, how did you meet Liam?" said Hugh.

Beli put the ball and pen aside and continued as if he hadn't stopped.

"Sometimes before sitting on my favorite dune with Jack to watch the sunset, I would walk a bit further into the open desert, lay on my back, look up at the endless blue sky. I imagined I was on a seabed looking through the ocean into the sky of another world. I don't know why I did that, maybe it was where my hope went, wishing to be somewhere else, where the sky was above a fairer world. It was in this moment of wistful artifice that I realized I couldn't stay a Priest a day longer. I needed another language. The language of my faith wasn't going to provide the answers I was seeking," said Beli.

"Did you know the language that would provide the answers?" said Hugh.

"Not really. I knew what I was seeking shouldn't have preconceived ideas. To put it another way, if it were a church, it shouldn't have a roof to limit what could be within," said Beli.

"I'm not sure I understand," said Hugh.

"Neither did I until Liam came knocking," said Beli picking up the ball and pointing to each of the dots in turn, "One dot for birth, one dot for death," he said, and then put it back down.

"When I returned to base I was told a package had arrived for me. I picked it up and returned to my quarters. A carton stuffed with packing paper contained a box, not too dissimilar to the jigsaw box you have been working with, and a letter. The letter was from the executor of Ms. Sawyer's will. She had passed away a few weeks back, leaving me the contents of the sealed box in her will. The box contained three things. Another letter, this one from Ms. Sawyer, a hand painted picture, also from Ms. Sawyer, and a page from one of my old comics, except the page had been cut up, neatly sectioning each of the picture boxes." Beli once again stopped talking to draw on the tennis ball. This time he connected the dots using a few straight lines and some squiggly lines that nevertheless connected the dots.

"Why do you keep stopping to scribble on that tennis ball?" said Hugh.

Beli held the ball up between them, "The lines represent the lives people lead, many paths..." Beli offered the ball to Hugh, which he took, "...that all start and end in the same places," said Beli.

Hugh examined the ball seeing nothing but an old tennis ball with black markings on it.

"Can you remember which dot was birth and which was death?" said Beli.

"No, I can't," said Hugh.

"Me neither. I drew on a ball just like that after I read Ms. Sawyer's letter," said Beli.

"She wrote that in a dream that was so real she couldn't believe it was only a dream, Liam had met her and told her about a 'place between', somewhere that people go when they die. If it was only the dream, I would have put it down to an old woman's synapses playing with memories of our conversations while she slept. Except she said Liam told her to go to my Mom's house and ask for one of my old comics. It was the one Liam was reading that last evening we spent together, the one that was now cut up in the box. Ms. Sawyer said Liam told her to tell me to find the 'place between', the answers I wanted would be there but first I had to put the pieces together to see the whole picture."

"And the picture in the box, what was it?" said Hugh.

"Any ideas?"

Instinctively Hugh knew, "The jigsaw you made me do."

"Correct..." said Beli and pointing to the ball Hugh was still holding, "...Ms. Sawyer's ball, who knows maybe her cat plays with a ball like that, wherever they are," said Beli.

"And how did you find the lake with the reflection from her picture?"

"In her letter she described the place where she met Liam. I knew this mountain, it wasn't difficult to find and with how I had come out of the desert that night, to get this message from Liam, because that's what it was for me, a message from my dead best friend from somewhere beyond. I knew I would find the place that Ms. Sawyer had drawn, that it was the guide to the Place Between," said Beli.

"So, then you met Gerald and he helped you find your hut?" said Hugh.

"Not straight away. I found a hut on a plateau, learned how to make jigsaws, learned to see the full picture of what Ms. Sawyer had painted, it was the start of the journey that brought me here to help people like you Hugh Mann."

Hugh gave a mirthful little laugh.

"Maybe you don't feel the help just yet, perhaps tomorrow when you finally complete the jigsaw."

"What makes you think I'll have more luck finding the piece tomorrow than I did today?"

Beli threw another piece of silver foil at Hugh before saying, "Clear pictures. We all have them but they're not all the same, individuals, families, friends, countries, we are tribal by nature, it's why we struggle so much to avoid conflicts and wars, our tribes don't share the same clear picture. Even for you in your tribe of three, you, Laura and Amber, there was conflict. No matter how close you get to someone you'll never share a thought, not from behind their eyes. If you're a parent, with so much more knowledge than your child, the toughest thing is when they start to see their own clear picture and it's not the same as yours. Something has got to give, or something breaks."

Beli stopped to drink more mead and made another silver foil ball.

"Are you going to throw that one at me too?"

"Well not now that you've said it," said Beli.

Hugh drank deeply from his own mead and felt the silver ball bounce off his head.

"If you want to have a chance of navigating all the clear pictures that there are in the world, you need to start with a clear picture of yourself. Hugh, there comes a time when the running has to stop, when there's nowhere left to hide. That's when you'll find your answers."

Hugh heard Beli say the words he didn't want to hear. As he scrunched Beli's silver foil balls into one large ball, all he heard was the water from a distance carrying the hiss of whispers,

'Why Dad? Why did you do it?'

'Close your eyes and see what you did.'

The water seemed closer. Hugh closed his eyes, an urge to fall in the water overwhelmed him, it was there just below the cloudscape, the water that would carry him away, and once again a strong arm from Beli stopped him from falling.

"Your journey continues up the mountain my friend."

Chapter Fifty-Three

Back at the hut Beli went lakeside for a final mug of mead. Hugh, having lost the race to keep pace with Beli's drinking about 2 bottles ago, opted not to join him.

He dreamed he was back at the cloudscape, alone on the precipice, this time he could jump into the unseen water. He did. Instead of landing in water he was by water, the lake to be precise, staring at his own reflection, which quickly changed to a reflection of a memory.

"Why am I always wrong?" Hugh sat at the dining table, steamed up, alone, feeling totally misunderstood.

Laura came back from the hall, "Can't you give her some space, let her have the time to work things out."

"Honey we need to fix this, the more time we give her, the harder it will be," said Hugh.

As he watched Laura stare at him for a long moment, he recognized her struggle to reconcile his comments with the man she knew him to be.

"Our daughter being gay is nothing to fix. If you can't understand that much then it's best you don't get involved," said Laura.

Laura left to take Amber to her swim meet. Hugh circled back to, 'Why am I always wrong?' except now he had the pitying look on Laura's face to add spice to his feeling sorry for himself.

The lake in his dream was momentarily dark before glowing silver as a large 'A' shape lit it from within. The silver 'A' resolved into an aluminum set of steps. A younger version of himself was climbing down the steps, paint tray and roller in one hand. He disappeared from view when he reached the floor. The steps stood alone for a moment before a toddler wobbled up to them. Amber, 2 years old. She looked so focused as she held onto the steps and started to climb. He remembered how it seemed so exciting to her to get to the top and see the world from a different perspective, the world in this case being whatever room he was painting. He remembered how he enjoyed her pleasure at standing so tall and also the even greater concern he had that she might fall, how he positioned himself to be certain to catch her if she slipped, the ladder toppled or it simply inexplicably disintegrated, he was going catch her, he was the safety net she didn't know she had. And in the dream, in the shadows of the lake he was there, ready to catch her but confident enough to let her climb, proud of his child who he wanted to lift to the highest heights as best he could, for her to then carry on going higher. 2 year old Amber reached the top of the steps and in the memory Hugh could see something he had never seen in real life, a determined look on his baby daughter's face, a look that seemed to go beyond whatever room she was in. Looking at her so proud atop the ladder, and he was there, ready to intervene but not getting in the way, he wished the safety he had needed to provide Amber could have remained a physical one, he would have been good at that. When it became the safety of an open-minded environment, of somewhere without prejudiced preconceived ideas about conforming to norms...and like a clockwork toy reaching the point of being fully unwound, Hugh came to a mental halt. *Conforming to norms* froze him on the precipice of haunted memories, where he was desperate to avoid that mirror of self-reflection, for fear of discovering he was the darkness at the heart of the haunting.

    The lake went dark as Hugh fell into the safety of deeper sleep.

Chapter Fifty-Four

AMBER

Amber stared for a long time at the door behind which Mia had disappeared. She hadn't expected Mia to leave so suddenly, but like a slow sunrise chasing shadows away, Amber realized she was the reason Mia had to leave. Amber knew she was her soul, Mia had helped her understand the mechanics of a soul leaving a body, The Places and circular time, how she was undergoing a transformation, but the most important point for Amber, the realization that was now making her feel stronger than she ever had, was that she was in control. Whether she fully grasped the minutiae of what was happening as she transformed into her soul, didn't change that it was happening.

But. Amber. Could. Make. Choices.

And Amber remembered a door. A door upon which she arrived. Amber saw this door as a way to her past. If these amazing particle things Mia had told her were real, then why couldn't she return home? Eternity, places before and beyond the Universe. Amber had chosen to believe finding her door was the key to finding her way back home. Amber was willing to believe everything Mia had told her, but she wouldn't believe she couldn't return home.

Amber set off up the mountain.

Chapter Fifty-Five

HUGH

Morning found Hugh hungry and staring at his reflection in the lake. Charlie was frolicking in the field of wildflowers, vainly chasing butterflies, seeming to enjoy the chaos of the hunt more than any need to catch her prey, which fluttered safely away from her happily snapping jaws.

Beli arrived with a plate of warm crumpets.

"You expecting to find the missing piece in the lake?"

"The lake was in my dreams."

"Good dreams or bad?"

"Memories of things that really happened, with Amber and Laura."

"Good dreams or bad?" repeated Beli, smiling as he proffered the plate of crumpets.

"What's to stop me packing some of these crumpets in my rucksack and carrying on up the mountain?"

"Nothing."

"What difference does one sodding jigsaw piece in a thousand really make?"

"Except a person won't get far in a desert without water."

"It's not a desert, it's a mountain."

"And it's not really water that you'll need, but you can be sure if you don't find the last piece the only way you'll go is down the mountain."

Hugh wanted nothing more than to grab the crumpets, pack them in his rucksack so he could leave Beli and his stupid jigsaw puzzle. His hand was reaching for the crumpets when he noticed, between the crumpets and the plate, was a sheet of silver wrapping foil. Something clicked; a clue and a silver ball. Hugh ran inside the hut looking for Beli's picnic rucksack. He couldn't find it, on a hunch he checked his own rucksack. Nestled at the bottom was the ball of silver foil from all the smaller balls Beli had been throwing at him yesterday.

Beli was nonchalantly chomping on a crumpet when an excited Hugh arrived in the doorway throwing and catching the silver foil ball in one hand.

"...when you see the picture clearly and yourself in the picture, only then will you be able to complete it," said Hugh repeating part of Beli's clue. He moved to the table tearing off a piece of foil as he went. He smoothed the foil out with a small smooth stone before folding it to roughly the size of the missing jigsaw piece, and then he squished it into the empty place in the jigsaw. It was only a few moments before he gave it a few triumphant tamps to smooth the edges into place.

Hugh felt like a shaken fizzy drink ready to explode free once opened, but something stopped him turning to Beli to crow about his success, he remained bent over the jigsaw as he heard Beli say, "The missing piece is the mirror that gives you the opportunity to complete the jigsaw Hugh."

Hugh could see his cracked visage in the shiny foil as though it were a reflecting lake. The reflecting lake that had shown him memories of the father he once was and the one he had become. For a moment the foil went dark, as though it was the real missing picture piece, in the darkness Hugh saw razor sharp teeth in salivating jaws above which red eyes glowered back at him. As though from a mousetrap snapping, he sprung back from the jigsaw, released from the hold of the silver and momentarily dark piece.

Hugh was breathing heavily as Beli clapped him on the back.

"I knew if I threw enough silver balls at your head and hid the foil in your rucksack you'd get the message eventually." Beli laughed and Hugh couldn't help but join in.

Beli packed Hugh some crumpets and insisted they share a final mug of mead before Hugh and Charlie left. In front of the hut with the cloudscape in the distance, they drank their mead in silence. The morning sunshine made the valley a golden crucible of light, a cool breeze perfecting the conditions for his hike up the mountain. Since Hugh had arrived in this beautiful valley all he had wanted to do was leave, continue with his search for Amber as fast as possible. Now that Beli's jigsaw was complete, now that he knew where to go to get the last piece of information to help find Amber, now he didn't want to leave. And now that he wanted nothing more than for Beli to keep replenishing the mead in his mug, Beli instead relieved him of his empty mug, placing it with his own by the entrance to the hut.
"I thought you'd be skipping away across the field."
"So did I."
Beli knew the look on Hugh's face, understood the power of self-reflections.
"At the end of my time with Lennie I saw a word in flames that I couldn't read. I had a feeling of wellness beyond anything I have ever felt, an uber-feeling I can't explain. In the missing jigsaw piece, I saw an image that gave me an uber-feeling of concentrated hatred. A feeling of repulsion I was more familiar with, it was like a dark repugnant place was calling me home."
"Once you see clearly, it's what you do next that counts. You have to go up the mountain to the Freedom Club if you want the final help you'll need to find Amber."
"I think what lives in the dark place is waiting for me in the forest."

Beli put a bear-like hand on Hugh's shoulder, squeezing it a little too hard as he said, "It's surely waiting for you, but it doesn't live in the forest."

Before Hugh could think about the meaning of what Beli said he was blinded by something Beli was handing him; the foil piece of jigsaw glinting in the sun.

"Keep this to remember our time together."

When Hugh was ready to leave Charlie led him along a path to the right of the hut, a path at 90 degrees to both the lake and the cloudscape. As he clambered up the bank of the valley's bowl, with Charlie waiting just in front of the forest, his thoughts were on Beli's assertion that what he feared was not waiting for him in the forest, and how confident he was in Beli's assertion. So, he wasn't going to stop and see what else Beli might have put in his rucksack. And he wasn't going to find Beli's letter nestled next to Gerald and Lennie's letters in the rucksacks' inner concealed pocket.

Chapter Fifty-Six

LAURA

Laura woke like a train whose brakes were desperately squealing, as the juggernaut of steel screeched to a halt. Heart hammering, she sat up deeply worried about the safety of a fragile butterfly from her dream. Heart rate calmer, fully out of her dream, Laura wanted to get to the hospital as quickly as possible. Ten minutes in the bathroom, she wasn't hungry so no need for breakfast, a thirty second interlude after opening the front door and a full fifteen minutes after waking from her butterfly dream, she was back in bed again; Laura had slept for a grand total of approximately four hours, the time now being midnight.

Her mad dash around the house only to be back in bed inside fifteen minutes had actually put a smile on her face. She and Hugh were notoriously bad time-keepers, most of their friends' made plans with them that subtlety incorporated the FMLF - Family Mann Late Factor. Only her parents seemed not to notice or more to the point, whenever they managed to arrive, the fact of having their company always outweighed any annoyance at their late arrival.

Fifteen minutes to back in bed and not much longer to dreaming of a lake and a swimmer searching for something that couldn't be found. Again, Laura was standing on the shore shouting to the swimmer she could barely see. Then it was Laura swimming in the middle of an endless sea, she was swimming with purpose but there was nothing in sight, until she saw the sea was hissing and steaming about fifty meters ahead, it was as though a firework was going off just beneath the surface. As she got closer the hissing stopped and the steam became a cloud hovering above the seas' surface. Head down, Laura swam hard to reach the cloud, as though her life depended on it. She splashed into a silent blinding fog, the cloud sinking a little, enveloping her entirely so that not even the sea was visible. Immediately tiny forks of lightning started firing like marbled veins throughout the cloud, and as lightning heralds thunder, so the lightning in Laura's personal cloud heralded a thunder of sorts; Hugh's voice croaked on a wind making a promise he vowed to keep.

'I'm going to find her.'

Part VI: WHY? PART I - FREEDOM CLUB

Chapter Fifty-Seven

Although the mountain path started in a forest, for a short while it was exposed, shielded by neither trees nor the circle of clouds Amber was walking towards. She was able to admire the dazzling endlessness of the Sea of Eternity. The clouds soon ended the breathtaking views with the finality of a light switch being flicked. Amber could feel the moisture of the clouds seeping through to her bones. The mountain became steeper, the clouds denser, their moisture like a fine shower cleansing her of everything that was below the mountain. Thoughts of doors faded away, memories of individuals morphed into feelings that shaped Amber, but the people concerned were lost in the mists of the clouds. Amber looked only at her feet, one foot in front of the other, following the path, there was nothing else to see.

The light switch flicked again, and Amber stepped from the clouds onto a plateau at the top of the mountain. The sun was incandescent, forcing Amber to shield her eyes as she heard a voice calling her name. A person made of liquid gold was striding towards Amber.

"Good morning gorgeous, pleased to meet you, I'm Deejon," said the liquid gold figure that, without the sun blinding her, Amber could see was a stunning brown person. Their hand was outstretched in friendly greeting, like the megawatt smile they beamed at Amber.

"And who might you be?"

"Am...Teal," said Amber.

"Am...Teal. Not a name I've heard before, but OK."

"No, just Teal," said Amber shaking Deejon's hand.

Deejon put an arm around Amber and lead her to a hut painted in vibrant rainbow colors.

"Well just Teal let's introduce you to the Freedom Club."

Chapter Fifty-Eight

Compared to its joyful exterior the interior of the rainbow hut was a somber space, old wooden furniture, all comfy and homely but not what Teal was expecting from something billed as the Freedom Club. As if sensing Teal's disappointment Deejon said,

"Honey, are you of a mind that this is the Freedom Club?"

"It's what you said."

"You'll get your intro to the Freedom Club, this is just my little welcome hut, somewhere I can meet the new arrivals before the technicolor roller coaster of the Freedom Club enchants you."

"That's good. I've never been to a club before and I was kind of hoping this wasn't going to be my first."

Deejon looked at Teal like something pulled from the back of the fridge, trying to gauge if it was still good or off. There was nothing unfriendly in the look, merely an appraisal.

"You look old enough to have been to clubs for some years," said Deejon.

"How I look and how I feel aren't exactly on the same page."

"No matter, time is something we got plenty of here, all the time you need to get those pages lined up."

"What is the Freedom Club?"

"It's a place to forget until it's time to remember."

"What do I need to forget?"

"Your walk in the clouds would have already helped you with that."

"What do you mean?" said Teal.

"Teal, always your name or did you have another name?"

"Teal, for as long as I can remember my name has been Teal."

Deejon took Teal's hand in theirs as they stood, "Well Teal, it really is time to take you to the Freedom Club."

As Deejon led Teal to the rear door of the hut she said, "Someone arrived yesterday. I think you two will get on just fine. I'm going to give you the room next to hers. Name's Erica."

Chapter Fifty-Nine

HUGH

As Charlie led them deep into the forest, Hugh was surprised they went neither up nor down. After at least an hour of following Charlie along a narrow twisty trail full of ancient roots and tree trunks as wide as a garage, they came to a rather odd small clearing about the size of a family dining table, the forest floor seemed as though it was swept and two old cut-off tree trunks were in the center, seats for passers-by in what Hugh imagined to be the most remote place on the planet. He was standing on the edge of the clearing when Charlie started to whine, she had heard something. By the time Hugh heard the rustle of leaves as something approached from the other side of the clearing, Charlie was barking loudly. He couldn't tell if she was excited or scared, only that he was definitely scared.

From the gloom of the forest trail the figure of Gerald C/Farer stumbled into the clearing.

"Hugh, how nice to see you."

"Surprising to see you," said Hugh as Gerald was vigorously shaking his hand.

"All part of the service. Take a seat."

As Hugh sat on one of the tree stumps Gerald was busy gathering rocks and inspecting sticks until he found some he liked. A few moments later he was sitting opposite Hugh.

"So, here we are."

"In a dark forest on two old tree stumps, all part of the service, you already said."

"How, What, Why. That's what I said you could get help with from my friends on this mountain. One little addition we need to discuss though."

"Let me guess, payment."

"In a way."

Gerald took a scruffy piece of paper from his jacket pocket, unfolded it until a flip-board sized piece of paper was on the ground between them, he placed a rock on each corner to keep it in place. Hugh recognized the drawn map from Gerald's hut.

"Commitment is a better word," said Gerald as he pointed to the map with his stick.

"You have a decision to make Hugh, you're more than halfway up the mountain, you have a lot of knowledge on how a soul might exist and what would be going on, the process as it were..."

"Actually I don't, I mean Lennie's stuff is as clear as a crash course in the history of the Universe, with a minor in quantum physics, can be. And I had this experience with a word in flames that was...was..."

"Not easily explained," offered Gerald.

"Yes, but somehow fitting with everything else Lennie showed me. I had a sense of closure with Lennie that fitted with the How," said Hugh pointing to the How on the map. "With Beli I did what he asked, I listened to his story, but process, what happens with a soul after a person dies, that was never clear."

"You say you did his jigsaw, which means you put 999 pieces together and then you found the missing silver piece."

"I know, I saw myself in the big picture..."

"Which is *what* happens with a soul after a person dies, they start to understand the big picture, they start to transform into the natural reality of a soul, I don't say physical because it's not physical in any way that you understand."

"I'm happy to be on my way to the final stop on your map, where I'm hoping I can find Amber, that's what you said."

213

"If you get to the Freedom Club then you might discover the answer to the Big Why, what does it all mean? Which will undoubtedly help you find Amber. First though, we return to commitment."

Again, Gerald pointed to a spot on the map just above Beli's What marker.

"If you go up the mountain it will be difficult for you to return to Laura."

"Difficult but not impossible," said Hugh.

Gerald could see the hope burning brightly in Hugh's eyes. He didn't want to throw cold water on the flames but fanning them would mean speaking an untruth.

"That's when commitment becomes more like price, and when you know the price you will wonder if it ever were really possible."

Hugh looked long at Gerald's open honest face, and the lie between his smile and the sorrow in his eyes. Hugh laughed, bitterly. He stood up, laughed some more as he walked around the clearing.

"How can you even ask if I'm going to continue up the mountain? From the beginning you've known all that matters to me is finding Amber's soul, why would I stop now?"

By way of response Gerald took a piece of chalk from his jacket pocket, knelt on the map and started to draw. Hugh's anger quickly turned to curiosity as he returned to his seat, with Gerald once again seated and the edited map between them, the edit being a crude curtain of clouds drawn between Beli's spot on the mountain and the Freedom Club at the top.

"Please don't be upset Hugh. Of course I expect you to finish your search for Amber, and she is here, I just wanted you to see..." Gerald was pointing to the Freedom Club with his stick as Hugh felt a word explode in his mind as violently as a kick to the solar plexus, he doubled-over holding his head.

"...the big picture," said Hugh, with his head closer to the map, seeing only the stick pointing to the Freedom Club and the space around it, Hugh understood what Gerald was trying to tell him. He sat back, exhaling long and deeply, focusing only on his breathing to avoid any chance of thinking about his decision, he knew if he didn't get up now, he never would.

"I'm going to take a walk in the clouds," said Hugh standing.

Gerald stood, put his hands on Hugh's shoulders, smiled the way a parent would when a child leaves home, then walked past Hugh taking the path back to Beli's hut, "I'm going to drink some mead with Beli, tell him we met."

"Say hi from me."

"Enjoy your walk Hugh."

Chapter Sixty

The picture-map Gerald had left on the floor was now occupied by Charlie standing there with Gerald's pointing stick clamped between her jaws.

"We're not playing stick; you have to show me the way."

Without dropping the stick, Charlie turned and trotted off down the path from which Gerald had come. Hugh dusted off the map, put it in his rucksack and then followed her along a path that quickly changed to nothing but dense forest. They were snaking their way around trees so tall Hugh could barely see the canopy above, the further they went the darker it became.

"Charlie, slow down girl."

Charlie immediately obliged and in an instant Hugh was lost. It was so dark he hadn't realized he was following Charlie by sound and not sight. He carried on walking for a few moments before he realized the only sounds he heard were his own footsteps.

"Charlie?" There was no response. All Hugh could see were dark tree trunks swimming in impenetrable darkness. Slumping down, back against the nearest tree, he called out to Charlie a few more times then listened for any sound from her, and thought of blancmange. He didn't know why from the shadows images of cream topping on pink mousse and red jelly assaulted him, except that at Beli's he had a disconcerting feeling his search for Amber was going to come crashing down, like a blancmange bowl on a hard kitchen floor, leaving nothing but a mash of messed up of stickiness and broken glass from which nothing could be recovered. What went on in his life felt more like the smashed blancmange bowl of his earlier imaginings, a happy mix of flavors promising a sweet tasty reward, presented somewhat untidily, while lurking within were shards of glass which would cut and tear the promised sweetness. The reality of many a family's life. He laughed to himself, wondering if he was discovering a talent for poetic metaphor or simply hungry. He heard Charlie making her way toward him, and they were soon making their way to the edge of the forest, Hugh knew, because the light was returning.

Chapter Sixty-One

The light was white, wet and dense, which was another way of saying it was the clouds bordering the forest. Hugh thought it seemed like a way-point on a board game, a spot from where routes could be chosen. He could see a rough patch of sand just about wide enough for him and Charlie to stand next to each other, the darkness of the forest was behind him, the dense whiteness of the clouds ahead. He was wondering how safe it was to go on with such limited visibility when Charlie nudged him with Gerald's pointer stick, which she was still carrying. She was holding it in such a way that Hugh could grab one end and be led by her through the clouds.

"Clever girl."

At first Hugh walked so cautiously, holding Charlie back, that she let go of her end of the stick and barked at him. Hugh was not much better when they started again, Charlie managed to growl even with the stick in her mouth, and Hugh slowly learned to let her lead.

As he walked, blinded by the white-out of the clouds, he thought of the irony of Beli teaching him to see the whole picture, when as he neared journey's end, he couldn't see anything. From Beli his thoughts wandered to Lennie and her teaching him about the Universe, which is dominated by empty black space, and here he was blinded by white clouds pressing in on him.

Ahead a yellow point of brightness, Hugh assumed to be the sun, penetrated the clouds. Maybe they were near the Freedom Club. Nearer to finding Amber. Hugh quickened his pace. Charlie picked up hers in response, forgetting she was much faster than Hugh and was still leading him.

"Charlie slow down!" Too late. Charlie was gone and Hugh had a mouthful of dirt.

Sitting in the dirt with nothing but a stick for company and of course his rucksack, Hugh couldn't see further than his outstretched hand. The sun was in the distance, but if there was a fall off the mountain between him and the sun, he had no idea.

"Charlie, where are you?" Silence.

Then someone was calling his name. Laura.

Laura was calling him.

"Hugh...

Hugh was up and running.

"...honey is that you?"

To a voice that, just for a moment, had sounded like his Laura's.

Chapter Sixty-Two

TEAL

Teal loved the simplicity of her room. Bare, white-washed floorboards bordered by white stone walls, a single wooden wardrobe, shower and toilet. The only thing she had changed was moving the square frame-less mirror from the bathroom next to the only window of her room. The lack of material possessions and overall sparseness always served to remind her of everything she did have, a life so full of what was important to Teal, that from the moment she woke and took in her empty room her happiness for another day started building. The sense of well-being that life at the Freedom Club gave her warmed her from the center of her being.

She took the few steps to the wall with the window and mirror. Teal played the same game every morning when she looked at what she considered to be her two windows, one showing herself, a young woman with short hair that fell naturally about her face, one step sideways and the other window showed the bluest sea stretching forever in all directions. Always straight ahead just by the horizon a shining patch of sea dazzling in the sun greeted her, a little wave of beautiful brightness that reminded her of something from a time long ago, from a place before. The memory wasn't concrete, it was more like a dream saying farewell as full consciousness entered the room of being awake. But this morning was different. The patch of brightness was absent, replaced by a shadow of darkness, shadow because it rippled under the surface. It was far away, on the scale of the endless sea it was but a dark dot, and yet it was all Teal could see. She didn't understand how her perfect view could be ruined by such a small detail, why she was allowing it to be an imperfection she could not ignore?

Teal didn't understand 99.9% complete jigsaw puzzles, how what was missing from the whole can be so dominant, can defile and destroy because it gives nothing through its absence.

She dressed quickly and went looking for Erica. Erica would know what to do.

Chapter Sixty-Three

ERICA

Erica's room, a few doors down the hall from Teal's, was similar in size and shape, but there all similarities stopped. Three c's described it best, colorful cluttered, chaos. Her walls and floor were various shades of blue, which she liked because it meant the sea-view from her window was an extension of her room, rather than something outside it. She too had an affinity for looking at the sea every morning, though she wouldn't claim to see a sparkling patch of sea greeting her, she did see the same dark shadow Teal was making her way to discuss with her. The shadow fascinated Erica because it was so other to the scene; the sea and the sky were normal, they belonged together, the shadow was at odds with the sunny seascape surrounding it, yet it was there just beneath the surface, resting, at home. And something else.

Malevolent.

Erica stepped back from the window, her heart racing, hand on chest. Nothing had happened but she was spooked, as though the dark shadow had reared up and reached out for her. Nothing had happened, the Freedom Club was a safe place, the best place, a place where dark shadows had no home. Erica took a step sideways and looked at the other half of her friend Teal's mirror, the empty frame. Erica had painted it all the colors of the rainbow and many more besides. Teal would joke that it resembled the palette a painter used to mix their colors more than an actual finished painted anything. The bare wall framed by Erica's version of a Jackson Pollock was all she needed for a 'reflecting' surface in her private space. She looked at the naked wall as she traced her bold broad lumpen features, features that in adult life had never known an affectionate touch. Erica would do her make-up and dress for the day in the club's changing room, where, as resident stylist, she looked after all the patrons of the Freedom Club.

As Teal's spartan room focused her on what she did have at the Freedom Club, Erica's routine of starting each day by staring into an invisible mirror and tracing her features, always ending on her eyes, was a result of the first conversation she had with the owner of Freedom Club, Deejon.

Honey Freedom Club is a place to see and be seen on your terms. It's the best place to be while a person works out just how they want to be.

That was the best thing Erica had ever heard. It wasn't about going to a place, it was about being, simply being Erica.

Chapter Sixty-Four

Teal sat on Erica's bed in the middle of what she thought of as Erica's bazaar. Kaftan's, shawls, scarves, pashminas and all manner of flouncy, flowing clothing covered the floor like a carpet of distressed undress. Erica was like a magnificent lighthouse in the midst of the color-storm that was her room. Erica had greeted her with an open door, a smile and no more. Teal approached speaking with Erica like she did a book of poems her Nana had given her. She would randomly open the book never knowing if she would get a 5 line single verse railing against the plight of downtrodden man or a 3 page monologue dripping with wonder at the nature all around us. So far it was looking like a 5 line day.

"You saw it too then?" said Teal.

"No."

"You just said you did."

"I felt it," said Erica.

"What does that even mean?"

Erica approached Teal, fresh from the shower in her white robe. Teal stood and took her friend's hands, black trousers and white shirt in sync with Erica, the lighthouse midst the riot of chaotic color.

"It means we speak to Deejon."

Chapter Sixty-Five

The Freedom Club had echoes of a saloon from the Old West or at least movies set in the Old West. The ground floor was for drinking and entertainment, rooms for guests on the first floor, accessed via stairs adjacent to the entrance, which lead to a balcony running around the upper floor in a large U.

From the balcony Teal and Erica could see Deejon in her favorite booth having breakfast. Spying them coming downstairs Deejon did what Deejon did for everyone at Freedom Club, she made them feel welcome. Deejon was all about the feeling. Her voice was like ice clinking in a sweating glass of fresh lemonade on a hot summer afternoon,

"Hey girls, come join us," they said, waving a long bronze arm. It wasn't bronzed as in a lighter shade that had been tanned, Deejon was a color that defied traditional labels. Teal thought of Deejon's color as warm, she had felt comforted and protected by Deejon from the moment they had first met. It was a feeling she and Erica shared.

"Good morning Beautifull's. Mercer could you bring some eggs and OJ for my Beautifull's please." A deep voice from the kitchen indicated Mercer was taking care of the eggs and OJ.

"Why are we seeing trouble on your faces?" said Deejon.

"We saw a dark shadow on the sea," said Teal.

"Clouds, a shoal of fish, a whale, dolphins, could be many things that mean nothing," said Deejon.

"The shadow had a feeling," said Erica.

"Aah." While Deejon stared deep into the eyes of Erica and Teal, Mercer brought their eggs and OJ.

"My Beautifull's what did I say to you on your first day here, two conversations, one message." Deejon flipped a pointing finger between them, ending on Teal.

"Freedom Club is a safe place, where we can just be."

"So why are you scared of a shadow?"

"The shadow had a feeling," said Erica.

"Feelings are everything my beautiful. They are like millions upon millions of rivers all running to one sea, a sea so wonderful you can't imagine, and whatever pebbles or boulders, dirt or debris the rivers bring into the sea, it is less than a single drop in the vastness of this sea. All the feelings become a part of this wonderful sea when they are ready, when they let go and stop being single drops."

"So, we are like the drops in the sea," said Teal.

"You, my Beautiful have seen the smallest shadow in the sea, it is nothing to fear. As to being drops, it's not something someone else can answer for you."

Deejon got up to leave, saying, "Shadows aren't real only the light that creates them. Be the light."

"As nice as that sounds it's not practically very helpful," said Teal.

Deejon looked from one to the other, the smile on her face betrayed by the worry in her eyes.

"I said something else to both of you when you arrived."

Teal and Erica looked blankly back at Deejon, not remembering anything significant from conversations that seemed a lifetime ago. A glass crashed to the floor in the kitchen and at the sound of shattering pieces a memory exploded to life for Erica.

"You said it's a place to forget until it's time to remember," said Erica.

As Deejon looked at Erica and Teal she shouted, "Mercer, bring my bag."

"How many glasses?" said Mercer.

Eyes intently on Teal and Erica, Deejon answered, "Three."

Mercer brought a beaten-up canvas duffel bag, which made an uncharacteristic clonk when he put it on the table. He also left 3 tall empty water glasses and a small coin, about the size of a dime.

Deejon loosened the drawstring on the duffel bag, rummaged inside before pulling out a heavy mallet hammer. She put the bag in the center of the table, the hammer to the left, glasses to the right, then picked up the coin.

"A place to forget until it's time to remember," said Deejon as she nonchalantly flicked the coin up with their thumb and caught it in the same hand.

"To remember particles so small, that if each were a person all the people that had ever lived could fit on one side of this coin." She slapped the coin down and moved the glasses between her and the duffel bag.

"If I broke one of these glasses and gave you all the pieces you could probably glue it all back together, a lot of time and patience, but it could be done."

Deejon put the three glasses inside the duffel bag, pulled the drawstring tight, picked up the hammer and proceeded to smash the glasses inside the bag. After a good ten thumps on the bag, she put the hammer aside and loosened the drawstring on the duffel bag. Deejon turned the open end of the bag towards Erica.

"As carefully as you can take out a handful of pieces."

Without questioning, Erica did as instructed. Her bloodied hand was full of broken shards of glass, blood slowly dripped between her fingers onto the table.

"Put the pieces in front of you," said Deejon, as she turned the bag towards Teal.

"Your turn."

Teal glanced at the bloody pile of broken glass in front of Erica, her bleeding hand resting on the table, and in her friends' eyes she saw something different, something that convinced Teal to put her hand in the bag too. She could feel the pieces of glass poking and piercing her skin, but the worst was the almost silent slicing of her flesh. It seemed that the pain slowly crept up her arm, weaving a remorseless path to a room in the farthest reaches of her mind. A room Teal did not want to open.

As Deejon put the hammer back in the bag and placed it on the floor, Erica and Teal simultaneously noticed a label on the bag which read, 'Property of Freedom Club.'

The three of them sat there with bleeding hands and piles of bloodied broken glass. The piles were different sizes with differing amounts of blood.

"This is what people's lives really look like. Everyone gets broken, even if only a little, people's lives intermingle, so that making ourselves whole again means we need to help others make themselves whole again too." With her bloody hand Deejon moved pieces of her pile into Erica's and Teal's, indicating for them to do the same.

"It's time to remember," said Deejon.

Chapter Sixty-Six

HUGH

"Hugh, hello, come on over here honey."

Hugh felt like a footballer running through the paper wall before going onto the pitch as he exited the clouds onto wide a plateau at the top of the mountain. The plateau was roughly the width of a soccer pitch and Hugh assumed, it was at the top of the mountain but couldn't be sure because there was a natural stone wall running the entire width. Backing onto the wall, dead center was a hut, just like Gerald's, Beli's and Lennie's but in one way, entirely different. The others had that gray lifeless color wood gets when weathered, a gray that might be OK on a sweater or a car but for a once living material, only has the look of death about it. Hugh hadn't actually given a moment's thought to the appearance of the other huts, they seemed perfectly normal, until he saw the Freedom Club hut. It was a riot of rainbow colors. The sun was blazing in the sky yet the hut somehow managed to seem brighter. These colors always suggested happiness. Hugh believed it was one of the reasons they had been appropriated by the LGBTQ+ community. Happiness was not what they suggested to Hugh Mann. These bright beautiful colors reminded him of his bright beautiful daughter, and all the things he had done to dull the color in her life.

The vibrancy of the small hut had distracted Hugh from Charlie barking excitedly and jumping around someone outside the hut, the someone who had sounded like Laura for the briefest of moments.

As Hugh approached the hut, striding out of the sunlight, hand extended in greeting, came the most beautiful person he had ever seen.

"Hi, I'm Deejon and you are Hugh Mann." Hugh was mesmerized by Deejon's beauty. It was not a physical attraction on any level, but a baser level reaction. He'd heard people speak of the beauty of Michaelangelo's David sculpture and wondered if what he was feeling was something similar. Except Michaelangelo's David, being naked, was clearly a He for all to see. Deejon made no such pretension to a binary description. Deejon wore cut-off overalls, sneakers, had short hair and no physical attributes that Hugh could use to navigate towards a female or male label.

"Are you gonna keep staring and holding my hand or do you wanna come in?" said Deejon. Even the voice, thought Hugh, didn't give a clue for male or female, it was just a tone that suggested comfort and warmth. Then the words of the voice made themselves understood in Hugh's head and he quickly let go of Deejon's hand, stammered an apology and followed Deejon into the rainbow hut.

Chapter Sixty-Seven

They sat at an old wooden dining table, the kind that had the history of many meals etched in the nicks and scratches on its surface, marks of good times shared.

"You made it. You've almost passed your driving test."

"Driving test?"

"Of course, you've done the theory with Lennie and Beli, now comes the practical, out on the road with real people. An analogy, it's good right?"

Deejon looked at Hugh as though nothing could be more important than his answer.

"Yeah, I guess so."

"Excellent," said Deejon slapping the table, "I used a Russian Roulette analogy once, and it did not work." Deejon stared at a space above his left shoulder for so long that he turned to see what they might be looking at. There was nothing.

"Oh honey, you'll need to do more than look over your shoulder if you want to see what we see."

"We? Who else is here?"

"We are us," said Deejon hooking a thumb to point at themselves.

"OK, OK," said Hugh, putting his hands up as though to push Deejon away. "I'm just tired after the walk. I can't...whatever. Deejon, I'll just call you Deejon."

"Well good, and if you're going to pass my little test..." said Deejon reaching over the table as they put a hand first on Hugh's right hand and then his left, "...the practical is gonna need some action from you." Deejon yanked Hugh up, swished his arms around and said, "Are you ready?"

Hugh shrugged off Deejon's hands, "No, nowhere near," he said taking his seat with a resounding thud. Deejon sat back down and waited for Hugh to speak.

"Not long ago Gerald told me I would find Amber here at the Freedom Club. He didn't mention any more puzzles, no practical tests. I would find Amber here, at the Freedom Club, he said that."

"Is that really what he said?"

"Up the mountain, at the Freedom Club, is where Amber would be."

"And that is an entirely different thing indeed. Amber *being* at the Freedom Club and you *finding* her, are not the same thing."

It was Deja vu with Beli's jigsaw. Hugh knew he was beat, that there would be no way round playing by Deejon's rules.

"At least you've told me upfront. Beli let me finish 99.9% of the jigsaw, to then find one piece missing."

Hugh sat back, resignation writ large in his slumped shoulders, Deejon's small kitchen seeming to push him down into his seat. Hugh noticed that he was dripping wet from his walk through the clouds. How could he have missed that? It was as though he had taken a shower in his clothes, yet he was completely unaware until this moment, when he sat back in the chair and was thinking for himself. Something snapped inside Hugh. Thinking for himself. Ever since he had met Gerald C'Farer he had been following instructions, scared that one misstep would cost him the chance of ever finding Amber. Nothing changed about needing Deejon's help, having to follow their rules, but how he followed them was still in his control. Hugh Mann was a man, he knew how to be on the front foot, how to control a room, how to lead, he could take charge when he needed to. If ever there was a time for taking charge it was now. He stood quickly so he could look down on

Deejon as he said, "I'll need some fresh clothes and somewhere to change, then I'll be ready.

Deejon was in no hurry to stand, in fact decided not to.

"Well look at you. Alright Hugh, ready to play the game. Time to take you to the Freedom Club."

Deejon was about to open the hut's back door when they turned to Hugh and said, "Just remember honey, you asked for the change of clothes." Hugh did not like the laugh they made as he followed them out the hut, but he was determined not to be pushed around anymore.

Chapter Sixty-Eight

The back of Deejon's hut was built directly into the wall that ran the length of the plateau. On this side of the wall Hugh could see that the plateau was indeed similar to a soccer pitch in size, with roughly 75% on this side of the wall. Most of the area was a riot of color, Hugh thought of Lennie's First Spark in microcosm, for it was here in garden form, a space where color and nature collided, combining to produce a jazz festival of beautiful fauna. Where there was a clear border between the end of Lennie's garden and the cloudscape, here it was more of a meeting point, the garden falling into the clouds, the clouds resting on the edges of the garden, like old friends gently hugging in greeting.

The Freedom Club occupied roughly a quarter of the plateau. It was difficult for Hugh to comprehend how apposite the building in front of him was to the joy that leaped from the walls of the rainbow hut and all around him in the garden. It was a drab two-story bunker of a building. There were no windows on the ground floor and only a few square windows on the second floor. There was nothing in its appearance to suggest freedom, prison would have been more apt.

A wooden door at odds with the concrete breeze blocks of the main structure, had a hand-painted 'Freedom Club' sign in scruffy gray letters above it. Inside the door Hugh stood with Deejon in a pitch dark entry foyer, a thick curtain separating them from the club proper. The only thing Hugh could see was a glint from Deejon's teeth.

"My advice to all first time visitors to the Freedom Club is always the same, 'just be before you see, just be before you judge, just be,'" said Deejon. She pulled back the curtain, and Hugh was instantly assaulted by light and sound. The light was from fast moving spotlights that were covering an act taking place on a runway stage in the center of the club's main floor. The sound was a combination of the cacophonous music accompanying the stage act and the buzz of the Freedom Club patrons. Hugh followed Deejon as she moved through the tables placed around the stage, heading toward one of the booths running along the wall adjacent to the stage. Lots of people gave Deejon happy greetings and smiled warmly at Hugh. Many watched the act, singing along to pop classics. Others were engrossed in their own conversations, and some simply held hands across their table, seemingly oblivious to anything else except each other. As the first impression of the club settled, Hugh started to see the people. He wanted to stop and stare, to stand on the spot, turn slowly and take it all in, because it felt oddly alien. It was the only word Hugh could find to describe his feeling, and he was actually slowing down to stare when he felt Deejon taking his hand, leading him to their booth. On the opposite wall, the other side of the stage, was a long bar, with mirrored shelves amplifying the size of the already impressive interior.

"You forgot my advice."

They were sitting in one of the vibrant orange and aquamarine booths running the length of the club, the booths giving Hugh the impression he was on some kind of coral bank for humans.

"Sorry, it's just so different from anything I've ever experienced," said Hugh.

"People in a club, enjoying a show, eating and drinking? What a sheltered life you've had," said Deejon.

"Not the club, the people," said Hugh. A waiter arrived to take their order. Hugh barely noticed her. Something had changed, there was something about this place that was different from Lennie's and Beli's places on the mountain. He sensed that Amber was close by, everything had been leading to the Freedom Club. The waiter was leaving, Deejon having placed an order for them, watching her disappear into the crowd Hugh recognized something odd about her; she was the least colorful person in the place, wearing a simple white shirt and black trousers. Her outfit served to remind him again that he needed a change of clothes.

"When Teal returns with our drinks she'll show you to your room where you can get a change of clothes."

"What is this place, it feels different to Lennie's and Beli's?"

"It's a place to be yourself, to find yourself, to wait for yourself."

"Well that's good and cryptic, how long does all this finding and waiting take?"

"How long is a piece of string?"

"Cute."

Teal returned with their drinks. As she served the drinks Hugh noticed her necklace was a piece of string with a simple gold ring on it. He also noticed she wasn't a particularly good waitress, spilling their drinks and in a hurry to leave and serve others.

"Teal honey, when we've finished our drinks would you mind showing our newest guest to his room."

Hugh could see the waitress did not look happy with Deejon's request. By way of response she about-turned and virtually ran away to speak with a colleague.

"Have I done something to upset her?" said Hugh.

"How could you, you've only just arrived," said Deejon.

Chapter Sixty-Nine

TEAL

A new guest at the Freedom Club is nothing new for Teal. Guests are always coming and going, some stay and become a part of the club, like Erica and her, others stay a month, weeks or just a few days and some not even a day. But this person didn't feel like a guest. This person made Teal think about the shadow in the sea from the morning. He was familiar to her but from a time so long ago, from before the Freedom Club and Teal didn't think about the time before the Freedom Club. The past had no place in her present, for Teal this person was viewed through the frosted glass of a front door, unclear and decidedly on the other side of a door only she could open.

"Deejon wants me to show him to his room," said Teal to Erica, who was tending bar.

Erica knew her friend was spooked by the arrival of the new guest. Even though she was too, after Deejon's hammer and glass 'thing' something changed inside Erica. She knew the pile of broken glass could be ignored for as long as she wanted it to be, the cuts on all 3 of their hands that had miraculously healed, seemed to suggest agreement. However, Erica no longer wanted to ignore the sharp dangerous edges of her existence. She wasn't fully sure who the new arrival was, like Teal, she didn't see him as clearly as she saw the others at Freedom Club, didn't see his colors, only the shadow of his colors. He wasn't the first guest to lack the vibrancy and warmth of most of the inhabitants of Freedom Club, but something told Erica he just might be the most important one for her.

She stopped making drinks and took Teal's hands in hers.

"What Deejon did with the glasses, what if he's the broken glass we need to fix ourselves?"

"Who said we need to fix ourselves?" said Teal.

"Apart from Deejon, no one has been at the club longer than you and me. It's a wonderful place *to be* but it's not a place to *stay*. I've never been surer of this, not since I put my hand in the bag with the broken glass."

Chapter Seventy

HUGH

"What is it about the people?" said Deejon. Hugh knew he was in trouble before he said anything. He knew it wasn't OK to say out loud what he was thinking but he didn't know how else to answer Deejon's question. Besides he was certain Deejon would know if he lied, and he felt deep inside himself being honest with his thoughts was more important than the quality of them. He had to stop lying to himself.

"This is not a bar for normal people..." Hugh paused, testing the foundation of his opening gambit, was he on solid ground or already on a rickety bridge? Deejon said nothing, showed no sign of offense.

"...It's a club for LGBTQ+ or whatever the right way to say it is, people," said Hugh.

"And that's not normal for you?" said Deejon.

"I think we can agree that normal is heterosexual, male-female couples and stick with your biological gender at birth," said Hugh.

"Honey I'm not agreeing with anything you say, I don't care what you say, not for now anyway. I want to help you start seeing what you are not seeing," said Deejon.

"I'm all for freedom of choice but some things are not meant to be chosen, they come as a basic part of who, of how, we are," said Hugh.

"What do you think this club is all about?" said Deejon.

"I think..."

"Don't think, take a walk, make a circuit and then tell me what you saw, then maybe you can think," said Deejon. As Hugh stood to leave the waiter arrived with their drinks, Hugh's bottle of beer and Deejon's Lovely

239

Sunset, which was a long-stemmed square cocktail glass filled with blue Curacao over crushed ice. Intricately curved ice-swans floated on the blue drink, one side of the glass had a thin sliver of watermelon with a smaller disk of pineapple skewered to it, giving the effect of a sun against a red sky. Deejon clapped with delight then shooed Hugh away so as to be left alone with her Lovely Sunset.

Hugh suspected Deejon was probably a transgender person, but he couldn't identify which way they had transitioned, and he didn't feel he had the sophistication to discuss it with Deejon. Although he had felt quite comfortable to tell Deejon that the people in the club were not normal. He decided to take Deejon's advice and make a circuit simply observing the people. He did. And he saw exactly what he expected to see. LGBTQ+ couples and groups enjoying each other's company and a wild trans singing show. Some couples/groups were more touchy-feely than others, some were like a long-married couple, comfortable in each other's company without the need for much communication. He didn't see anything inappropriate for a public place. Except for the general group vibe some tables gave him, and every set-up that wasn't heterosexual. Of course, that was inappropriate.

The sun had definitely set on Deejon's drink when Hugh returned, and his beer bottle was sweating in a most thirst-inducing way. Deejon let him take a long swig before saying, "What did you see?"

"The people are enjoying themselves, the guys or gals on stage can belt out a tune while dancing in crazy heels, but it's not right. We're not meant to have same gender, multi-gender, multi-partner/multi-gender relationships at the same time. Let alone changing gender and then revisiting all the options from the new gender," said Hugh.

"I'm guessing your views have a lot to do with..."

"I'm not a religious fundamentalist, you can't put me in that box. I might be looking for my dead daughter's soul, but I've never said this has to be about God," said Hugh.

"I was going to say your views have a lot to do with how we procreate, you know, man and woman make baby, so there's a kind of Mother Nature's way about how we should do things," said Deejon.

"Exactly," said Hugh, feeling immensely satisfied that someone had finally understood him.

The waiter arrived with another round of drinks. As she shuffled the empty and full glasses between tray and table Hugh noticed she was wearing a pin badge on her shirt. On closer inspection he saw that it was a flag in the shape of a jigsaw piece. He assumed he was looking at the LGBTQ+ Rainbow Flag in the shape of a jigsaw piece, and then it felt as though everything stopped as Hugh saw the real colors of the flag; seven horizontal bars, top and bottom black, next top and bottom were gray then two white sandwiching a green bar. Beyond the waiter Hugh noticed dots of bright light all over the club, as though for a fleeting second everyone in the club had a badge that flashed. Then everything was moving again, the noise and color was back, and the loudest thing was Deejon finishing off another Lovely Sunset.

"What are the badges all about?" said Hugh.

"Flags of identity. Teals', our waiter, represents agender."

"Meaning she is a gender," said Hugh.

"Meaning she doesn't identify with any gender," said Deejon.

Hugh shook his head, as a parent might to a child that was earnestly demonstrating belief in something that was patently childish and would soon enough be put aside with the wisdom of living longer.

Deejon was giving Hugh exactly the same look.

"Your puzzle has two parts. Part One itself has two parts. Part One A is for you to visit the Freedom Club dressed up appropriately, to be a part of all this 'inappropriateness' you have been telling me about. Part One B is for you to perform on stage in whatever you decide is your favorite costume..."

"Hang on..."

"I'm not finished, let me tell you about Part Two before you protest, which will be a waste of time, let me tell you that now. Part Two is a question. The question is, can you tell me why this is not The Freedom Club?"

Hugh folded his arms, like a child facing a meal he didn't want to eat.

"I don't want to do any of Part One and Part Two doesn't make any sense."

"Very good. Why don't you let Teal show you to your room, where the costumes can be found," said Deejon paying no attention to Hugh's protest. She got up to leave as Teal made her way over to the table.

Chapter Seventy-One

Teal was leading Hugh through the club to the backstage changing area. They went down a small spiral staircase which lead straight into a large open dressing room. Performers were everywhere in all states of undress, from clothes to wigs to make-up to simply having a shower, in what resembled a 5 star hotel version of a communal prison shower on the far wall. Hugh had stopped on the last step of the stairs to take in the smorgasbord of people and their tangible excitement at the prospect of performing, or flush with the pleasure of having performed already. But there was something else, a resistance to participate, to step into the light with the other performers, the others whom Hugh judged inappropriate.

While Hugh simultaneously admired and rejected what he saw, Teal returned to chaperone him to his room. She stood in front of Hugh, smaller, as he was one step off ground-level. She was so different to Deejon, whose character Hugh couldn't imagine the room it couldn't fill, dominating the space with its pride. Teal, Hugh imagined, would be difficult to find in a half-empty room even if she wore a bill-board sign proclaiming; I am Teal, I am here. Hugh felt sorry for this poor mouse, wondering how she survived in a place like Freedom Club.

Stepping down to her level, he realized they were similar in height, she was in half-shadow between the harsh brightness of the changing room with all the blazing make-up mirror lights and the darkness of the stairwell entrance. Behind her was like a movie running at 1.5x normal speed as people changed; costumes on, costumes off, faces painted, faces cleansed, hair netted, wigs wild and afire with color. The noise was more akin to a memory Hugh had of being backstage at a circus as a child, except here it was only human artists preparing to sing and dance. Teal was between him and this carnival of people in various states of change, Teal in her black trousers and white shirt with her stripy jigsaw pin-badge, seemed barely present.

"I need to show you the way," said Teal as she turned and walked away through the colors of the changing room.

Chapter Seventy-Two

Over her shoulder Teal said, "Your room doesn't have a bathroom, so when you've chosen an outfit, you bring it here to change. If you need any help with your look, just ask Erica."

"Look. Jeans and shirt are hardly a look," said Hugh.

The only 'look' Teal cared about was being away from the look of this the new guest. She didn't share Erica's certainty about needing to leave the Freedom Club. To leave somewhere, you needed to have somewhere to go, and Teal had nowhere she wanted to go, needed nothing more than her life at the Freedom Club. She knew it was silly to think the new guest had anything to do with the shadow in the sea, but his presence annoyed her in the same way the shadow did; once you knew it was there you were drawn to it, no matter the vastness of the surrounding beauty, one blemish rendered the whole imperfect.

"Whatever, that's between you and Deejon." Without waiting for a response from Hugh, Teal about-turned and went to another spiral staircase, this one by the side of the showers. As Hugh followed Teal a dazzling flash of light pierced his vision. He stood alone at the bottom of the stairs, rubbing his eyes vainly hoping to accelerate the return of sight. As his vision returned Hugh saw a large person in a blood red kaftan bent over a chair shaving one of the performers with a naked razor. It was the movement of the razor reflecting the bright lights of the make-up mirror that had blinded Hugh. The person in the kaftan wore a yellow bandanna to keep long hair pulled back while working. Even bent over, wearing what amounted to a red tent, Hugh could tell the person had a big frame, the face had large flat open spaces separated by what looked like a sitting cow for a nose and two dark caves housing eyes so deeply blue they were almost black. Everything was big and bold about this person, and Hugh was struggling to reconcile the delicate flowing movements of her hands as she shaved the person in the chair, with the fact that the giant was a woman. As the thought that he was looking at a woman punched its way to the open spaces of his mind, the object of his staring stopped shaving to stare back at him. It was as though the snow in the snow globe melted away and all Hugh could see was the woman, nothing but this bold woman challenging him to look away.

"Hugh, are you coming?"

Teal's question broke the spell.

Teal led Hugh to a room on the opposite side of the balcony to hers and Erica's. The rooms on this side were for the short-stay guests, those that came for a show or two and then moved on. Deejon always seemed to know who needed to stay on which side of the balcony. It gave Teal a lift that she had put the new guest in one of these rooms.

Hugh wasn't sure if he had a room with a large closet or a closet with a bed. There was a small bed for sleeping in the middle of the room. The rest was closet. The two long walls had entire racks dedicated to outlandish dresses and outfits, which Hugh imagined only the most extrovert drag queens would entertain wearing. The far wall had a rack with what, on first glance, looked like regular suits, but it was a deception relative to the wild outfits on the adjacent walls. In their own right, the suits were more Liberace than Armani. The walls behind Hugh, either side of the door, had vintage outfits from 1920's sequined flapper dresses to 1970's floral hippie clothing to 1980's power dressing. Above the racks on all the walls were rows and rows of shelves housing shoes, boots, shirts, tops, jumpers, hats, smaller racks with scarves, boas, shawls, ties, bow ties, cravats. He heard a click, turned to see that Teal had left.

He locked the door, stripped from his wet clothes and stood naked in a room full of clothes, with nothing for him to wear.

Chapter Seventy-Three

Laying on the bed Hugh wondered why Teal had left so suddenly, it was as though she didn't want to be near him. It bothered him more than he wanted to admit because it reminded him of what was left unsaid between him and Amber, of intentional avoidance to keep the family happy. The clothes in this room told the story of everything Hugh thought about the gays, about the LGBTQ+ community, they were loud and proud and in his face, and he didn't want them there. He rested his head between his knees and got what felt like a punch to the face from a conversation remembered.

"Dad I'm not ill, being gay is not something to be cured," said Amber.

"It's not normal either, normal is girls liking boys and boys liking girls. If you're lucky you find the right person and you make a life together. It's simple and normal," said Hugh.

"So I'm abnormal according to you. You're like someone who believes the earth is flat, you can't imagine that the world is not how you believe it to be. It's not normal to not love your children. How about that?"

"What? Amber, honey of course I love you," said Hugh.

"I'm not asking whether you think you love me, I'm telling you how I feel," said Amber.

"I just want what's best for you honey. Not being gay is for the best."

Amber left the dining table in a whirlwind of frustrated anger, tipping over her chair before the inevitable teenage door-slam.

Hugh started to clear the mess when Laura stopped him, told him to sit, they needed to talk.

"I know you love Amber but what you're doing is not going to work," said Laura.

"Oh come on, a teenage tantrum about not being understood, a version of the 'I hate you' speech and a door slam. It's pretty standard."

"What is standard is our daughter finding and growing into who she is, and she is a young gay person. What is not standard is your lack of understanding, your bottom-line belief that this is a phase, something she will grow out of. Being gay is not a debatable position for Amber."

Something snapped inside Hugh. It felt like he'd spent the last year being Mr. Wrong, on being on the wrong side of every discussion where Amber was concerned. His views were normal, he was a part of a massive majority of normal heterosexual people, yet in his own home he was Neanderthal Man with his so-called backward thinking.

"I'm sick and tired of feeling like the last asshole in this conversation. Is it so wrong that I wished for my daughter to be straight, that I had the crazy idea she would get married, have kids, we'd have grandkids. Can you honestly tell me you didn't want the same?" said Hugh.

It took Laura a while to answer, like a painter unsure which brush to use, after a moment she had her chosen brush, something to give bold, clear strokes, this was anything but a delicate water-color.

"I think you need to look at this picture differently. You told me the story of what a moment it was for you when you saw me holding Amber for the first time in the birthing room."

"Nothing has changed about that," said Hugh.

"I know, but while you were having your moment I was too, holding the life I had carried inside me for all those months, a life that was a part of me but was now starting its journey apart from me. When I looked at Amber for the first time something beyond the physical bond was born, a feeling from a place so deep it felt almost primal. It was more than love for our child, it was a base commitment to nurture, to protect and for her happiness, that the world would be good to her, and she would be good to the world."

"You think I don't have those same feelings?" said Hugh.

"Your idea of normal seems to be more important than her happiness right now. Her wellbeing comes before any wishes we have for grandkids, not that it's an issue anyway."

"So, you're telling me you're OK with everything," said Hugh.

"Not everything..." she came and sat by Hugh, took his hands in hers, "...my wellbeing only hits top gear if that fiery teenager of ours is OK, and the man I love is OK too. We walked down paths that were well-trodden, new for us but not new paths. The kids today are off the map we know, they are making the charts..."

"But why do they need new maps, the old ones worked," said Hugh.

"Only if you want to see the same places," said Laura. Hugh went to speak again, Laura put a finger to his lips.

"If you want to go on this journey with Amber, you'll need to learn to read her map. And you really have to try my love because the journey is her life," said Laura.

The memory was bittersweet; arguing with Amber, Laura's wisdom and his ever so flawed response, which to use Laura's map analogy, was to ignore any new maps, grab the oldest, dustiest map he could find and set off for the old world, full steam ahead. Hugh flopped back on the bed, embracing the weariness of sleep that crept from his toes to his head, wishing for the oblivion of blessed unconsciousness, foolishly thinking the deep would be safer than the shallows.

Hugh's dream had no scenery, only a feeling of hunger so intense it was like a wound from which the blood of his life was gushing. He could hear it splattering on a hard floor, globs of blood pumping from his body. The wound could not be staunched, only eating would stop the bleeding. He was on the floor slick with his blood, and he was sticky too. Lights came on. His blood was not red, it was pink and white and orange. His blood was blancmange splattered about the floor. He greedily scooped handfuls into his mouth. It was the most satisfying taste he had ever had, it was beyond food, it was heaven in his mouth, if the perfect summer's day had a taste, this was it. He was scooping so fast and so much, he could feel it dripping down his chin. He wiped his chin with the back of his hand and screamed as he saw his hand covered in his blood, a scream that was choked silent as his mouth filled with blood. He slumped to the floor surrounded by the messy pretty blancmange, full of broken glass.

Hugh sat up in his dream, broken glass and blancmange long gone. He was sitting cross-legged in the middle of a road, a road that ran through the darkness of space. Above his road in space was a patch of blue sky with a cloud in it. Sitting on the cloud was his daughter waving at him. He felt as though he could jump from the road to the patch of sky above. He stood ready to make the jump, when he noticed Amber was waving *something* at him and pointing with her other hand to him. It was a phone and when he looked in his own hand, he was holding a cell phone with a screen as dark as the infinite space around him. He looked back to Amber, hoping for a clue, maybe she could call him with her phone, that must be it. The patch of blue, the cloud and Amber were gone. The phone vibrated. It was Amber contacting him, he knew it. It vibrated again, this time there was a tingle in his hand, like a faint electric shock. Hugh knew with certainty it was not

Amber. From the depths of the screens' darkness words were spat onto the screen, *Remember what you did.*

The darkness started to fall away from the screen, revealing a picture. Hugh didn't want to see the picture. It was as simple as that, with every fiber of his being he knew it would destroy him, and if he couldn't control the screen, he could control his eyes, he squeezed them shut and heard a truck approaching fast.

Hugh woke breathless. The room was silent and dark save for some of the outfits glinting in the moonlight that fell through the window. As his breathing settled the images from his dream played in his head, and like any good director, he cut them to show the movie he wanted to see; no sharp objects, no blood, no hard to answer questions, just a girl waving to her father, inviting him to come to her.

Hugh jumped up from the bed, dressed in his own damp clothes keeping the light off, not wanting to see the bright ridiculous clothing on offer in the room. He exited to a wall of sound coming from the club floor below, but he heard nothing other than the call of Amber from his edited dream.

Chapter Seventy-Four

AMBER. IS. HERE.

It was the soundtrack to the movie in Hugh's head. While a carnival of happiness played out around him in the Freedom Club, he saw only enemies to his own happiness, people who weren't Amber, people who were in the way of him finding Amber. He rushed between tables, startling people enjoying the karaoke show, people enjoying their own company.

Hugh felt like a rock in the middle of a fast-flowing river, all rough surfaces full of fissures and sharp edges, water flowing around his heavy immovable body. Though he made the water go around him, it did not change course, its flow was never broken, instead it embraced him as it moved on. And Hugh embraced this idea of himself, he liked it, his heaviness, the ugliness of his solidity that prevented him from moving. There was strength in weight, in convictions that didn't change because they didn't need to change. There was an empty booth, Hugh half walked half fell into the booth, his still damp clothes squelching on impact with the leather seat.

Chapter Seventy-Five

"Well, that's a first, never seen anyone sleep in here before," said Deejon.

Hugh woke from his slumber feeling like he'd spent an evening drinking mead with Beli, except he hadn't the pleasure of doing the drinking, only the hangover.

"I saw you running around looking everywhere, seeing nothing."

"Please, no riddles, no puzzles. I know Amber is here, just tell me where I can find her."

"I already told you she is here. To see her you're going to have to see her."

Hugh slumped back in the booth.

"That's what you call no riddles?"

"You thinking it's a riddle says more about your lack of understanding of the situation. What I said is as plain as the nose on my face. Give me your map."

Hugh pulled the folded somewhat damp map from his jacket pocket and gave it to Deejon.

"How did you know I had a map?"

"Everyone Gerald sends here has a map, they don't all look the same, but they all tell a story," said Deejon as they smoothed out the map on the table.

"If you can't tell me how to find her, can you at least tell me what the Freedom Club is all about. It's got to be more than a gay club."

Deejon snapped their gaze from the map to Hugh.

"It's not a gay club Hugh." Their eyes were like lasers burning their words directly into his head. When Hugh looked away, they returned to the map.

"So, what do we have here? Gerald's hut, Lennie's hut, Beli's hut and our little Freedom Club, with you right in the middle of it." As Deejon said the last words they removed a rope necklace from their neck. Hugh could see that like Teal's, it had a gold band hanging of it. Deejon placed the rope necklace over the Freedom Club on the map. They waggled the ring around the rope a little and said, "You."

"Teal has a necklace like that."

"Everyone does, it's a simple symbolic thing. See, the rope represents circular time, because it has no beginning, no end, it's an infinite loop of time. The ring represents a person, in this case, you." They moved the ring around the loop of rope.

"And you can go round and round taking as long as you need to work things out."

"But I don't have as long as I need. Gerald and Beli both said I had to hurry."

"They weren't lying. Things always get completed when more than one person is involved."

"Then tell me now, where can I find Amber," pleaded Hugh.

"I'll tell you how you can find Amber," said Deejon as they turned the map over. On the reverse side was Hugh's equation, his conditional logic for finding Amber;

- *She was dying in my arms*
- *I could see her in the sky*
- *I could hear her*
- *Therefore, I can find her*

"A sound piece of reasoning Hugh." Deejon turned the map so it faced Hugh.

"You asked us what the Freedom Club is really about. Hope. This is a place where Hope lives. If a person is set in their ways, say like a stone that doesn't change, they will never understand the Freedom Club, never find what they are looking for in the Freedom Club."

"I could if you told me where to look."

"You don't look for Hope with your eyes Hugh. Hope is something wished for, something yet to come, Hope lives in the present while it is directed at the future. A person that doesn't want to see things differently can't understand Hope in the Freedom Club." Deejon turned the map over to show the huts on the mountain.

"You might think what I say next is a riddle, but it's really the question that will help you find the answer to understand Hope. The question you must answer for us Hugh Mann is, Why is the Freedom Club not the Freedom Club?"

Hugh didn't have the energy to question anything Deejon had said. He simply stared at the map wondering if it would be more accurate to call it Hugh's Folly.

"One last thing. A little dance might help you get a feeling for this place, help you with the question."

Hugh smiled ruefully, he was falling fast, didn't know how long the fall would be, only that it wasn't a fall you walked away from. When he looked up the large woman from the changing room was sitting at the table with them.

"I'm Erica. If you dress, I will sing with you." She left without waiting for Hugh to respond.

"Looks like you got a cross on your dance card," said Deejon laughing merrily.

Chapter Seventy-Six

TEAL

In the changing room Erica was shaving one of the guests, recumbent with a hot towel over his eyes, while Teal busied herself tidying Erica's already perfectly tidy make-up table.

"I saw you talk to him you know," said Teal looking at Erica in the mirror.

Erica continued shaving the guest.

"Why did you talk to him? He doesn't look like he belongs here."

Erica stopped shaving and looked at her friend in the mirror.

"Maybe he could belong here if we help him."

"Why? He looks old and angry, makes me uncomfortable."

"He's broken. I know what that feels like," said Erica.

Teal couldn't say why she wasn't happy with her friends' intentions towards the stranger, she only knew that while Erica saw someone to help, she saw someone dangerous.

Chapter Seventy-Seven

HUGH

Hugh didn't know how long he'd been staring at his so-called map before an iced water was plonked on the table, spilling some of its contents on the map.

"Sorry."

Hugh looked up to see Teal not looking very sorry.

"You looked like you were thirsty."

"Thanks, I guess," said Hugh as he used his still damp sleeve to mop the spilled water.

"Are you going to dance with Erica?"

"I wasn't planning to."

"It's what I thought," said Teal before turning and walking quickly away.

Hugh moved the map aside, pulled the glass of water close, something new to occupy his attention. A large cube of ice bobbed in the water, it's all there was to see, the main attraction. Hugh didn't know if time sped up or he simply stared at the ice in the glass longer than he realized, but before his eyes it gradually became smaller and smaller until it vanished, consumed by the water, into the whole. He took a sip of water and sat back. He wasn't an ice cube, he wasn't a stone in a river, he was an old grizzly bear, too slow to hunt, too big to survive. What good were bears anyway? Maybe he was being unfair to bears, but as animals go an old bear seemed to sum him up, fat on glories past, slow to keep up with times that had raced ahead of him, he was too old, too expensive and the wrong gender for his job. Wrong gender. Hugh looked around the club considering this last point and his inability to understand it. How could gender be so complicated? If anything was ever binary it was gender, boy or girl, girl or boy, there was no other way to look at it. People could feel differently in their heads but they had the body they had. Hugh sat back, he felt something with that last thought, like a seed stuck in his tooth, so small, but its presence occupied all his attention.

Across the club he saw Teal. Agender. What could that even mean? He could see a young woman, she could have whatever sexual orientation worked for her, but she clearly had a gender. Agender. Non-binary. How could that possibly work?

Deejon slid back into the booth.

"Thought you'd be getting ready for your dance with Erica."

"Thought you'd be more helpful."

"Touche," said Deejon smiling.

"Can I ask your gender?"

"Only if you can tell us why it matters."

"Of course it matters, I mean you can see that I'm a man but I'm not sure if you're a man or a woman."

"Or neither."

"Don't do that," said Hugh.

"Don't think with your eyes," said Deejon pulling the map to the center of the table and flipping it over to show Hugh's logical reasoning for searching for Amber.

"Look at your first two statements,"
- *She was dying in my arms*
- *I could see her in the sky*

"So what did you see, her soul. What were you holding, her body. The soul is not the body, it's something else. Lennie taught you about the scale of the Universe, the magnitude of what is unknown, and about the quantum realms. We've got the quantum realms going on inside our heads, the spark that gives us consciousness. As the candle exists in different forms, so do we. Emotions are what make our souls, at the most basic, fundamental level of existence, we are emotions in a form that is beyond the way people approach understanding the human soul."

"What do you mean by approach understanding the human soul?"

"Like your views on gender, views of the soul tend to be binary. It either doesn't exist because science explains everything we know and will, given enough time, explain everything we don't know too. Or the soul is a subject of spirituality and religion, where it's more of a concept, sometimes evidenced by a sense of inner well-being. But what if the answer to the existence of our souls is a combination of science and spirituality? We can understand the nature of our souls through knowledge of the quantum world, while their purpose is to be found under the umbrella of spirituality. Not that it matters if you don't want to see it this way."

"How can it not matter," asked Hugh.

"Because it's not something that needs to be studied, even if it could be studied. You saw a word in flames, it touched you deeply, it was the tiniest glimpse into the world of souls and you were overwhelmed. You will need to be your soul if you want to understand the language of souls and the language of souls is emotions."

"I don't want to be my soul just yet, I want to find my daughter's soul, have some sort of connection, so I can share it with Laura."

Deejon reached over the table taking Hugh's hands in their own, "Embrace this place Hugh, let go of the thoughts that are holding you back, the soul has no gender."

Chapter Seventy-Eight

Hugh returned to his room, unable to stay in the club where Deejon said he could find Amber, and where he felt further away from her than at any time on this crazy journey. There was a knock on the door. Hugh opened it expecting it to be Deejon with more confusing advice.

"Are you ready to sing with me?" said Erica, wearing the same kaftan and headband from earlier.

"Why is it so important to you?"

Erica pushed past Hugh, into his room and immediately started looking through the racks of outfits.

"We're not singing together and I'm not wearing anything from this room."

"I can help you find your daughter."

"You're not the first person to say that, and apart from knowing more than I ever wanted to about the Universe and completing a jigsaw, I'm no closer to finding Amber."

Erica continued rifling through the outfits, putting some on an empty rack, presumably for Hugh to try on.

When Hugh realized Erica wasn't going to say anything else he asked, "How can you help me, a crash course in chemistry or some new board game?"

Erica ignored him as she went through the last rack of clothes.

"You don't say much."

"Sometimes words can be like wrapping paper, hiding what's really important."

"OK, so what's important?"

"What you do," said Erica as she turned, offering an outfit to Hugh.

Her smile was like a mouse sniffing the air for threats, and in her barely upturned lips there was a question,

Will you? Hugh was trying to work out if she had spoken the words out loud when she approached him, stood close so he had to look up to fully see her face.

"We can help each other, I feel it..." Erica took Hugh's hand and placed it on her heart.

"...here."

A surge of electricity shot up Hugh's arm as Erica held his hand to her chest. He tried to pull away, but Erica's big hand clasped his as a mother's would a child's when crossing a busy street. And like the child who initially fights the restraint before realizing he wants to go where his mother is leading him, Hugh stopped pulling away from Erica and felt something that was beyond any description that made sense; Hugh felt color, burning, bright, vibrant, glorious colors. He thought the tears he could see gently tracing their way across the expanse of Erica's cheeks were blurring his vision until he realized it was his own tears.

Chapter Seventy-Nine

'Embrace this place Hugh...'

Hugh had reached the bottom of his fall only to be caught by a strange woman who believed they could help each other by singing karaoke together. Hugh thought he would go insane if he dwelt too long on the idea that his search for Amber's soul ended with him in a sing-along with Erica. But Deejon, man or woman or neither, had told him to embrace the Freedom Club, and when you're out of options even the craziest idea is still something to do. More than anything else, he had felt a connection to Erica that was beyond anything he had ever experienced in his life. It made the wonder of seeing Laura holding Amber for the first time seem like nothing more than a smile at a fond memory.

Which explained why Erica was now holding a razor to his throat. A razor she was using to shave him. After the moment of 'seeing color' when Erica held his hand to her heart, he decided to follow Deejon's advice, so when Erica suggested a shave and freshen-up, he quietly agreed. As Erica's razor followed the contours of Hugh's face, he traced the story in her big bold face, the story behind the makeup, behind the 4 o'clock shadow making an appearance, the story of the man Erica once was. *'Why?'* bounced around his mind, like a bird in a storm, flying with no control. Erica stopped shaving, her blade at the bottom of a stroke down his jawline. It was as though she had heard Hugh's unspoken question.

Hugh noticed Erica's jigsaw-piece shaped pin badge, two pale blue horizontal stripes at top and bottom, each next to a pale pink stripe and a single white stripe in the middle. He didn't ask what it meant for fear of what his reply might be.

From a distance Teal watched. From a distance Hugh and Erica appeared mid-embrace, a freeze-frame of motion about to explode, emotion that started on a journey long ago, a journey that was soon going to conclude. From a distance Teal could see Erica holding a razor to Hugh's throat.

Hugh closed his eyes and spoke, "Finish what you have started. Please."

Chapter Eighty

TEAL

Teal had fled the changing room when she saw Erica holding the razor to Hugh's throat. She hadn't fled because of what she might see, it was because of what she wanted to see. She was hiding in the cellar underneath the bar when Deejon found her.

"There you are, drink this honey," said Deejon proffering a shot glass filled with a clear syrupy liquid.

"Will it help?" said Teal, knocking it back before Deejon could answer, feeling the liquid like a kick to the gut as she bent over, dry-coughing hard.

"It's called Firewater, Portuguese farmers use it to kick-start their early mornings, warm their bellies and chase the sleep away to face the work ahead."

"It's not morning."

"Doesn't mean you're not waking from some kind of sleep," said Deejon helping Teal to her feet.

Deejon brought Teal up from the cellar to her booth.

"Why were you hiding in the cellar?"

Teal was clutching her iced water glass as if her life depended on it as she said, "It felt like the furthest I could get from myself."

"You know it's impossible to hide from yourself?"

Teal looked at Deejon with red-rimmed eyes for a long moment, "It's him. He makes me wish for horrible things and I don't know why. This place used to feel like home, I was safe here..." She snatched her glass to her mouth, drinking deeply as the water spilled over her face. Glass empty Teal roughly wiped her mouth with the back of her hand.

"...not anymore."

The lights went out.

Chapter Eighty-One

HUGH

Hugh followed Erica from the changing room to the main room of the Freedom Club. A small set of stairs to the left lead up to the runway stage. Erica hit a switch on the wall next to the changing room door and all the lights in the Freedom Club went out.

"For Saturday Night Specials," said Erica as she took Hugh's hand to lead him up the stairs.

Hugh was in shock; as the lights went out and he felt Erica's touch, memories flashed like a strobe in his mind.

Getting dressed for dinner.
Amber excited.
Rainbow colors.
A smashed bowl of colors.
A cell phone with a broken screen.
Hugh falling into the black hole of the broken screen.
'Remember what you did!'
The owner of the voice waiting for Hugh in the darkness

Luckily for Hugh, before he could fall too deeply into the tricks of his memory, Erica was leading him up the stairs onto the stage.

"We call it Saturday Night Special, but it just means whenever a main event is going to happen, can be any night," said Erica.

As they stepped onto the stage a spotlight picked them out and tracked them as they made their way along the stage. Murmurs of appreciation and applause rippled through the audience.

Hugh didn't know how to describe how he felt. A moment ago on the stairs he was drowning in memories that had finally caught up with him, and just when he was about to be overwhelmed, Erica rescued him. Now walking beside her, dressed in an identical red kaftan, yellow bandanna, Kohl-lined eyes, ruby red cheeks, blood-red lipstick, he felt gloriously alive, the bliss of utter freedom, like a dolphin swimming for nothing but the pleasure of swimming.

Then the music started.

Chapter Eighty-Two

Hugh recognized the melody instantly, Diana Ross's I'm Coming Out, he suspected it was a fan favorite in the Freedom Club. The mainly instrumental intro seemed extended to Hugh, the percussive ching ching of the guitar persisting longer than he remembered. The lyrics presented on a monitor by the stage, a hush swept across the club as Erica started to sing. This big, ungainly trans-woman sang with the voice of an angel, Erica channeled Diana Ross so well, that if your eyes were closed, you would believe Lady D herself was in the house. But Hugh didn't close his eyes, couldn't take them of Erica, singing with her own eyes closed, she was beauty personified, and like a switch being flicked Hugh was lost in the glory of the moment, the dolphin was swimming faster than any dolphin ever had, jumping, twisting, squealing with pleasure, alone and at the same time connected to everything. His arms went out by his sides, something like rhythm, a distant cousin perhaps, took a hold of him and he danced. Hugh Mann wiggled, he shook, he shuffled, he grooved, he freaked out. The music stopped. Hugh opened his eyes, he was half-way down the stage, a stage that only he occupied. Erica was sitting at a table on her own. How long ago had the music stopped? Then a new sound hit Hugh; applause, whooping and cheering. And it was all for Hugh. He slowly walked to the front of the stage, embarrassment creeping over him at the thought of what he must have looked like. Then he saw the joyous faces of the people, they were happy for him, happy with him, there was music and they danced around their tables, most better than him but not all, and no one cared, there was a simple joyful abandon in their group movement.

Hugh felt free in a way he never expected. When he decided to follow Deejon's advice and embrace the Freedom Club he had let Erica choose an outfit for him and paint his face so that he could hide, just be a person in drag singing a quick song, get it over with, maybe Erica could help divine an answer to Deejon's question. In his attempt to hide, Hugh found an unexpected freedom, a rounding out of the squared-off edges that had allowed him to fit into the box of Hugh Mann, binary male, who saw the world of gender in either pink or blue. As Erica belted out the lyrics of 'I'm Coming Out', Hugh was decidedly not coming out. As he twisted and twirled to the beat of the music, Hugh realized it wasn't about being one thing or another, it was just about being, and in that moment he was a person dancing to the beat of the color he felt in the music.

Erica was waiting for him at a table not far from the stage. As Hugh joined her she pushed something across the table to him. Her badge, except now it was a blank white badge.

"I don't need this anymore."

"It doesn't have the colors it used to." As Hugh looked from the badge to Erica he took in everything about her; heavy make-up couldn't hide the heavy-set masculine features beneath. The effort to present female wasn't really working for Erica, Hugh couldn't stop himself from seeing her as ugly. But. Her face kept falling off. Hugh blinked. Ugly Erica. Blink. Something else. Before his eyes Erica was changing. But Erica was not changing. It was Hugh. His brain, pre-wired to see beauty in a certain way, was applying frameworks to Erica, which couldn't hold, couldn't fight the real beauty of Erica, her voice, her kindness. The pre-wired templates kicked hard against Hugh's eyes wide open moment, and then for the briefest moment, Erica exploded in light. Hugh didn't know if it really happened or he imagined it, but for half a second he saw her soul, it was beyond a beautiful voice, beyond physical appearance.

Hugh was breathing heavily. Sensing something had changed in him, Erica placed both her hands in his and smiled. Hugh had never seen anything so beautiful. Erica looked exactly the same, Hugh simply didn't see her with any judgment.

"You must decide what colors your badge has Hugh."

HUGH. Erica had never said his name before and now she was looking at him, really looking at him as though she knew him. And suddenly Hugh knew Erica from another time.

"Alvin."

Chapter Eighty-Three

"I have to go, I'm ready to move on," said Alvin.
"I'm sorry Alvin, I never meant to hurt you."
Again, Alvin took Hugh's hands in hers. "We always think only the nail feels the blow of the hammer, but in the striking, there is pain on both sides. Spending time with you helped me realize this. This does not excuse the hammer, but to understand it, allows me to go beyond."

Hugh froze, did a mental rewind to the beginning of the conversation with Alvin, and got lost in a black hole of utter confusion.

Breaking free from Alvin's grasp he said, "How are you...Why are you here?"

"Don't you know what happened..."

"Where is here?" said Hugh frantically looking around as though seeing the Freedom Club for the first time.

"...after I left the restaurant?"

"Restaurant?" But the word didn't conjure a memory of an evening at Pride restaurant. Instead, Hugh saw an image of a broken cell phone screen upon which the image of a beaten face was resolving pixel by pixel. Hugh was transfixed by the developing image, like passing the scene of an accident, knowing you shouldn't look but unable not to, Hugh was powerless to tear his internal gaze from the image revealing itself on the screen.

Alvin grabbed his hands again, thrusting her face across the table to get Hugh's full attention.

"Look at me Hugh."

Hugh snapped out of his grim picture-reveal moment and looked at Alvin's close-up face.

"It's not just what you do, it's what you do next that matters most." The Freedom Club seemed momentarily silent as Alvin's words screamed into his head. Alvin was standing, then moving away, Hugh desperately wanted to stop him, he needed more time with him. Hugh lurched after the disappearing Alvin and then stopped. In moving away Alvin had done all that was needed to find Amber.

Chapter Eighty-Four

TEAL

"I always thought Erica and I would sing together," said Teal.

"But you never did," said Deejon.

They had watched Erica and the new guest sing together from Deejon's both.

"Doesn't mean we couldn't have," said Teal, her 25 year old face making a little pout as she stared at the back of Erica sitting some tables away with the new guest.

Deejon smiled to herself, enjoying the glimpse of the 16 year old she knew Teal to have been when she arrived in the Place Between. It was because Teal didn't want to let go of where she started, was unwilling to fully grow from that point of entry, that she was still here at the Freedom Club.

"The new guest repulses you but Erica is drawn to him, he gives her something she needs..."

"What could he possibly..."

"Don't ask, because I don't know. Maybe it's her time to remember."

As Deejon spoke Erica left her table and Teal was staring into her past, into a memory of watching a man holding the dying body of a girl holding a broken cell phone. Of her Dad, holding her as died.

"Dad...how can it be?" Teal was a sparrow in a tornado.

"Deejon how could I not see it was him before, how did he not recognize me?"

"Souls don't see the way a person does, and you have been presenting as an older version of the person you were when you arrived on the Sea of Eternity."

"I need to leave. Now. I want to leave the Freedom Club."

"Are you sure you don't want to talk with him, your friend Erica did?"

"I have never been more certain of anything. I have to find my door, and I know how to get to it from here."

Teal looked at Deejon one last time.

"Thank you."

"Honey, you're welcome."

Chapter Eighty-Five

HUGH

As Erica left, Hugh had a clear view to Deejon's booth. To Deejon sitting with Teal. Teal who no longer looked vaguely familiar. Teal who looked explicitly familiar. Teal who was not Teal.

Amber.

And then Hugh was another sparrow in a tornado of destruction, emotional winds strong enough to lift houses from their foundations, smashed at the fragile birds as they stared at each other.

Hugh suddenly gasped for air, almost passing out, momentarily shocked that he hadn't been breathing. He was up and running to Deejon's booth. A booth in which Amber no longer sat. Frantically Hugh whirled around looking for her, saw Amber leaving through the main entrance. As he went to give chase, Deejon was suddenly in front of him.

"You have a question to answer."

"I don't need to answer your stupid question, I found her, I saw Amber, it was Teal and then Amber."

Hugh was moving away from Deejon who was making no effort to stop him, when she said, "And what did she do when she saw you?" Hugh slowed but didn't stop.

"You can chase her up a thousand mountains, but if you don't answer my question you'll never have the conversation with her that you really want to have."

Hugh stopped. He honestly didn't have a clue how answering Deejon's question could possibly help him, but he couldn't deny the brutal truth of Amber running away from him.

Chapter Eighty-Six

Hugh was sitting where only moments ago Amber had been. He was still struggling to breath, his emotions washing over him like waves on a beach.

"Why couldn't I see them?"

"Beli tried to teach you to see the whole picture and the importance of understanding yourself in the picture, really understanding with an honesty that allows for no brushing of things, big or small, under the carpet."

"I've been seeing this place, all of it, even dancing in the center of it."

Deejon carried on as though Hugh hadn't spoken.

"Lennie taught you a little about the Universe and the quantum world but mainly how much remains a mystery..."

"None of that helps me now. Amber was just here and the longer I sit here with you the further away she gets."

"From everything you've learned do you really believe the distance you need to travel to find Amber could be measured in miles?"

Hugh had no answer. In the odd statement he knew there was a kernel of truth, that everything that had happened from the moment he met Gerald C'Farer was less about the physical distance of going up the mountain, and more about a journey that needed to happen inside himself.

"Why is the Freedom Club not the Freedom Club?"

Hugh idly played with Erica's badge as he looked in vain for Amber. Deejon pushed another badge across the table to him.

"That was Teal's."

"You mean Amber." Deejon merely nodded, smiling warmly at Hugh. He looked at the two badges, one plain white, the other with the black, gray, white and green stripes of the agender flag. Hugh was drawn to the white flag, although it was Erica/Alvin's, it reminded him of his Amber, of a picture frame around a blank poster in his teenage daughter's room. He turned his attention to the agender flag. This is what Teal/Amber wore here in the Freedom Club.

Hugh thought once more of what Beli had said...*the missing piece is a part of the whole picture, in that which is missing lays hope, in that which is missing is where our souls await.* Hugh smiled partly at the memory of his friend Beli and their mead fueled conversations, but mostly because he had the answer to Deejon's question.

"Why is the Freedom Club not the Freedom Club?" said Hugh as he slid both badges to Deejon.

"Because there should be nothing to be free from. This is a place of sanctuary but not freedom. No one should need a badge to be recognized. Being recognized should be a right for everyone, and we all should be seen without judgment. It's why you made me get up on stage isn't it?" said Hugh.

"You needed to taste the freedom this club offers to be able to understand what we need to be free from," said Deejon.

"And the scales literally fell from my eyes when I sat with Erica and really saw her for the first time," said Hugh.

Deejon dropped the badges in her empty glass, "No badges. I don't wear one because I shouldn't need to, but some statements need to be made, positions achieved and maintained before situations can be remade."

"Sounds like the language of war," said Hugh.

"Not war, of righteous passion," said Deejon.

"Amber once spoke to me with such passion about those flags. I thought it was teenage temper at a Dad who just wasn't with it," said Hugh.

"Do you see it differently now?" said Deejon.

"Yeah, you wouldn't believe how much I see differently," said Hugh. Deejon smiled sadly, waiting patiently for Hugh to join the dots.

"It still doesn't mean I can find her though, does it?"

"It means you don't need any more help."

"My time here is finished isn't it," said Hugh, it wasn't a question, and he wasn't talking about the Freedom Club.

Chapter Eighty-Seven

Outside the Freedom Club the mountain plateau was a rectangle of silvery shadows as the moonlight let all be seen while hiding all detail. The only way Hugh knew to go was back through Deejon's rainbow hut and down the mountain. Finding Amber in the forest would not be easy but it was also the only way she could go. He was making his way to the rainbow hut when he heard a dog barking.

Charlie. It must be. Charlie his guide, ready to lead him to Amber. He followed the sound of her barking through the wild garden next to Freedom Club until he found her barking excitedly at Alvin, who was standing on the precipice of the mountain, the cloudscape stretching away in all directions, its size an expression of power, dwarfing the mountain, covering the sea and yet it offered nothing, no support, only a masking of what lay beneath.

"What are you doing here Alvin?"

"Waiting for you. I knew you'd come looking for Amber."

"Did you see her, where did she go?"

"It's where she's trying to go that you need to understand."

"Tell me, please just tell me."

"Come and stand next to me Hugh." Alvin held out her hand to Hugh.

Standing on the precipice Hugh and Alvin held hands while Charlie sat quietly next to them.

"My future is through these clouds but so is my past. Everyone who comes to the Freedom Club comes through the clouds, it's like shedding a skin, where things about you can be temporarily left in the clouds."

"Things. What kind of things?"

"Emotional things that hold people back, stop them seeing..."

Hugh roughly let go of Alvin's hand as he said, "...the big picture. I know all about the big picture, and here I am on a big mountain with big clouds everywhere and even though I see things differently, I still can't get to Amber. A big nothing is all I've got."

Alvin gently took Hugh's hand again.

"Listen and try not to follow old roads to old answers. Neither of us has much time. Think of the clouds like a cloakroom for all the emotions that make up you, Hugh Mann. You leave in the cloakroom whatever emotional-clothing you choose, your soul, which is all your emotions, is doing this, it's you but you haven't fully become your soul, it is part of the process. You come out of the cloud-cloakroom and spend time in the Freedom Club. The Freedom Club which is like pausing a movie you've never seen before; everything up to that point you know, the movie will resume when you decide to press play. When you do press play, you go back to the cloakroom put on those emotions once more but now *you wear them differently.*"

"What makes you know when to press play again?"

"When I first saw you at the Freedom Club there was the tiniest memory of the 'clothes' I had left in the clouds, like a first grader at the back of a class of seniors desperately trying to be seen by the teacher. The more I saw you, that first grader grew in confidence, until she was not only at the front of the class but was actually teaching the class. The point is, I had all the necessary knowledge, that which held me back didn't matter anymore, I had taken it in, made it mine, overcome it and moved on."

Hugh laughed ugly.

"I've heard so many analogies and metaphor's it's driving me mad..." Hugh laughed again adding manic to the ugly, "...if I'm not already."

It was Alvin's turn to push Hugh's hands away.

"OK, you want a true story about something Amber did, something that made her cry?"

Hugh had no time to answer before Alvin continued.

"When I met Amber I was having lunch. She joined met at my so-called table. We were sitting on a pallet in the corner of a big warehouse. Amber was so excited, and I couldn't understand why until she said she imagined it was like being on a raft in the middle of the ocean, she said it made her feel safe. It wasn't difficult to understand that her story was about escaping something."

"I know and I see it differently now."

"That's not what made her cry. It's what she killed. A beautiful butterfly flew in through the open loading doors and was fluttering around us. It was quite special, this little thing of beautiful colors, staying by us. Amber watched it intently, mesmerized by the oddness of its natural beauty in a warehouse that was a cathedral for man-made stuff, where everything was gray concrete, dull metal, dark fixings or dead wood."

'It doesn't belong here,' she said.
'It will find its way out," I answered.
'No. It won't be able to survive here.'

Before I could do anything she squished it with her sandwich box. Tears were running down her cheeks when she said, *'It's for the best.'*

Alvin turned and jumped off the mountain.

"Alvin, Alvin..!" No response and Charlie was completely unmoved. There was a splash, a distinct body-breaking-water splash. Immediately rainbow colors rippled outward from where they stood across the entire cloudscape, then the sea of clouds was a carpet of rainbow colors that pulsed brightly for a few seconds then faded, and in the last moments of the fading Hugh saw a word in golden flames in the clouds, a word that he almost read before the clouds moved and the flames were the last fire of Alvin's rainbow.

"Hugh honey, you forgot your rucksack," said Deejon as they approached through the wild garden.

Chapter Eighty-Eight

Giving Hugh his rucksack Deejon said, "I've put some supplies in there for you, don't look now, put it on your back, think of it as a mental parachute and use it when you get to where you're going."

"Where am I going?"

"Where you've always been going Hugh, ever since you started to run across that road to save your daughter."

After Deejon left with Charlie, Hugh sat on the precipice, his legs dangling into nothingness, looking like a school child with his rucksack sitting on an enormous bench. Of everything that he had been told and shown, not least the cloudscape lit like a glorious rainbow carpet stretching to infinity, nothing stuck more clearly in his mind than the idea of Amber and Alvin in the corner of a warehouse sitting on a pallet, eating sandwiches and feeling safe.

Sitting on a pallet and feeling safe.

Hugh knew where Amber was and had a crazy idea on how to get to her. There was no need to ask Deejon if it was the right thing to do. The time for questions was over. The time for answers was over. What Hugh did next was all that mattered.

Hugh pushed himself off the mountain.

Chapter Eighty-Nine

Hugh Mann fell through the white darkness of the clouds, wind lashing his face as he raced to the bottom. A voice gave chase, hissing on the wind,
Remember
What
You
Did
Hugh was falling so fast he could barely breath. He was close to passing out when the hiss became a roar,
I AM WAITING
Hugh smashed into the Sea of Eternity.

Chapter Ninety

LAURA

Laura woke to the sound of breakfast commotion from her kitchen.

"Mom is that you?"

"No, I'm a burglar that's decided to make you breakfast, how do you want your eggs?"

"Funny. Scrambled. Down in a minute."

"You got ten until breakfast is served."

Ten minutes later Jean was amazed at the difference between the Laura she had found crying in her car yesterday morning, and the one sitting in front her devouring eggs and toast, humming a melody she couldn't quite put a name to.

"You're in a good mood."

"I had a dream that helped me remember some important things."

"Which were?"

"Which were all the good things about Hugh, how he loved us, made us laugh and how..." she paused to swallow a mouthful of egg, then using her fork to emphasize her next point, continued, "...how he would do anything to protect his family."

"Honey, you don't need a dream to tell you those things."

"No Mom, I mean yes, I don't but the dream reminded me of the last thing Hugh said to me," the phone rang cutting Laura off.

"Hadn't you better get that, might be the hospital."

"They can leave a message, you need to hear what Hugh said."

"OK, I'm all ears."

"He said he would find Amber."

The next moments, mere seconds, were amongst the hardest in Jean's life. Her daughter beaming with what she believed was wonderful news, and Jean trying to feign enthusiasm as she realized the trouble her child was in. She was saved by Laura refocusing on her eggs and starting to hum again.

"What's that you're humming?"

"From a Distance, it was popular many years ago."

The phone rang again. Dr. Midler's office left a message urging Laura to come to the hospital as soon as possible.

Jean was driving them to the hospital when she said, "That song you mentioned, From a Distance, had a bit of a religious angle as I remember it, God is watching you or something,"

"God is watching us from a distance."

"You believe that?"

Laura's answer was stillborn as she realized where her Mom had driven them.

"Mom this isn't you, this isn't us."

Jean had stopped the car in the shadow behind a big church, where its garden was a dark green apron pockmarked with headstones and crosses.

"I know, but it seemed to me that you wanted to do the impossible by living in the past or believing the possibility of Hugh finding Amber," she knocked on the window indicating the church, "This is a place of impossibilities, it's not something we've ever had much time for in our family, but if there ever was a time, it's probably now."

They sat in the garden in the last of the sunlight, it wouldn't be long before the church put everything in its shadow. The church was on a hill, in the distance Laura could see the lake of her perfect picnic and her dreams.

She had been expecting questions on her approach to faith and was surprised when the young Priest started by saying, "I don't believe a lot of what it says in the Bible."

Jean spoke up while Laura was still processing the Priest's words. "It's quite a commitment you've made for something you don't fully believe in."

The Priest smiled like a teacher comfortable in the knowledge the class were going to follow her to the answer, without getting to it before she was ready.

"You can be certain that I'm committed to something I fully believe in, you just need to understand the difference between wrapping paper and what's inside."

Looking directly at Laura she continued, "I could tell you God has a plan we can't understand, that more angels were needed in heaven. Some people like to hear that, and there's nothing wrong with offering such words if it gives comfort to the grieving, but my house is not about these words, it's about hope in the unknown."

"People can hope without needing religion," said Laura.

The Priest held up her left hand, crossing the index and middle fingers.

"Fingers crossed for luck, maybe to win a raffle or for your team to win a game. You get it. Fingers crossed for a young child having their first ever injection. How about fingers crossed for a major operation, for giving birth." Laura wanted to say something, but the Priest wouldn't be interrupted.

"Here's a good one, fingers crossed that the soul of your stillborn baby is in heaven."

Laura and Jean had nothing to say as the Priest retrieved something from her trouser pocket with her right hand, the left still having the fingers crossed. She placed a plain gold cross on the table between them.

"Millions of words have been written about the meaning of that Cross, millions of people believe those words, there are rules and ceremonies concerning that Cross, and it's all wrapping paper. Inside that Cross is Hope, that's its greatest power. I was close to leaving the church when I met a couple who had just lost their child 8 months into the pregnancy. I was terrified before meeting them, I had no words, no thoughts, and nothing I did gave me any sense of being prepared. None of the other Priests had words, wise or otherwise, that calmed me down. So I made a call I really didn't want to. I called my Mom. I knew she could help, but she was not happy with my planning to leave the church. Moms know when to ignore the noise and focus on what's important. She said two sentences, a total of sixteen words, *"Be a mirror for their hope. Come for lunch on Sunday to tell me your decision."*

By now the Priest had uncrossed her fingers, she held the cross lightly in her right hand.

"Those people had had their lives destroyed as clearly as if a hurricane had torn through their home and destroyed everything they owned. Because what had happened to them was the same in a way. They had dreams of a future as a family, of a child growing..." she stopped, took a handkerchief from her pocket to wipe the tears she couldn't stop.

"I'm sorry, of course you understand what I'm saying. These people were clinging to the Hope in this Cross for all their broken lives were worth, and they saw me as a part of that, just being there helped them. I don't know what I said, but it was a little comfort in a sea of pain. Three days later I told my Mom I was staying in the church. I had chosen to not let the wrapping paper get in the way of the real gift of Hope."

Jean took the young Priest's hand in hers.

"Thank you for sharing that."

She nodded before saying, "When you called it reminded me a little of my Mom, direct, brutally honest, you said you don't believe, it's most likely all mumbo jumbo but it might help your daughter if I could find some comforting words. I thought my Mom would have liked you, she passed 3 years ago, so here we are. I get you might not be church people, but it doesn't mean you can't have Hope."

Part VII: WHY? Part II - Finding Home

Chapter Ninety-One

The sea spat Hugh to the surface and rolled him on white crested waves to the shore. Face down in the surf, Hugh coughed and spewed sea water as he came back from the brink. Standing on legs that screamed at him to sit down and stay down, he managed to stumble a little way up the beach before falling again.

Using what little strength he had, Hugh shrugged off the rucksack and retrieved Deejon's supplies; a zip-lock plastic bag containing a post-it note stuck to a sealed envelope.

The post-it note was from Deejon, where they had written, 'Some pictures to help you remember your friends from the mountain before you return Home. Your Friend Dj. (who wears no badge <smiley face>). On the back of the post-it note was a pencil sketch of a butterfly. Underneath the sketch was written, *Fill It In.*

The envelope was labeled, *Your Helpers.* Inside were five photos.

The first photo was a black and white of a group of plantation slave workers. The group huddled together, haggard and bent, broken individuals taking strength from each other, looking as though the camera's act of capturing them could harm them even further. One young man stood aside from the main group, arms hanging loosely by his sides, head slightly uplifted, something between a smile and a grin beneath eyes that looked right into the camera, eyes of defiance that said, 'I see it all and I'm still standing tall'. On the reverse of the photo was written,

Gerald C'Farer c1798.

There was no hope in my world except that which a person created for themselves. I don't know why, but I was always able to see beyond the bond others put on me, I was always free. I could feel The Word even when the chains

were making me bleed. Now I help others find their way to The Word. You've seen The Word Hugh, and now you have climbed a mountain only to jump off it. When you go 'Home' remember the toughest mountains to climb are the ones inside us.

The second photo was also black and white, the inside of a hall where a young woman was being presented an award. The stage was full of somber suited men, the only smile coming from the young woman shaking hands with the man about to give her the award. On the reverse,

Leonora Kostas, Athens Institute of Science, 1954.

I received an international science award along with the advice to make the kitchen my laboratory and making kids my specialty discipline. I could see it all even then, something inside me told me about Places, magical Places that were real. No one wanted to look for the Places I could feel inside me, vast Places populated by the smallest of things. Now I am the telescope and the microscope, helping people navigate on the most important journey of all. When you go 'Home' remember that an address is never really a destination, it's a label for a place where things can happen between people, between you and those you care about. Emotions, however they are shared, are the currency of our lives.

The third photo was a color photo of two boys, arms around shoulders, one with a bloody nose, the other with a bloody fist, bodies looking like they had lost whatever fight they were in, faces full of jubilation. On the reverse,

Ben & Liam, Michigan, 1967.

*We were 10, best friends, we lost the fight but we lost it together, and if we were together we never really lost. We were inseparable. Until I let Liam go to war without me. I spent a lifetime looking for my friend who never came home. Beli, **Ben**+**Liam** became Beli. Now I spend my time helping people see that they are a part of the*

Bigger Picture. *When you go 'Home' try to see all your colors in the Bigger Picture.*

  The fourth photo was of a dog caught in freeze-frame bounding through a lake. Her ears were flat against her head, lips blown up revealing a crazy dog-smile, water splashed all around her. On the reverse,
  Charlie, 2005
  Nothing else was written. Nothing else was needed. The photo perfectly captured the wild joy that was Charlie.

  The fifth photo was also color, a young teen wearing a too big football shirt, legs bare, in one hand a ripped pink shirt, in the other a torn blue shirt. The child stared coldly into the camera, giving nothing away. On the reverse,
  Deejon, 2014.
  We were born into a world that gave us no choices, only two options, boy or girl, and we couldn't even choose from those for ourselves. Labeled and assigned a gender path from birth. The external world was two kinds of nightmare for us. One because how we were meant to look was not who we were, and two, because of how the external world looked at us, judged us, ascribing 'less than', 'abnormal', 'freak'. So, we got to know us, ourselves, the internal we that is us. And We could feel two truths, truths that are as old as anything Lennie taught you, two truths that are so important for you to see in the silver jigsaw piece of Beli's, two truths that you need to understand if you want to conquer the mountain Gerald told you about. Two Truths Hugh Mann; We were a soul, and souls have no gender. We just had to BE. And so do you.

  The pencil butterfly was drawn again with *Fill It In* written underneath.

Chapter Ninety-Two

LAURA

They drove in silence all the way to the hospital car park. As Jean went to get out, Laura put a hand on her arm, stopping her. "Mom, thanks for calling the priest, it was..."

"...it was a hopeful thing to do," said Jean, not letting her child stumble over finding the right words.

Laura smiled sadly before saying, "I dreamed Hugh told me he was going to find Amber. It was one of those dreams that seems more real than others..."

Jean watched as her daughter stared into the car park, seeing a life that would never be lived.

Laura had tears in her eyes as she said, "...I think it was a dream that seemed more real than others because of Hope."

Chapter Ninety-Three

"Mrs. Mann I'm sorry, it's not good news...".

"Wait...wait," Laura didn't know what to say next. She only knew she didn't want to hear the doctor's next words. Her arm was outstretched, as though she wanted to hold back his words.

"Your husband protected her from the impact of the truck, but they were knocked some distance, the impact on her cranium..." Laura's hand gripped the doctor's desk, nails gouging the dark wood.

"...there's no sign of..."

"I want to see her."

The doctor looked from Laura to her mother, who gave him the slightest of nods. In that movement the doctor understood now was not the time for words. It was a time for people, for emotions, and in this case, terrible pain.

"Nurse Seaport will show you the way." He buzzed his intercom to call Nurse Seaport.

Chapter Ninety-Four

HUGH

Kneeling in the sand clutching the photos, Hugh watched his rucksack float away, and with it any chance of seeing Amber again. The notes on the photos all said he was going home; Amber had run away from him, and he was on a beach where he seemed to be the only living soul. He put the photos in his pocket and decided to walk along the beach. The sun was still rising, the air was fresh, and for the first time since meeting Gerald C'Farer he felt no pressure, the race was run. He knew souls existed, how they were able to travel from a person's body to another Place, and how the essence of a soul was a person's emotions. There was a word in flames that spoke to his own soul even though he struggled to read the word. He had seen Amber in a club at the top of a mountain. Even if she had run away from him, it was enough to know that she was somewhere and there would come a time when he, Laura and Amber could be reunited. For now, he would walk along this beach until he worked out how to find his way home.

As Hugh set off along the beach he briefly saw a dark shadow on the horizon. There were no clouds or anything else in the sky, he assumed he imagined it. For once, things hiding in the dark didn't worry him.

He walked until the sun was at its' zenith and he was going to have to walk inland into the forest to get out of the heat. As he started arcing his path towards the forest he saw what looked like a hut in the distance, it was half on the beach and half in the sea. Hugh had met all of his Helpers in huts and before he knew what he was doing, he was running to this hut that was half on the beach and half in the Sea of Eternity.

As he got closer the similarities to the other huts on the mountain were clear, except this one had raised decking at the back, which the sea was lapping up against without quite reaching the back door. Hugh ran round to the front door and stumbled, almost cracking his head on the lower of the two steps leading to the door.

The door was identical to his front door, the home of his family. Number 117, brass knocker, peephole and wonky letter box that he never got around to fixing. The hut was like Gerald's, Lennie's or Beli's but it was the front door to the place where Laura, Amber and Hugh lived. Hugh pushed the door and walked into a memory.

Chapter Ninety-Five

LAURA

Laura said goodbye to memories of perfect picnics as she stepped into the reality of the room where her family lived. Amber in one bed, Hugh in another, their broken bodies hooked up to monitors, drip feeds and ventilators. She took a chair and placed it between the beds, took her seat and held their hands. Friday night and the family was together.

Holding their hands Laura Mann made a decision to let Hope live in her.

Chapter Ninety-Six

HUGH

He was in their front hall. Hugh put his arms up against the wall making it look like he was holding the wall up, when it was the other way round. He took deep breaths. He could hear movement in the kitchen, he needed to get himself together. Too late.

A pretty face with a bright smile poked around the doorway.

Seeing him, Laura's smile became a look of concern, "Honey you look like you've seen a ghost."

"Just stretching out my back, think I spent the day sitting in one position," said Hugh."

"Oh, OK. So long as you can still make the pizzas. Dough's already rising."

So, it's a Friday night thought Hugh.

Laura laughed a little as she came up to him.

"Funny that ghost comment, I've never seen a ghost so how would I know what you'd look like if you really did see one."

"Hugh gave an unconvincing laugh and said, "Maybe you're not so wrong."

Laura pecked him on the lips, "If the first ghost I see looks like you I'll be alright."

She walked off shouting over her shoulder, "Now hurry up, Amber's hungry and the wine won't pour itself."

Hugh looked in the hall mirror. He was wearing his work clothes and new shoes, which he remembered being angry about scuffing the first time he wore them. This was a memory of his, he was in it looking like his remembered self but with his current awareness of having walked into this memory-hut from a beach after his travels up and down the mountain. He took a few more deep breaths then walked into the living room.

There was Amber sprawled on the sofa, headphones on, giggling at something undoubtedly useless on her cell phone, wearing her standard black jeans and white hoodie.

"Where's my greeting? said Hugh.

"I'm hungry," said Amber.

"I've got a great film for us to watch tonight,"

"Ham and pineapple," said Amber.

Her eyes never left the cell, but Hugh was well used to this style of teenage greeting and was mainly happy there was at least some interaction. He turned to go upstairs and was almost knocked over by the force of the bear-hug Amber gave him, as she quickly whispered in his ear, "I bet the film's rubbish," and ran off upstairs giggling. Laura was waggling her empty wine glass at him from the kitchen while she checked a message on her phone, Amber had already decamped to her room, on the stairs, he was between them both. The smile on his face was not so big, the one in his heart could have filled the Grand Canyon ten times over. He thought about the photos, wondered if he still had them in his pocket, there was something he urgently needed to check.

Upstairs he went into the bathroom and locked the door. He still had the pictures. He checked the notes on the back of each. Four mentioned home but two had home written inside apostrophes and two had home with a capital H. Out the window Hugh could see the Sea of Eternity stretching away forever, and from downstairs he could hear Laura calling,

'Hugh honey, where are you?'

Where was he? That really was *the* question. As he looked out the window at the waves gently washing part way up the decking, something tumbled from the waves and stayed on the decking, which continued to wash over it but not move it.

Hugh couldn't be sure, but he thought it looked like a cell phone.

"I'm coming, just give me a minute to change," he shouted down to Laura.

Hugh put on jeans and a T shirt he didn't mind getting covered in flour, then sat on the bed. He pulled at the T shirt laughing without joy. Why would he care about getting flour on this shirt or any other? He lay back on the bed and closed his eyes. A wall of incandescent light immediately flared in his head. Written on the wall a word in flames burned brighter still, a word he couldn't read but was starting to understand. Hugh jumped up, looked at the photos again, he put the two with lower-case h's on the bed and the two with capital H's by the window. He understood his two homes now, at least that there were two, the memory one that he was standing in, and something out there, beyond the sea. He walked to the window, apart from the decking with the cell phone on it, the sea was all he could see, calm and peaceful. He knew Amber was out there, that what was happening inside this hut was for him alone. As if to confirm his understanding Laura came into the room.

"What's keeping you slow-coach?" she said, handing him one of the glasses of wine she was carrying.

"I had to pour these myself and you know it's in our marriage contract that you are the wine-pourer."

They clinked glasses.

"Happy Friday my love," she said.

Hugh was dumbstruck. Laura had not noticed the photos or the sea outside the window.

"Something wrong?"

"No...everything is perfect."

Laura smiled and said, "You have a hungry daughter waiting who would beg to differ."

As Hugh followed Laura downstairs he couldn't help thinking about,

Amber.
Waiting.
Somewhere outside the hut.

Chapter Ninety-Seven

Laura sat at the kitchen table with her wine and cell phone, smiling at the shared memes, gifs and messages she liked to catch-up on at the end of the day, her work for pizza night done until Hugh called for help getting the pizzas out of the oven. As Hugh looked at his wife he knew he couldn't do it, couldn't knowingly spend a last evening with her. If this was somehow based on his memories, then better to walk out now and go looking for Amber. But his memory of Amber was upstairs, and he could also spend some time with her again, in a place and time before all the trouble he had caused.

"Pizza's not going to make itself honey," said Laura, for a moment not looking up from her phone. Then she did. And Hugh knew he could spend the rest of forever lost in that smile. It was a perfect moment catching Laura's smile in his heart, like the final piece of one of Beli's jigsaws falling into place. Hugh remembered the suggestion of light he had seen in Lennie's Nowhere Room, the light that was a tiny piece of the first spark of the Universe. He understood it here, near to Laura, as a moment of emotion on the infinite loop of circular time as explained by Deejon, moments that will combine into the emotion of The Word that he couldn't read. Outside the window it became so bright Hugh thought the sun had exploded. Hugh was starting to understand the Big Picture and his place in it.

Chapter Ninety-Eight

Making the pizzas was the usual affair of Hugh getting worked up about getting no help from Laura and Amber. In fact, they always did everything that was asked of them, Hugh was simply disorganized in the kitchen, and grumpy because he always made and ate his own pizza last. He was never really upset, more worried that what little process he did have could be disrupted and result in him serving burnt pizza. It happened occasionally, and Hugh absolutely hated to ruin Friday Night Pizza.

Hugh felt the experience of this living memory was like driving a car. He was driving the memory, it was coming from him, but working the pedals, steering wheel, gear-shifter, it was all on auto-pilot, and he was able to have his own thoughts while the memory played out, while he was a part of it. He could watch Laura laugh at one of her own jokes while he and Amber shrugged shoulders at the non-event of her joke, which only made her laugh more. He could listen to Amber complain about his poor choice in music, groan with Oscar-worthy feeling when he went to his go-to upbeat play-list. Or simply watch her chomp on her pizza, happy in herself, happy at home with the family. He could simply revel in the boring, priceless details of a Friday evening with his family.

He raised his glass to make a toast, "To Family Friday Nights."

Laura clinked her wine glass and Amber her soda can.

"Dad, you do know that I will go out on some Friday nights, right?"

"Some is OK, just not all, because you know, being home with Mom and Dad in da house is da bomb, right," said Hugh making some kind of finger/fist gesture, as yet unseen by anyone.

Laura laughed while Amber shook her head in mock embarrassment.

"Dad you are so uncool. Promise you will never do that in front of any of my friends."

"Only if you do one thing for me."

"Anything to stop 'da bomb' happening again."

"Close your eyes, you to honey."

Hugh reached across the table taking a hand from each of them and asking them to link hands too, then closed his eyes.

"OK. Think of the night sky with a bright full moon, and all the people in so many different lands, with so many things going on in this world, millions and millions of little things, important things for all the people in all the world. You can open your eyes now."

They were holding hands awkwardly across a table with half eaten homemade pizza.

"One of those millions of things is us, around this table on our family pizza night." He let go of their hands and continued, "I love our little tradition and I hope you might one day do something similar with your own family, maybe even impress them with some da bomb hipster speak." He smiled and blew Amber a kiss as Laura raised her glass, saying, "To Dad who makes the nicest toasts," glasses clinked, Laura, blew Hugh a kiss mouthing, *Love you.*

"Will we ever see you in anything besides black jeans and a white hoodie?" said Hugh.

"It's who I am, I feel good in them," said Amber.

"You are way more than what you wear but I get it, it was only a question."

"Anyway, you should be grateful, you don't have me chasing all those expensive brands."

"I am grateful, always for you two," said Hugh.

Amber blew him a raspberry-kiss, which was one of her ways of showing affection without it being too much for her teenage standards.

"Why so sad?" said Laura.

"It's nothing." He topped up their wine glasses.

"I hope you've chosen a good film, not an action or superhero movie," said Laura.

"Mom you always make us watch something you like then fall asleep after 20 minutes."

"But I always see the end," said Laura smiling to herself as she started to clear the plates. Hugh lingered on his wine and silently wished that Laura wouldn't see the end tonight.

The film delivered more moments of priceless banality for Hugh. It had nothing to do with the quality of the movie, only the laughter of the two loves of his life. No sooner had the movie ended than Amber sat forward, gave Hugh a comedy smile, jumped up, gave him a peck on the cheek, "Great pizza Dad, laters," and bounded upstairs, eager to connect with her friends. Halfway up the stairs she turned and said, "Hey Dad, would it be alright if I brought a friend, Michele, for pizza night sometime..." Hugh felt himself become fully in the moment of the memory, no autopilot.

He stared at Amber halfway up the stairs, casually awaiting his answer, no sign that it meant so much to her. His beautiful daughter, a life full of colorful potential, dressed in her favorite black and white.

"That would be perfect honey."

Big smile from Amber, "Thanks Dad."

The living room was dimly lit but enough for Hugh to see their reflection in the now off TV screen. They were comfy on the sofa, of all the wonders and riches in the

Universe, a seat on a sofa next to the person you've made a life with can be all you need. Laura slept, head resting on his shoulder, that she had chosen to let her head fall asleep on his shoulder for all these years remained a miracle to Hugh, and the love it spoke of, his greatest treasure.

    He thought about putting the TV on and looking at photos, he knew Laura would sleep through but there was no need to look at more memories, everything was here in this moment. He knew he had to get up now or he would never leave. He made the well-practiced move of extricating himself from under Laura while gently lowering her onto the sofa, cushion under her head.

    He went to the stairs where he could hear Amber's voice amid squeals of laughter coming from her room. He listened for a while, until all sound was gone, and he was conscious of his white-knuckled grip on the banister. He didn't want to turn around, didn't want to see what he had to say goodbye to. He had been so focused on finding Amber, he had never thought what he might end up losing. Letting go of the banister Hugh slowly turned, taking in the room where they ate together, celebrated birthdays, holidays, where they lived and laughed together and there she was, his Laura, as beautiful in sleep as at any other time. He walked to her, wiping his tears away for fear they would wake her. A soft kiss on the forehead, a last look, "Goodbye my love."

Chapter Ninety-Nine

Hugh left through the back door onto the decking of the hut, the sea lapping at its edges and just beyond the salty reach of the waves, a cell phone.

He picked up the phone. The make and model familiar, the red marks he didn't want to think about.

'Why Dad?...

Hugh's hands started to shake. He gripped the phone tighter, like a bar of soap it slipped from his hands straight into the lapping waves which gently deposited the cell phone back on the decking.

Holding the phone again, the screen started to fill with a picture. Alvin's bloodied and beaten face filled the screen with the tag line; queer man found dead in alley. Hugh couldn't believe what he was seeing. The main article suggested a sexual encounter in an alley had turned violent, resulting in the death of Alvin Schwartz, 29 years old, next of kin unknown.

...Why did you do it?'

Hugh fell to his knees, head in hands and wailed with the cries of a guilty man.

In the distance a shadow rose from the depths.

'Now you remember Hugh Mann. I'm coming for you.'

Hugh stood and stared out to sea with tear streaked cheeks. He threw the phone with all his might in the direction of the shadow.

"Come then. I might be guilty but not of the crimes you think."

Hugh dove into the sea, swimming like a man possessed to meet his destiny.

Chapter One Hundred

    Hugh's muscles were screaming for him to stop swimming, the voice in his head screamed louder for him to swim until he finds Amber, to swim until he can silence his accuser. And like a child fighting sleep, everything slows, his body, his thoughts. He can't go on, the sea is all around him, the only way is down.
THE ONLY WAY IS DOWN
    The thought exploded in his head like a firework. The last image Hugh Mann saw was Amber sitting on a door on an endless sea. He smiled at the thought of it ending where it all began.

Chapter One Hundred One

AMBER & HUGH

"Why can't you leave me alone?"

Hugh opened his eyes. Blinked. Coughed up sea water. Blue sky. More blinking. More sea water expunged. Blue sky with a big dark shadow in the middle of it.

"Can you tell me why?"

The shadow spoke. The shadow moved back, and Hugh sat up, and from the shadows he was looking at Amber.

"Answer me!"

"You pulled me from the water. I really did see you."

Hugh felt the tiniest spark of hope; Amber had pulled him from the sea onto her door, she was angry, but he could work with that. He had hope.

"Tell me Dad, why won't you leave me alone, just why?"

"Because I needed to tell you I'm sorry."

"Sorry for what, do you even know?"

"For Alvin. He ran out of the restaurant because of what I did. I didn't do anything to him in that alley, but he was there because of me."

"He didn't deserve to die like that," said Amber.

"No, he did not. He didn't need to live a life hiding who he really was either."

"Nothing to be done about it now."

"Maybe not, but we made our peace, at least Alvin told me he had overcome what happened to him, moved on," said Hugh.

Amber stared out to sea, saying nothing. Hugh did likewise, keeping a sideways watch for any change in her demeanor. He hadn't expected to be doing anything that challenged leaving Laura for making him feel like an emotional punch-bag so soon, if ever again. Yet here he was with another mountain to climb. Thoughts of Laura brought the tears to his eyes. He started to speak, choked, looked down, then roughly wiped the tears from his face, missing his daughter seeing her father in a moment of emotional tension most children never witness in their parents.

"What I did in that restaurant not only lead to Alvin's death, it lead to yours too. You stopped in the road when you saw his picture on your phone. What I did in that restaurant started long before we were there. I had stopped listening to you for a while, your Mom tried to tell me, I wasn't listening to her either."

"Why Dad?"

"Because there's a way I thought things should be. People can be tribal about the silliest of things, like sports teams, or things that are more serious like religion or fundamental things like family. When children don't want to fit into the way parents think things should be, parents can feel rejected and disrespected. So they double-down by enforcing their values because they have the unquestioned wisdom of their own history, it worked for them, so it will work for their children. I had some stuff going on at work, which didn't help. Still, no excuses, and it's not really more complicated than me wanting you to do things my way."

"What was it with work?"

"Lost my job, 44 years old, no job, no prospects, it's what it felt like anyway."

"Gender politics took you by surprise when you were feeling down."

"Surprise doesn't begin to describe."

They sat in silence again, but this time Hugh felt they were not so far apart. Hugh took a chance and did something that scared him more than anything he had ever done. Hugh slowly put his arm around Amber. She didn't pull close...but she didn't pull away.

"Surprise doesn't excuse either. The parent-child contract covers all eventualities, you know why?"

He waited for Amber to ask, "Why?"

"Because it's a bond of love. If it could be written down it would say, I loved you from before you were born, for all the days of your life and beyond."

"Mom always said you were good at speeches." She sniffled, he pulled her closer, and this time his daughter rested her head on his shoulder. Hugh's heart soared.

"Did you have a Helper?" said Amber.

"Helper's. Four, five if you include Charlie."

"Five! I just had two, Mia and Deejon."

"I think we can both agree, I need more help than you," said Hugh.

"So you know about the Places, that this is the Sea of Eternity?"

"I didn't know this was called the Sea of Eternity, but I sort of understand what souls are made of and how they can move between the Places," said Hugh.

"Emotions..."

"...at the quantum level, or very very small, for people like you and me," said Hugh.

"The big headline is transformation, that's what this place is all about, and us being here means were not going home. Mia, my Helper, said there's no going back."

Another firework went off in Hugh's head, *THE ONLY WAY IS DOWN*

"But I don't want to transform. How can I become something else when I hadn't even become myself? I'm going to stay on this door until..."

Amber was interrupted by a wave unsettling them.

"Where did that come from?" said Amber.

It was a fair question, there were no other waves apart from the single undulation that had passed beneath them. Hugh was relieved that Amber seemed to have lost her earlier thought until she said, "I wish we could see Mom."

He couldn't say anything. Not Yet.

Then mountains exploded. That's what it sounded like.

Holding hands they stood on the door. At the horizon geysers of water hissed and steamed as they shot skyward. The sea foamed and frothed as a black shadow emerged.

"Dad...what's *that*?"

Hugh had been scared of *that* for as long as he could remember. Not anymore.

"It's me."

"How can it be you?"

"Amber, listen to me, we are in the Place Between becoming our souls, a lot of things can be in a way we don't understand."

The shadow had emerged, as big as a house, it rested on the water's surface, water hissing and steaming where the shadow touched it.

"I need you to trust me. Forget about the darkness, I'll deal with that. Do what I say, no questions, just do. OK?"

Amber didn't answer, she was staring at the darkness which was taking shape before her eyes; the creature was bear-like, with blood-red eyes, smoke steaming from its nostrils and flames dripping from its maw over rows of razor teeth.

"OK!" Hugh was shaking Amber to get her attention. Amber snapped into the moment.

"Yes, do as you say, got it."

"Good. Remember your favorite game when you were little?"

Amber blanked, the question too left-field to sync with the impending danger of the creature.

"Come on, try to remember."

"Airplane?"

"Good girl. No questions now," said Hugh as he lay on the door, legs bent, arms ready to support Amber. It wasn't the same as on their living room floor, but Amber managed to lay on her Dad's feet and hold his hands as he pushed her up.

The beast roared, reared up on its hind legs before smashing them down and charging.

And Hugh smiled at two-year old Amber pretending to fly from the safety of his hold. He closed his eyes and heard Laura's voice, *Don't drop her.*

Never my love, he whispered back.

He opened his eyes and saw Amber as Teal, the young woman she would one day become.

The beast was getting closer. Eyes closed again. The beast sounded even closer.

Eyes open and there she was, Amber, 16 years old, fearful and full of life, that's how Hugh saw her.

The waves caused by the beast crashing over the sea were making it difficult for them to stay on the door. It would be over soon; the beast was almost upon them. They could hear the water roiling, hot splashes on their faces. Amber started to look.

"Amber, stay with me."

Something in her Dad's voice made her look at him and forget everything else.

"I got you..." Hugh let go of Amber dropping her straight onto him.

"...always."

The beast smashed into the door.

As Hugh held his child close and rolled off.

Chapter One Hundred Two

AMBER

Amber had no time to react as Hugh fell into the Sea of Eternity holding her tightly. She expected the dark beast to come diving after them, but its fight remained above the water. She didn't understand this plan of her Dad's, they would have to resurface, but she knew he wouldn't hurt her, so whatever was happening, she would trust him. Amber looked at Hugh clutching her close, his eyes only on her, air bubbles fast escaping his mouth as he spoke.

What, why was he speaking? They were still sinking, and her Dad wasn't holding his breath. Amber started shaking her head vigorously, urging him to stop talking. She managed to free her arms as the bubbles became less and less. She held his head in her hands, his eyes still on her. Amber heard his voice.

I had to find you because I love you.

It was so dark now she could barely see him. His voice again but from further away, even though she could feel his head in her hands, see the whites of his eyes.

Be yourself and live the life you want.

Amber couldn't see anything, couldn't *feel anything.* Where was her Dad? Amber felt her lungs burning, she knew she didn't have much time left when she heard her Dad's voice for a final time, like a whisper on a summer breeze,

Say Hi to Mom for me

It took what little breath she had left away.

Then Amber saw the light.

Chapter One Hundred Three

LAURA

The doctor stood in the doorway, watching Laura sitting between her husband and daughter, holding a hand from each. She didn't want to hear what he had to say, and he wished he didn't have to say it, but he had learned through a long career that between medical realities and medical miracles, the truth of the human body always won.

"You can come in now doctor and tell me what I need to hear," said Laura without turning around.

The doctor entered the room, approached Laura and gently put a hand on her shoulder.

"Your husband suffered major trauma to his spinal column as you know, and significant internal bleeding. But there was sufficient brain activity to suggest he would regain consciousness. However, over the course of the last 24 hours his brain activity has reduced to minimal levels. Right now machines are keeping his body alive, but consciousness has gone. That he was even conscious when we got him to the hospital is beyond anything I've ever seen."

Half a sob convulsed Laura's shoulders as she remembered Hugh managing half a smile as she rushed into the emergency room after the accident, his voice a raspy whisper as he said, *'I'm going to find her.'* A moment as he fought back a wave of pain, then a long look and the second to last squeeze of her hand, *'Goodbye my love.'*

Laura, straightening to face her fear head-on, said, "And?"

"And your daughter's readings have, I'm sorry to say, also significantly degraded."

"But what was there before was enough to keep monitoring, to give her time," said Laura.

"Yes, and if her readings stayed the same or degraded only slightly, I mean it's not black and white, there are many factors..." the doctor paused, it was the closest thing he had found to softening the hammer blow, allowing people the time to take a moment to prepare to hear the worst, because there was nothing that could soften a real hammer blow.

"...Amber's brain activity has stopped. The respirator keeps her breathing, but she will never regain consciousness."

Laura almost jumped out of her skin. Not because of what the doctor said. Hugh had squeezed her hand.

Chapter One Hundred Four

AMBER

Monitors beeped as Amber slowly opened her eyes, Laura put one hand to her mouth as Hugh's grip loosened on her other hand. More monitors beeped, this time from Hugh's bed. Doctors and nurses rushed in, but Laura knew there was nothing they could do.
"Oh Hugh," she whispered to herself.
"Mom..?" Laura turned to her daughter.
"Dad says Hi."
"I know honey, I know," said Laura, holding Amber's hand as her tears flowed.

Chapter One Hundred Five

HUGH

Hugh was falling. Faster. Faster. He sensed Amber was no longer with him. That was good. The speed threatened to make him pass out, it was so fast he couldn't breathe.
Breathe
He didn't know who spoke.
Breathe through your soul.
Breathe and let go.
It wasn't a voice; it was an urging from deep inside him.
Break Free
The speed was like a weight crushing him as he pushed his arms up, fighting an unseen force pushing him back, this unseen force that was only his own power as his soul sped from the depths of the Sea of Eternity towards the light above.

Hugh Mann's soul burst from the Sea of Eternity, a needle of brilliant white light with Hugh at its center. The light twisted as it shot straight up, with the sun blazing behind Hugh, he twisted at a dizzying speed. Then all was abruptly still. Hugh didn't float, he just *was* in the sky, he felt like himself but he had no body save for this light, but something was coming. Something BIG. Hugh felt the suggestion of light for an instant, the first spark, and then The Word was upon him, filling him from his center, Hugh Mann was transforming into his soul. What felt like wings exploded out-wards from Hugh, enormous, luminescent butterfly-like wings of purest light. Hugh Mann's soul was present, and it was fabulous. But it was not complete. The

Word that Hugh couldn't read, The Word that overwhelmed him was like light dancing in him and around him, it was a blind feeling looking for direction. Hugh understood the problem was him.

From below Big Bad bellowed as it smashed Amber's door into pieces. As one Hugh and Big Bad turned to the beach, the beach where Hugh's memory hut sat, a dot on the otherwise empty beach. Big Bad started a slow ponderous gallop towards the hut, looking up and roaring at Hugh as it went. Big Bad seemed in no hurry to get to the hut before Hugh got to Big Bad. Hugh was happy to oblige.

Hugh swooped down crashing into the side of Big Bad, bouncing off it as a fly would a charging bear. Hugh realized Big Bad wasn't waiting for him, it simply didn't fear him. Hugh picked himself up from the surface of the sea and sped ahead of Big Bad, stopping on the surface of the sea directly in Big Bad's path. The beast trampled right over Hugh pushing him beneath the surface. Hugh lay on the surface watching Big Bad bear down on memories of what he loved more than anything else in the world, and he saw ALL OF HIMSELF in the beast and the hut. As he realized this was not a battle he could win, Hugh Mann took the last step of understanding towards becoming his soul. He jumped high and flew away from all that was him in the beast and in the hut.

Chapter One Hundred Six

Big Bad was emotion pure, fueled by the ugliness in Hugh Mann's life. Big Bad was an aspect of Hugh's developing soul, an aspect with purpose.
To Destroy.
The Hut Where Love Lived.
Big Bad was almost upon the hut, a blunt instrument of destruction set free and ready to fulfill its purpose.
The sun went out.
A darkness so deep swept over the Sea of Eternity that Big Bad had to stop.
Big Bad looked up as glimmers of light filtered down from the edges of the sun. In silhouette, blocking the sun was The Heavy Butterfly; Hugh Mann as his soul.
The Heavy Butterfly dropped weightlessly, turning to face down, speeding toward the seas' surface, pulling up at the last second, speeding along above the surface, contrails swirling above its powerful wake.
Sunlight blasted across the land and Big Bad felt something it had never known before; fear.
Big Bad turned and charged for The Hut Where Love Lived. Big Bad was close but would never be close enough. Not when The Heavy Butterfly has arrived.
To Hugh it seemed he was on the beast as soon as he thought it. Big Bad, as huge as a house, was dwarfed by the enormity of Hugh's soul. He folded the beast into his wings, shooting arrow-like up towards the sun. When he was high and far away from the hut, Hugh unfurled his wings and in so doing, ripped Big Bad to shreds.
Big Bad fell towards the Sea of Eternity as masses of wispy dark entrails. Hugh swooped beneath all of Big Bads' remains, letting them fall onto his wings. As each piece of dark matter touched his wings, color sparkled and

rippled through them, then settled into a pale multi-coloring on his wings as Hugh's soul absorbed all the emotions that made up Big Bad. Hugh felt The Word as feeling taking hold of him once more, and again there was the knowledge of being incomplete. The Word in his soul pulsed and Hugh knew what to do.

He flew away from the beach as fast as the very first First Spark, like an ocean in space the Sea of Eternity stretched away forever. The Heavy Butterfly banked in a turn as wide a football pitch throwing up a wall of water in its wake and sped towards to its destiny, to the completion of Hugh Mann's soul and the beginning of The Place Beyond.

The Heavy Butterfly grasped The Hut Where Love Lives in its wings and flew as high as the stars, and when it seemed there was no more space to fly into, it flew on some more, dancing at a speed greater than the speed of light. Hugh Mann, The Heavy Butterfly, opened his wings tearing asunder The Hut Where Love Lives releasing the dark matter of all his remaining emotions. He flew and caught them on his wings, color radiating from every touch, a kaleidoscope of colors so bright only a soul could see them, could be them.

At the end of time the soul of Hugh Mann flew to The Place Beyond.

The Word in the center of his soul pulsed and filled him.

HARMONY

Chapter One Hundred Seven

EPILOGUE

"Hugh Jnr., come get a drink," Amber called to her son as he played on the beach.

"M can you get him a juice box from the bag." Hugh Jnr. arrived panting, covered in sand, desperate for the drink he didn't know he needed.

"Where's Nana?" he asked.

"It's Friday and you know what Nana always brings for dinner on Friday's, no matter where we are?"

"Pizza!" said Hugh Jnr. laughing with happiness the way only children can at the simplest of things, in this case, thoughts of his favorite food.

Laura was returning from her car bringing cold home-made pizza in sandwich boxes.

"Nana was Granpy a good swimmer?"

Laura set the pizza on the beach blanket, raised her sun hat and looked at her grandchild.

"He could, but it wasn't one of his best skills," said Laura.

"What was then Nana?" said Hugh Jnr. as he plonked himself on the blanket by her and grabbed a slice of pizza.

"He could make me laugh, your Mom too."

"I often think of Granpy like a beautiful butterfly because when I see one they always make me smile," said Amber.

"Your Granpy was a good man," said Laura.

"And he made the best pizzas," said Amber.

Hugh Jnr. took a big bite from his slice and around a mouthful of pizza said, "I'm going to chase the butterflies," before running off to where the wildflowers grow.

<<◇>>